ON STONY GROUND

AN ALEX RIPLEY MYSTERY
#3

M. SEAN COLEMAN

RED DOG

UK

Paperback
ISBN 978-1-913331-06-1

eBook
ISBN 978-1-913331-07-8

www.reddogpress.co.uk

You will listen and listen, but you will not understand.
You will look and look, but you will not see.

Matthew 13:14

1

REVEREND THOMAS BAINBRIDGE stooped to pick up a small duffel coat from behind a chair.

"Don't forget your coat, Connor," he called after the young, ruddy-faced boy walking out of the room, chattering excitedly to his father.

"Thanks Tom," Connor's father said, turning back to grab the coat and thrusting it playfully at his son. "He'd forget his own head if it weren't screwed on."

"Too hot," Connor complained, dragging the coat along the ground behind him.

"Put it on," his father said. "It's cold outside, you'll need it. Imagine your mother's face if she saw you out without your coat on."

"See you next week then, Connor," Reverend Tom called as the pair left the church hall, Connor shrugging his coat reluctantly over his shoulders.

Connor turned and waved. He was a sweet kid, and an enthusiastic member of the Boys Brigade group that ran every Thursday in the church hall, though you could almost guarantee that if something was left behind, it belonged to Connor Heath.

Tom smiled as the door slammed shut behind them. Scooping up the last few plastic cups that had been left abandoned after the usual refreshments of squash and biscuits, he dropped them in the bin.

Tom had been leading the Boys Brigade for three years now and loved every minute. Though it ate into his evenings, it was always worth the sacrifice. The boys who attended were enthusiastic and confident, and he'd learned early on that he needed to get them moving and tire them out if they were to understand any of the spiritual guidance the organisation was supposed to provide.

Tonight, being Ascension Thursday, had been a more spiritually focussed group than their regular fun and games, but it was important, he felt, for the boys to understand that today kicked off a period of nine days dedicated to spreading Christ's word. Tom had sent them all off with promises that they would share His message with at least one friend, though they'd probably all forgotten that promise as soon as they'd left the room.

"Oh, Tom?"

He looked up to find Morris Hanson, the headmaster of St Michael's – the local Church of England school – poking his head round the door. He often stopped in after Boys Brigade, ostensibly for a chat, but Tom knew he was seeking any bad report on his boys' behaviour. He ran a tight ship at that school.

"Hello there, Morris," Tom said. "Just locking up."

"I'm glad I caught you," Morris said. "I won't keep you long. I just wanted to check that we still have your support for the Whitsun Parade. It's going to be a good one this year."

"Oh, I wouldn't miss it for the world," Tom said. "And anything you need – help setting up, or keeping the baying crowds back, you just let me know. I'll be there to work."

"I knew I could count on you, Tom," Morris said. "Do you have time for a quick half then?"

"Not tonight, Morris, sorry. My tea's already in the oven, so I'd best be off to enjoy it before it spoils."

"Fair enough," Morris said. "I'll see you at the parade then, if not before."

"Goodnight, Morris," Tom called, stacking the last of the chairs with a scrape. He was pleased the headmaster hadn't pushed him to have that drink. He was feeling uncharacteristically weary today, and all he wanted to do now was finish up and go home for a late supper and a good drink.

Tom flicked the lights off and locked the door to the hall as he left, grateful that he didn't have to spend any more of the evening at work. The cleaners would be in early to sweep and mop before the flower-arranging group was due in, so all he had to do was lock up the church and he could be off.

His wife was out for the evening, staying over at her sister's as she did most Thursdays, and he was looking forward to being in the warm of their small cottage, in front of the fire, with a nice glass of wine and a belly full of Janet's delicious stew that she'd have left warming in the oven. It had been a long day, and he was keen to spend some time in peaceful reflection.

Walking back through the church grounds, he noticed that one of the floodlights up-lighting the side of the church was not working. He would have to tell Roger, the maintenance man, in the morning. Roger prided himself on keeping everything around the church in good condition, and would hate to think part of the building he loved so much was in darkness.

Tom made his way quickly along the path towards the main entrance of the church. He always locked up on a Thursday, since he was staying late anyway. It meant the vicar could get home at a reasonable time for at least one evening a week. Right now, he was regretting not having a coat with him. The night had drawn in and it felt surprisingly cold for an early June evening.

Pushing the main door to the church open, Tom was struck, as always, by the beauty of the inside of this ancient building. The body of the church was broad, with the surprising addition of a balcony level made of dark wood, contrasting dramatically against the bright crimson ceiling.

The balcony gave the place the feel a public meeting hall, rather than a church that, Tom felt, made it more welcoming. In daylight, light flooded the church, streaming through the stained-glass windows in each bay along the building's length. It never failed to make him smile, despite having known this church all his life.

His footsteps echoed on the flagstones as he crossed the nave to check that all was closed up through the back of the chancel.

"Hello?" he called out. "Anyone still about? I'm locking up."

No reply. No sound, save his own steps. Good.

Tom checked and locked the door off to the side of the chancel and turned back into the nave. There were no other open exits from the church to the garden. Rubbing his hands together against the cold, he headed back to the main entrance, humming gently to himself.

He stopped short of the entrance, noticing that the door to the storeroom was open. It was unusual that Roger would leave the door unlocked, given that the church remained open to the public, often unmonitored until long after nightfall. Roger was cautious about leaving his precious supplies unprotected, especially after they'd had a couple of items go missing in recent months.

"Roger? You in there?"

No reply, but it definitely felt like someone was there. Tom crossed quickly to the door.

"Roger?" he asked again, pushing the door open.

The small storeroom was dark, but the light from the main body of the church filtered in behind Tom, revealing a figure standing there in the darkness. A black cloak, hood up, face concealed.

"Hello?" Tom said uncertainly.

The figure didn't move.

"Can I help you?" Tom asked, a little more tersely. The church may be open to the public, but there was no reason a member of the public would be in the storeroom unless they were up to no good. Was this their robber, returned to snaffle more supplies?

Tom took a step closer, reminding himself that if a person had been reduced to theft, especially from a church, they must be in a fairly desperate state.

"Do you need help?" Tom asked. "I can help you. Just come on out and we can talk. There's no need to be afraid. You're not in any trouble."

He opened his arms, trying to show that he was no threat, and sensed a movement. It was always better, he thought, to appease than attack.

"That's it," he said, reassuringly.

But the strange, hooded figure seemed to grow taller, suddenly standing upright, before rushing at him, cloak billowing, hands out, aiming for his throat. Tom raised his own arms instinctively to defend himself but he was too late. His attacker was too fast and too strong.

Before he knew what was happening, Tom had been turned around, right arm bent up high behind his back. He cried out as pain tore through his shoulder. Hot breath rasped, ragged in his ear and a strong smell of camphor assaulted his nostrils.

"Please," he implored, as he was propelled across the nave, half-lifted, half-pushed towards one of the smaller, open-sided chapels lining the wings of the church.

There was nothing he could do to stop the momentum – his attacker was much stronger than him. *Why was this happening?*

Tom was forced to his knees on the hard stone in front of the small altar, sending pain shooting up both legs. The figure of Christ on the cross leaned out from the wall, angled to look down on those praying here. The bright gold of the altar glinted under the soft, purposely angled lights he'd always found so pleasing. Instantly, this once restful chapel had been transformed into a place of pain and terror.

"What do you want?" Tom asked, trying to look back over his shoulder to catch a glimpse of his attacker. *Did he know this person?*

"I want you to see the truth," the voice said, soft and menacing, close to his ear. Alcohol. Stale breath. All muted under that pervading smell of camphor. Like old moth balls. "Start praying."

"Please," Tom begged again.

"Pray. Now," the instruction was accompanied by a sharp blow to the back of his head, something hard and metallic splitting the skin at the base of his skull, sending light bursts across his eyes. Tom lurched forward, hands out to break his fall, but his attacker caught him by the hair and pulled him back upright, knees grinding against the stone floor.

Tom clasped his hands together, quickly muttering the opening lines of the Lord's Prayer.

"He can't hear you."

Tom raised his voice, hoping someone – anyone – would hear and come to his rescue, but fearing no one would. He lifted his eyes to look at the figure of Christ, repeating the short prayer at the top of his voice, beseeching God to intervene.

Just as he reached the final *amen*, his attacker gripped his hair again, pulling his head back. Something cold ran across his throat. It took a second for the pain to come, and the warm flow of blood to follow that. His throat had been slit. He felt the man's lips right against his ear.

"Do you see the truth now?" he asked. "Your own God did this to you. He let this happen. Do you see?"

Tom slumped to one side as his attacker let him go. His face hit the stone floor. His heartbeat pulsed in his cheek, fading as the blood flowed out of him. Dying, he watched his attacker's feet step away as the pool of blood – *his blood* – neared them, and an anger he had never felt before overwhelmed him. *How dare you kill me, here, like this, in this church?*

Reverend Tom Bainbridge let the anger fade along with his last breath. God would be there to receive him. *Wouldn't He?*

2

DR ALEX RIPLEY approached the reception desk on the psychiatric ward of the hospital with the same trepidation she'd felt for the past six months. She hated hospitals at the best of times, but the small unit on this military base felt particularly haunting.

"Good morning," the guy on reception said, as cheerful as ever. He had a great smile and he always made her feel welcome, but Ripley couldn't help feeling he was always just a bit too enthusiastic.

"Morning Justin," she said, taking the proffered ballpoint pen from him and signing in on the register, noticing again that she was one of the rare regular visitors to the ward.

"Good trip?" Justin asked, as he always did.

"Not bad," Ripley said, likewise.

The military hospital where her husband, John, had been a patient ever since his extraction from Afghanistan was not close to their home in Manchester, but it was the best the army had to offer, and after what John had been through, he deserved the best on offer.

"Who's on the ward today?" she asked.

"Doctor Lister," Justin said, checking his forms.

Good. She liked Dr Lister. He was a no-nonsense kind of guy, who didn't peddle false hope, but always found a way to focus on the positives. And, by God, they needed positives.

Ripley's husband, John, had been brought here after having been missing in action in Afghanistan for three years. Before she'd got the call to say that John had been found alive, Ripley had all but given up hope of ever seeing him again. So, when his former colleague, Neil Wilcox, had got in touch to say they were bringing him home, she had genuinely thought she'd had a miracle of her own. But when she finally saw him, she wasn't so sure.

Of course, she'd expected his experiences in hellish captivity for three years to have changed him, but she hadn't been prepared for the extent of that change.

All that the army would tell her about his time in Afghanistan was that he had been captured by hostile forces, held in appalling conditions and tortured both mentally and physically. They'd warned her he may never be able to talk about what he'd been through. But they'd assured her he was in the best hands, getting the best possible care and that they would do everything they could to return him to her in some recognisable form. It was going to be a long and difficult road. They all had to acknowledge that much.

The hardest part for Ripley to come to terms with had been that John hadn't wanted to see her at all for the first month. She had been so desperate to see him, to hold him, to reassure herself that he was actually alive, and yet she'd had to find a way to respect his wishes and keep herself away. He just wasn't ready for her to see him so reduced.

His colleague, Neil Wilcox – Coxy, as they knew him – had been in to visit him first and had come out of the room ashen. He'd warned her that it was probably better for now that she didn't see him. She hadn't understood until she'd finally been allowed in. He was no longer the man she had married. No longer the man she'd known.

His body was emaciated, even after a month of recuperation. He was broken and twisted. He'd lost three fingers from his right hand, apparently removed during the torture, and she could see the strange bends in his limbs where broken bones had been left to set badly. His eyes had been damaged by months in the dark without any light, his lungs had been burned by smoke and his body peppered with shrapnel and lead pellets where they had taken pot-shots at him for fun.

Ripley had sat with him, that first time, and just held his hand as he wept. It was the first time she'd ever seen him cry. She didn't know what to say. Neither did he. He was home, but he would probably never be back. And so it went on, day after day as she came back to visit him. Sometimes being allowed in, and other times being turned away by apologetic nurses.

"He's had a bad night," they would say. Or *"He needs his rest."* But what they really meant was: *"He can't face seeing you. He can't stand to look at the life he could have had. You're setting him back."*

He couldn't talk to her about what had happened or where he'd been, so more often than not, they simply sat in silence. She found herself talking gently to him about what was going on in their old world – things she'd changed in the flat, something she'd seen on her travels, or tales of friends and family. She did her best to keep away from difficult topics, but it all felt so mundane and patronising – not at all how they had ever talked. More than anything, she wanted him to talk to her. John had clearly suffered a great deal, but she was his wife – surely they could talk it through together? She, of all people, should be able to help him through this.

The doctors had told her to keep their conversations light, but that had never been the way they communicated, and Ripley had to admit to finding it hard. She wanted to talk to him about her work, about their future and where they went from here. She wanted to help him see that he could come back from whatever brink he was on.

Slowly, as the weeks had passed, she'd begun to see glimpses of her husband in the shell of a man she visited. The faintest trace of a smile at a fond memory of a time before all of this. But she could also see, far too clearly, in his hollow, terrified eyes that he had seen things he would never recover from. It was almost as though every small step towards recovery reminded him how far away he'd gone, and how lost he'd been. And the clouds would rush back in.

Sometimes, out of nowhere, he would become angry and frustrated. Ripley had learned to recognise those as her cues to leave him alone, much as she hated to do so. She couldn't fight his demons for him. The doctors had told her of frequent nightmares, insomnia, paranoia, headaches. She had seen with her own eyes the sudden panic at a sharp sound beyond the doors, felt his hands shaking in hers.

She knew the doctors were helping him with medication, sedating him if he became too distressed, slowly easing him into the journey through therapy that would probably continue for the rest of his life now. She wished she could do more, but this was beyond her skillset, even as a loving partner. All she could do was stay level, keep coming to visit, hide her trepidation and hopefully, slowly, reel him back from the edge.

The nurse manning the desk in the ward looked up and smiled at her.

"You're early," she said, sounding impressed.

"It was a clear run today," Ripley replied. "How is he?"

The nurse looked sympathetic; she knew what Ripley was really asking: *Will he let me see him today?*

"He seemed brighter when I went in this morning," she said. "A better night last night, by all accounts. Dr Lister's been in to see him. He's on his rounds now, but he wants to talk to you before you leave."

Ripley liked this particular nurse. She was sympathetic without being overly bubbly and upbeat, and Ripley was grateful for it. One of the other nurses was incessantly cheerful, and it just made Ripley want to punch her. She knew the woman was only doing her job, but the enforced cheerfulness made her feel patronised – like everything was being glossed over with this superficial veneer so that she wouldn't worry. Her husband was very sick and she couldn't stand anyone treating it like he'd just fallen over and scraped his knee.

"He even managed to eat some breakfast this morning, which is a good sign, isn't it?"

John had been struggling to eat properly since he'd come back. They'd often had to resort to a drip, slowly rebuilding his strength, acclimatising his body to proper nutrition again. The doctors were gradually pulling his physical form back into some kind of shape. His mind, on the other hand, was a far trickier entity.

She was so grateful that John was home and alive, but she wondered whether he would ever be able to live as they had done before. He would have to leave the forces, that much was clear. When he'd been captured, he'd been on his last tour before he was due to begin riding a desk, anyway. But he would be retired out of the service now, and that would be yet another mountain for him to climb.

John *was* the army; it was all he'd ever known. No one had broached the subject of leaving with him yet. It was far too early for any of those kinds of conversations. But Ripley knew he would struggle to find any peace outside the service. They taught you how to be a soldier – how to kill and how to survive – but they didn't teach you how to be a civilian again. Right now, she wondered if he'd ever even get to leave this hospital.

"Is he up for a visitor?" she asked, hating that note of forced cheerfulness in her own voice.

"I'll go and check, shall I? Take a seat."

It was the same each time. The nurses had to see what kind of mood he was in before anyone was able to go in. This was so far from any life Ripley had ever imagined for them, it was all she could do to remain positive. At least he'd come home alive. *Right?*

Ripley checked her phone was switched to silent while she waited. She'd once forgotten and the bright ringtone piercing through their conversation had thrown John into a frenzy. If he'd been stronger at the time, he could have hurt her quite badly the way he'd launched at her. She knew it wasn't aimed at her – it was the trauma – but it had scared her more than anything she'd ever experienced. The look in his eyes had been feral, and it had eroded another part of their relationship – her blind trust that he would never hurt her. She wouldn't make that mistake again.

She looked up as the nurse emerged from John's room.

"He's ready for you," she said, smiling. As she passed Ripley, she gave her arm a little squeeze. "And I think you'll notice a real difference in him today."

Ripley frowned. *What did that mean?* She gathered her things, took a deep breath and walked into John's room.

The curtains were open, casting a nice pale light into the room for once. She couldn't remember ever seeing the curtains open in here before. It made the room much brighter and more positive. John was propped up on the bed, surrounded by pillows, waiting for her. She stopped dead as soon as she saw him.

John had come home with a long, thick beard and thinning, shoulder length hair – both greyer than the dark brown he'd left with. He'd let the nurses shave his hair back to the military buzz cut he'd always had, but for some reason he'd refused to get rid of the beard. It had looked so strange on him, ageing him and changing the shape of his face. Ripley now realised that it had been hiding just how sallow and sunken his cheeks were.

Since she'd last seen him a week ago, John had shaved off the beard. He smiled when he saw her surprise. Her heart skipped. For the first time since he'd come home, she saw the man she used to know.

"What do you think?" he asked, as she crossed the room and stood beside his bed, staring at the transformation.

"I was just getting used to that beard," she said, smiling. "But this is much better."

"Coxy talked me into it," he said. "Said I needed to smarten myself up."

That was another thing Ripley had to thank Neil Wilcox for, then. John's colleague had been one of the few who'd kept in touch while he'd been missing, the only one who'd been able to look Ripley in the eye and understand her pain. And, of course, he'd been the one to break the news to her that they had finally located John, and that they had managed to get him out alive.

"It looks good," Ripley said. "And I hear you managed some breakfast this morning."

"Baby steps," he said.

Today was a good day. John had been very open about accepting his diagnosis of PTSD. She knew he'd seen enough other men returning with some degree of the disorder, but she hadn't expected him to accept the diagnosis in himself. The problem was that knowing what you had didn't stop you having it. When the panic hit, there was no point trying to rationalise it with explanations or diagnosis. They had agreed that every positive step, no matter how small, was a step towards recovery. *"Baby steps"* had become something of a mantra between them.

"Besides, it was a Full English," he said. "You know I can't resist a bit of bacon."

Ripley had a flash of comfortable Sunday mornings at the kitchen table, papers spread in front of them, the smell of bacon, eggs and sausage hanging in the air. Simple times they might never get back.

"Lucky you," she said. "I had a flapjack from the petrol station.

"Nice," John smiled.

"So, when did you see Coxy then?" asked Ripley. The problem with the unofficial visitor rota they'd worked out was that she never got to see Coxy anymore. And she would like to catch up with him at some point to get his view on John's marginal progress.

"He was in last night," he said. "He's signed me up for some new therapy group they're trialling."

Ripley frowned. She wasn't sure John would be in any state to join in with group therapy yet. He was still so volatile in his responses to any interventions.

"Oh yeah?" she asked. "What group is that?"

She saw him frown. One of the many side effects of his condition was erratic memory loss. He could sometimes shut down mid-sentence, forgetting what he was talking about, and the frustration would trigger another outburst. She hoped she hadn't just provoked one. He shook his head.

"Somewhere up North a bit. It's a residential thing. Pretty intensive. He left a flyer for you on the unit there," he said, clearly relieved to remember.

Ripley crossed and picked it up. It was a single page leaflet talking about a residential group therapy unit in a purpose-built home in the Lake District. Designed for returning soldiers with PTSD, it was designed to be a safe place where all thoughts could be openly discussed. The words intensive and effective featured a lot in the brochure, with suggestions of a speedy resolution to facing the future. Perhaps it was a good idea after all.

"Looks interesting," Ripley said, eyeing John over the top of the paper. "You going to try it?"

"Shouldn't think so," John said. "You know what I think about sitting around in groups sharing our feelings. Besides, places are limited."

Ripley wondered why Wilcox had even suggested it? John had always been incredibly dismissive of group therapy – saying it just reinforcing self-pity.

"But Coxy thinks it's a good idea?"

"Yes. He's just trying to help, I guess," John said. "He said it wouldn't be as bad as I thought, anyway. There's apparently only a handful of guys there. Coxy says they make me look normal."

"Charming," Ripley said. Gallows humour. The default fallback between John and his army mates. Take the piss first, worry about the consequences later. She decided to talk to Wilcox about the group and see what it was all about.

"Still," she said, putting the leaflet down again. "Can't hurt to try."

"We'll see," he said.

"I'm heading to the lakes to see Emma this weekend. I could drop in, if you like, check it out?"

"You don't need to do that," he said. "I don't think it's that kind of place, anyway."

He was shutting the conversation down already. She knew better than to push him on it further. She crossed to the window, looking out on the landscaped lawns and garden, perfectly designed for their calming influence. The hospital ran all the way around a central square, so that most rooms had a view of the gardens.

"Nurse says it's better for me to let the daylight in," John said, explaining the open curtains.

"She's probably right."

"I don't really like it," he said. "It makes me feel exposed."

"You want me to close them?"

"Not right now," he said. "Maybe when it's time to go."

She drew up the chair and sat beside him, taking his hand and feeling the quivering slow. He was trying so hard to come back. She'd forgotten just how tough he actually was. He must have gone through hell in the last three years, and just because he was home, didn't mean it was over yet. *Baby steps.*

3

DC DANIEL COTTER locked the squad car and cut back through the trees on the side of the church car park to meet his colleague, DS Helen Dunn, in the gardens at the front of the building.

They'd had the call moments after getting into the office this morning. A dead priest. Murdered. Discovered by a cleaner. Though murder was always a shock, Cotter was actually secretly pleased to have something big to get his teeth into.

He was only a few weeks into the new job here in Penrith, having transferred to the bigger Cumbrian town from his small village of Kirkdale. He had jumped at the chance of moving from a village where everyone knew his name, and where the victims of crime were all people you knew everything about.

He hadn't thought he'd get the promotion to detective, but he'd had the support of a local forensic officer that he'd worked with on a previous case, Emma Drysdale. Whatever she'd said in his favour had worked – he'd got the job.

"Where did you leave it this time?" Helen asked, eyebrow raised. His partner still hadn't let him forget the last time he'd been left to park the fleet car and had blocked an ambulance bay outside the health centre.

"There's a car park round the side," Cotter said.

"Lucky for you."

Dunn was supportive and open, but took every chance she got to rib him for being a boy from the backwaters. And, while he often felt out of his depth here, she was a good boss who had really helped him settle in. Of course, she took the mickey out of him herself, but she hadn't let any of their other colleagues get away with it yet.

"You ready?" she asked.

Cotter nodded. "Let's do it."

"It's quite a grim scene, apparently. You're not going to freak out on me, are you?" She was half-smiling, but Cotter knew it was a serious question. This would be the first body they'd processed together – she needed to know he wasn't going to panic or throw up.

"Don't be daft, I grew up on a farm, remember?"

It was becoming something of an in-joke between them. She'd nicknamed him Farmboy from day one – shortened through overuse to Farm, which is what had stuck. He didn't mind. He still had a lot to learn about policing a big town, after being a lowly constable in the small village where he'd grown up.

"Besides, this isn't my first murder case. You don't need to worry."

He hadn't talked much to her about his last case – it still made him shudder. A spate of teenage deaths in his own village, all linked to supposed angel sightings. The case had uncovered some dark secrets too close to home, and Cotter was much happier now he'd left.

"Okay," she said. "But it *is* your first one with me, so follow my lead, do as you're told and this should all go smoothly."

"Yes, boss," Cotter said, clicking his heels.

He looked up at the church as they approached. He'd walked past it a few times since moving to Penrith, but only because it was a handy shortcut through the gravestones from the shops to his flat. He'd had more than enough religion growing up, and he'd been enjoying the distance from scripture that his new life here was giving him.

Stepping inside, he realised this building was a world away from the small and oppressive little church he'd grown up attending. This place was incredible – filled with light, and much larger than he would have imagined. Somehow churches often seemed smaller inside, but not this one. This was open and impressive, usually filled with a steady stream of tourists coming to view the many unique features. Not so today.

Apart from a couple of uniformed officers and the forensic team working at the front of the church, the place was empty, making it feel even bigger than perhaps it was. He and Dunn exchanged a grim nod, and walked down the central aisle to where the focus of the action was.

The beautiful light streaming in through the stained-glass windows seemed at odds with the scene at the front of the church. Cotter may not share the religious fervour of most of the inhabitants of his childhood village, but he couldn't fail to be moved by such an impressive monument to faith. It was all he could do to tear his eyes away from the stunning interior of the building to focus on the body ahead of him.

An elderly man lay on the stone floor, at the foot of a small altar in one of the side chapels. He was completely naked apart from a sash of deep crimson cloth draped over his crotch and, strangely, a ceremonial hat – a mitre – shoved awkwardly on his head. It was the kind of ornate head-dress a Bishop might wear – deep burgundy with a golden cross spanning the front – it looked as though it had been placed on his head after he'd died.

He lay splayed across a stain of blood, his legs folded up behind him as though he'd already been kneeling before he passed out. His right arm was bent up behind his back, his shoulder twisted at an unnatural angle. A thin slice, the full width of his neck, left the skin open and puckered. Blood below, pale blue skin above. His mouth was open, his thin grey hair matted with blood on the side where it had rested in the dark pool now drying on the stone beneath him. His left hand extended behind his head in a straight line, fingers outstretched, grasping for something unseen.

"Jesus Christ," Dunn said, earning her a sharp nudge from Cotter. "Sorry."

A young guy in full forensic gear handed them their own protective suits. He smiled at Dunn and nodded at Cotter.

"Stick these on for now," he said. "We're nearly done here."

He stood back, appraising an oblivious Dunn as she slipped easily into her paper suit. He paid no attention to Cotter at all. Cotter was getting used to the effect his partner had on people. She was tall, strikingly attractive with a sporty build that she owed to her passion for triathlon. Her pale green eyes beneath dark brows seemed to draw you in, and Cotter had even found himself staring at her awkwardly at times, though he had realised early on that he would be lucky to make it to the Friend Zone with her. Men were not her thing.

"Enjoying the view there, fella?" Dunn asked the forensic officer, pointedly, and Cotter grinned at the blush that flushed his cheeks as he closed his mouth and turned away from them. She winked at Cotter. *Not that oblivious, after all.*

Suited up, they stepped closer to the body. Another forensic officer crouched beside the man, examining his hands.

"What've we got?" Dunn asked, taking the lead as usual.

It was only when the officer looked up that Cotter realised who it was.

"Emma?" he said.

Of course. Emma Drysdale was a forensic officer for Cumbria Police, so it made sense that she would be here, but he hadn't been expecting to see her again quite so soon. She had been the one to recommend him for this job, after they'd worked together last year.

"Dan," she smiled, genuinely pleased to see him. "You got the job then? I'm so pleased."

"I did," Cotter said. "Thanks to you."

Emma stood up, stepping away from the body and turned to Dunn.

"I don't believe we've met," she said, and there was something about the way she said it that inferred she would have remembered.

"DS Helen Dunn," she said.

"Doctor Emma Drysdale."

They looked at each other for a moment, a slight smile playing on both of their lips.

"So, what's the score?" Dunn asked.

"He's the Assistant Priest here. The cleaner found him like this first thing this morning. As you can see, he suffered significant blood loss, which would have stopped his heart. Judging from the angle of the cut, he was on his knees when it happened. The attacker standing behind him, slicing left to right."

Dunn stepped back towards the chapel, bending to look at the body.

"So, he was praying then? Somebody steps up behind him and slits his throat?"

"Would that it was so simple," Emma said. "He has bruising on his right wrist, and a dislocated right shoulder. There is also a contusion at the base of the skull."

"So, a fight, then?" Cotter asked.

"A struggle, certainly."

"Why is he naked?" Cotter asked. "Where are his clothes? And what's with the hat?"

"That's one of the stranger things," Emma replied. "We found his clothes neatly folded and piled at the foot of the altar, shoes below the pile, scarf on top. There was a note tucked into the fold of his scarf."

Cotter looked at her, head angled inquisitively.

"A note?"

Emma led them both over to a pew where the forensic team had gathered and stacked a number of transparent bags of evidence from the scene. She picked up the bag with the note in it and handed it to Cotter. Dunn leaned over his shoulder as he held it up to the light to read it.

"*Nulla est Redemptio*," Dunn read. "What the hell does that mean?"

"I know this," Cotter said – he'd heard it enough times in his childhood. "No rest for the wicked."

"You think this is some kind of revenge killing?" Dunn asked. "Perhaps the Reverend was not so holy, after all?"

"I'm not sure," Emma said. "It's very precise, isn't it? Leaving him naked like this and making sure that we found the note. It seems too planned, too clinical for a revenge killing. But I'm no psychiatrist."

"Any idea when this all happened?"

"Hard to say," Emma said. "The church is cold, and he was lying naked on the stone floor overnight. Vicar says he should have finished with a group at about seven-thirty. She'd already gone home, so she didn't see him. The group meets over in the hall around the side of the building. He'd probably come back over here to lock up for the night."

"What do we know about the victim?" Cotter asked, realising that he couldn't look at the body properly. He desperately wanted to cover the man up, feeling the indignity of his death acutely in this beautiful place.

"The cleaners found him this morning, confirmed him as The Reverend Thomas Bainbridge, Assistant Priest. He's the guy who runs – ran – most of the community groups, Boys Brigade, flower arrangers, Messy Church, that kind of thing. His wife was out for the night, visiting her sister, she'd left him some dinner warming in the oven. She got home this morning to find it burned to a crisp, so we know he didn't make it home."

"Poor guy," Cotter said, looking at the body again, a rising feeling of sickness stirring in his gut. The naked corpse lying on the stone floor in this beautiful church made a gruesome image, but he had a strong stomach and had seen his share of blood, guts and gore on the farms of his youth. But it was these little details of the life lost that made him feel sick to his stomach.

"Where is she now? The wife?" Cotter asked, swallowing.

"She's through there with the vicar having some tea. They're both understandably shocked."

"We'll need to talk to them both," Dunn said. "See if they have any idea who would want to do something like this. You got any thoughts on that, yet?"

"No," Emma said. "But whoever did this, did a good job of cleaning up. So far, we've found no prints, no trace evidence, nothing. Except for the deliberately placed clues. We might find something when we're back in the lab, but it looks pretty clean so far."

Emma led them over towards the storeroom entrance, where a couple of yellow plastic markers identified other potential clues.

"It looks like the struggle started here. We found some scuff marks on the floor there which could be from the victim's shoes. Perhaps he disturbed his killer doing something in this storeroom."

"You think this was a robbery gone wrong?" Dunn asked, incredulously.

"No, I don't," Emma replied. "The scene is too constructed. I think whoever did this came here with the intention to both kill and shame. What I don't know is whether Reverend Tom was a premeditated victim, or if he just happened to be in the wrong place at the wrong time."

"To my mind," Dunn said. "It looks like the Reverend here has been a naughty boy sometime in his past, and his victim finally snapped. They come here to get their revenge, kill him, strip his clothes off and write the note so everyone will know what he did. Job done."

Cotter walked slowly back towards the body, trying to imagine the scene that had played out. A struggle. The elderly vicar forced across the body of the church, pushed to his knees in front of an altar while his throat was slit from behind. That much was plausible, but he didn't understand the rest. The killer staying after the event and taking the time to undress his victim, fold his clothes into a neat pile, place a note on top for others to find. A note which created a suggestion of motive, but didn't provide enough detail to explain anything.

"I don't think that's right," Cotter said.

"Oh, really?" Dunn asked, intrigued.

"Well, it feels a bit obvious, doesn't it? Priest does the dirty, victim turns attacker."

"It wouldn't be the first time there was some sex scandal involving a priest though, would it?" Dunn said.

"No, but if you'd been a victim of something like that, and you've come here to kill him, the last thing you would want to do is see him naked again, is it?"

"He's right," Emma said. "Unless there was mutilation, why strip the body? The murder and the note would be enough, wouldn't it?"

They all turned at the sound of a throat being politely cleared behind them. A woman in clerical vestments stood beside one of the pillars watching them, unwilling to step closer to the scene.

"Are we able to cover him up at all?" she asked. "Tom would hate to be exposed like that."

"You know the victim well?" Dunn asked.

"I'm the vicar here," the woman said. "Judith Clay. Tom was a good friend. This is just awful."

Cotter could see she had been crying. Her dark, shoulder length hair tucked back behind her ears, her cheeks still tinged with a red puffiness. Cotter placed her in her late thirties, maybe early forties. Tall, straight-backed, kind face.

"Pleased to meet you," he said, stepping forward. "DC Daniel Cotter, and this is my colleague DS Helen Dunn."

She smiled gently, sadness fighting with politeness.

"Would it be possible to have a quick word, while the other officers finish up here?" Cotter asked.

"Of course," the vicar said.

Cotter nodded to Dunn. He'd already established that she was not great at lending a sympathetic ear. She had a more direct approach to policing, which was effective most of the time, but she recognised his ability to coax small truths out of witnesses without them realising what they'd said.

They hadn't tested the split of forces on anything as serious as murder yet, but Cotter saw that she was willing to give him a chance. He left her leaning over the Reverend's body with Emma, deep in conversation.

COTTER SLID INTO the pew beside the vicar and angled himself round to face her as much as the high-backed seat would allow. She smelled faintly of perfume and baked goods. Her head remained bowed for a moment before she turned and looked at him, eyes still glistening.

"Sorry," she said. "It's all been rather a shock."

"I can imagine," Cotter saw. "It's awful."

Judith Clay nodded.

"How long have you been vicar here?" Cotter asked, knowing that he should give her time to breathe between the difficult questions.

"Three years now," she replied. "I moved here from Yorkshire."

"How did the community take to you?"

"What? With me being a lady vicar?" she asked, slightly defensively. "Most of them were more than happy to welcome me."

"I meant on account of you being from Yorkshire," Cotter said, and she managed a weak smile.

"Oh, they're still getting used to that," she said.

She waved a hand, dismissing it.

"You said you were friends with Reverend Bainbridge?"

"Yes," she replied. "He was delighted when I accepted the position. He'd been doing the bulk of the ministerial duties for almost six months and was quite tired of it – he liked all the community activities, but the sermons were not really his thing."

"What was he like?"

"Tom? Just delightful. A charming man. Kind, thoughtful, caring." Her voice caught. "I just can't understand why anyone would want to hurt him, let alone…"

"So, there were no disputes that you knew of? No history that may have come back to haunt him?"

"You'd have to ask his wife about any history," she said, and then shook her head. "No, it's just ridiculous. Tom was a pillar of the whole community, not just the church. He spent all of his time helping people, raising money for all sorts of causes, volunteering for various charities. I don't know how he found the time. There is no way a man like Tom could have any enemies."

"And he was married, you say?" Cotter asked.

Judith nodded.

"Yes, poor Janet. She's through the back with Di and Jane now – the cleaners. It was Di who found him. I just don't know how poor Janet will cope without him." Her voice cracked again. Tom had clearly been very dear to her.

"Would you say it was a good marriage?" Cotter asked, feeling awful for even broaching the subject, knowing the insinuation which would inevitably follow.

"One of the better ones," Judith said, honestly. "They've just celebrated their fortieth anniversary. As far as I know there were no problems between them at all, barring the odd night of heavy snoring forcing Janet into the spare room."

"What about children?"

"They had two, a boy and a girl, both grown up and moved away, but they always come home for Christmas. I've met them a few times. They've always seemed like a happy, normal family. Their son's a bit of a wild child, but nothing serious."

"There was no family animosity, in your opinion?"

"No. Lord no," she frowned, thinking about what he'd just asked. "You can't possibly think one of his family did this?"

"I'm just trying to establish a picture of the victim. What happened to him was awful, but the way his body was left seems to be sending a specific message."

"Because of the mitre?" she asked. "Why would they put that on him?"

"What significance does it have to you?" Cotter asked. He had to admit to being a little stumped by the hat himself.

"I'm not sure," Judith said. "It's used in some churches for more formal ceremonies, but not here."

"It's not from this church?" Cotter asked. For some reason he assumed it had been.

"No," Judith replied.

"Can you think of any reason someone might think the Reverend was a wicked man?" Cotter asked.

"*Wicked?* No, why do you ask that?"

"His clothes, deliberately removed, were left in a neat pile, with a note tucked in to the top. Tom Bainbridge's attacker wanted us to find the note, and know that it had been put there, rather than having fallen out of his pocket."

"A note? What did it say?"

"*Nulla est redemptio,*" Cotter replied. "No rest for the wicked."

"No *escape* for the wicked, technically," Judith said, distractedly. "From hell, that is. It's a quote about the Last Judgement. *In inferno nulla est redemptio* – there is no redemption in hell."

She fell silent, clearly considering the repercussions of the words.

"We wondered if, perhaps, something Tom Bainbridge had done, you know, in the past, maybe…" Cotter began.

"No," Judith said sharply, her voice loud enough to silence the rest of the room momentarily. She hushed again, but lost none of the insistence. "What happened to Tom last night was disgusting and despicable. Plain evil. He was a good man. There is absolutely no way that he was ever involved in anything sordid. No way."

"How can you be so sure?" Cotter asked.

He didn't want to push her too hard in her time of grief, but he was well aware how easy it was to be deceived by those good at hiding their past. It had happened to him with people he'd known all his life.

"Because I knew him," she said, looking Cotter in the eye. "I worked with him every day. I saw the way he was with everyone he met, young and old, male and female. I saw the way people responded to him. People trusted him. People loved him. Whatever you think that note means, it's got nothing to do with scandal, or sex, or abuse. I'm sure of that."

She breathed deeply.

"I have to ask," Cotter said, quietly.

"I know," Judith admitted, shaking her head. "But that line of questioning is a waste of time, I can promise you that much."

Whether or not that was true, Cotter realised there was no point pursuing it with her. He didn't get the sense that Judith Clay was hiding anything. She seemed genuinely shocked by what had happened to her friend.

"Do you think it could be a case of mistaken identity?" Cotter asked. "Is there anyone else who works here who may have made any enemies along the way?"

"Look," she said, turning to face him fully. "I may not have been here long, but I know my team. There is nobody I can think of who would deserve to be treated the way Tom has, and there has never been any hint, as far as I am aware, of any scandal or crime connected to the parish or any of its staff. It may be boring. It may even sound unrealistic, but please bear in mind that anything you may have read in the press about members of the clergy is not representative of the majority of us. We are good, kind people. And what happened here was nothing short of evil."

"Perhaps the note refers to the killer, not the victim," Cotter said, thinking aloud.

"Hmm?" she questioned.

"I don't know," Cotter said. "I'm sorry. I'm just trying to make sense of it. Can you tell me a little about what was going on at the church last night? I understand there had been some kind of group that Tom Bainbridge was running?"

"The Boys Brigade," she replied. "It's a bit like the scouts. Only it's all boys. They're a good bunch, get on well with Tom. It was only the young ones last night, as the older boys are all rehearsing for the Whitsun parade. They would have finished around seven. The parents usually come in for the last few minutes to see what the boys have got up to. Tom likes to get them doing stuff, you know? Building things, or making circuits, carving, drawing, painting. You name it, Tom can explain it."

She stopped, the realisation that he would no longer be there hitting her again.

"I'm so sorry," Cotter said, automatically. "I know this is hard, but the more we know, the quicker we can catch the culprit."

"You think you will?" Judith asked, eyes filling with tears again.

"We'll do our best," Cotter replied.

"I can give you the names of the boys in the group, maybe their parents will be able to shed more light. Perhaps someone saw the killer but just doesn't know it yet."

"Perhaps," said Cotter, thinking it unlikely. Nothing about this seemed incidental. The more Cotter heard, the more he felt that Reverend Tom Bainbridge had been deliberately targeted by someone who had been studying his routine for enough time to know when he would be alone in the church, and even when he might not be missed at home for several hours.

"A list of the names would be very helpful," he said. "And, of course, if you think of anything at all that may help – someone odd hanging around recently, any arguments, upsets, anything at all – please let us know."

"Of course," she said.

"Do you think his wife would be able to talk to us?"

"Not today, I shouldn't think," Judith said. "It's been a terrible shock."

"Of course," Cotter said. "We'll finish up here as quickly as possible and get Reverend Bainbridge moved to the coroner's office. There's a family liaison officer on the way to go through everything with Mrs Bainbridge. Would you be able to stay with her until they get here?"

Judith simply nodded. There was no question she would do everything she could to help. After running through a few more questions, Cotter stood up, thanked her and went to join the team.

He found Dunn and Emma Drysdale deep in conversation about the significance of the hat they'd found shoved onto Reverend Tom's head. They both turned to him as he approached.

"What did she say?" Dunn asked.

"That he was very much loved, hugely respected, and there is no way that he could have been involved in anything sordid."

"Of course not," Dunn commented.

"Actually, I believe her," Cotter said. "Or at least, I believe that it's her opinion of him. She's giving me names and details for the kids who were here at the scout group thingy last night. We can see what their parents have to say."

"Good stuff," Dunn said. "What about the wife?"

"Too devastated to talk for now. I said we'd let the Family Liaison Officer take care of her, maybe we can talk to her tomorrow."

"Fair enough. What else did you find out?"

"The hat," Cotter said. "According to the vicar, it's not theirs. She's never seen it before. So, it might be worth focussing some effort on where it came from."

"The killer brought it with him?" asked Dunn. "What the hell for?"

"It must be part of the message," Emma said. "Buggered if I know what, though."

Tom looked at the deep red mitre hat, wrapped in an evidence bag, balanced on top on the Reverend's clothes. There was definitely a message here, but they were all missing it.

"You know who'd love this, don't you?" Cotter said, grinning at Emma.

"Dr Alex Ripley," Emma smiled back. "And I'm seeing her this weekend."

4

DC DANIEL COTTER leaned back in his chair, dunking a chocolate digestive in his mug of tea. Dunn sat opposite him, her feet up on the desk, skimming through the folder of papers in her hand. Their desks were pushed up against each other, so that they could face one another while working.

"You worked with her before then?" Dunn said, looking up from the paperwork. "Dr Drysdale?"

"Yes, she ran forensics on the last case I did. She's very good. She was the one who put me up for this job."

"I must remember to thank her for saddling me with a farm boy as a partner." She winked at him playfully. "What's she like then?"

"She's great," Cotter said. "I mean, as far as I know, but then I've only really worked with her on that one case, and I hadn't worked with many senior forensic officers before that. But she cares about the victims, which I think is a good thing."

Dunn nodded.

"Strange one this, isn't it?" she said, looking at the report she'd made of the crime scene. "What do you make of the note?"

"I don't know," Cotter said. "I mean, on one hand it's really literal – *no escape for the wicked* – but then, according to the Vicar, Reverend Tom was absolutely *not* wicked, so why leave those words with his body?"

"Yeah, well, I know the Vicar is convinced he was a good man, but people can hide a lot, even from those closest to them. We see it all the time."

Cotter had seen that only too recently in his own village – people he'd thought of as good men and women, who had turned out to be killers, liars and cheats.

"Perhaps it's self-referential?" Cotter suggested. "What if the note is about the killer rather than the victim?"

"Sure, it's another option," said Dunn said. "But I'm not ruling out my Dodgy Reverend theory yet," Dunn continued.

"Even though the Vicar said he was a good man, a pillar of the community, Scout leader, all of that? Even his wife couldn't think of anyone at all who would want to hurt him."

"I'm just saying we should ask around a bit before we rule it out, okay?" Dunn said. "Usually those closest to the bad guys are the last to know."

She stood up and lifted a few sheets of paper off the printer – photographs from the crime scene, sent through by Emma Drysdale.

"He could also just be a random victim, couldn't he? Maybe the killer didn't care, so long as it was a man of the cloth" Cotter mused.

"Hmm," Dunn said, spreading the photographs across the desk. "I don't know, though. If it's just some straight up killing, even if it's the wrong guy, why go to the trouble of stripping the body, and putting on this ridiculous hat. I mean, it's not even the right religion this, is it? Isn't this kind of get up more of a Catholic thing?"

"No, I think Anglican bishops can wear them too," Cotter said. "But I'm no expert. Either way, it's not something an Assistant Vicar would ever wear, and it wasn't theirs, anyway."

"True," said Dunn. "So bringing it along is a lot of effort to go to, with a huge risk of being caught in the act, just to send a message. And who are they sending it to?"

"What are you two looking so confused about?"

The question had come from another detective in the team, Andy Rowland. A tall, solidly built guy, and a bit of a joker with a filthy tongue. Despite finding him a little intimidating at first, Cotter liked him. He was straight-up, helpful, and didn't seem to be point scoring at all, even with the inexperienced newbie. Rowland walked over and looked at the photographs on Dunn's desk.

"Jesus," he said. "Something go wrong at the tarts and vicars party?"

Dunn scooped the photographs up and turned them over.

"Have a bit of respect, will you?" she said, tersely.

"All right, keep your hair on," Rowland said, rolling his eyes at Cotter over Dunn's shoulder. "This your new case is it?"

"Yeah," Cotter said. "He was found like that this morning at the parish church."

"Murder?"

"Looks that way," Dunn said, not giving anything away.

Cotter hadn't seen her so snippy. He wondered what had gone on between the two of them in the past. Rowland clearly got Dunn's hackles up.

"Seems like a bad time to be a religious type," Rowland said, turning away. "Dropping like flies, they are."

Cotter stood up.

"What's that?" he asked, louder than he'd meant to.

Rowland turned back to them, looked at Dunn who hadn't responded, and then back at Cotter.

"Very end of last year, remember Dunn? That nun they found in the park. Hadn't she also been stripped naked?"

"Not quite. Her clothes were torn, but she wasn't naked. It was a completely different murder, anyway," Dunn said dismissively. "Besides, they arrested someone for that."

"Ah, but they had to let him go, though. Not enough evidence. Ask Meeks, it was his case."

Cotter looked quizzically at Dunn. Was this a pattern? She shook her head.

"It's completely different," she said again.

"And don't forget the boy at St Whotsits, the fancy school up the way. He was a choirboy, wasn't he?"

"Ever the conspiracy theorist," Dunn said, tucking the images of Tom Bainbridge into a new folder and slipping it under her arm.

"Don't blame me if you can't see a pattern."

"There is no pattern. Just leave me alone to get on with my own case," Dunn snapped.

Rowland smirked, head tilted facetiously, hands raised in mock defence. There was definitely history between these two. Cotter wondered if she'd tell him what it was.

"Come on," Dunn said to Cotter. "We've got to go."

Cotter frowned, surprised. He'd thought they were desk bound for the rest of the morning.

"Where are we going?" he asked, trotting to catch up with her as she stomped out of the room.

"Away from that wazzock," she muttered under her breath.

"What's the matter?" Cotter asked. "He seemed like he was just being helpful."

"You've got a lot to learn," she said. "The only person Rowland helps is himself. He can see that this is a good case, and he wants to get in on it. He's eyeing up a promotion."

"So, you don't think he's got a point? Could there be any connection with these other two cases?"

Dunn pushed the doors open to lead them out of the building into the cold drizzle. Cotter lifted his collar to cover his neck. If he'd known they were leaving the building, he'd have brought his coat.

"Of course I think there's a connection, but I wasn't going to give him the satisfaction of admitting it in front of him, was I?"

She strode across the car park and opened the driver's door of one of the squad cars.

"So, should we look at these other cases?"

"Absolutely, but not here," Dunn said. "I don't want to make a big thing of it until we have a bit more to go on. He'll just try to nick it off me. Come on, hop in," she said.

"Where are we going?"

"Dr Drysdale wants to see us over at her office," she said, smiling. "And there's every likelihood she'll be able to dig up most of the pertinent facts about those other two deaths from there, if we ask her nicely."

RIPLEY FOUND HERSELF wandering listlessly around their spacious, city centre flat more and more these days, restless and anxious.

Here in the flat, the radio was her constant company, burbling away in the background, filling the silent corners with noise, an echo of life. She felt like she was in some interminable hiatus. She couldn't concentrate on work, let alone think of what she should focus her investigations on next.

Her latest book – an investigation into Faith Healers – had come out at the end of last year, and she hadn't promoted it as much as she usually would. Not least because she had almost lost her life investigating a fraudulent faith healer after the book had come out, and now she wasn't so sure she wanted to get into anything else. Not now John was home and needed her support.

For now, she was keeping her mind occupied delivering a class once a week at the university in Manchester, and it was all she could do to keep focussed on her preparation for that.

The alarm on the oven pinged, and Ripley took her reheated lasagne to the table with a fork, a bag of salad leaves and a glass of wine. There was no point dirtying a plate, she thought, eating straight from the oven dish, and picking her salad out of the bag with her fingers.

Ripley flicked through a copy of the morning paper as she ate. The same old news filled every page – inefficient politicians covering their own backs and scrapping among themselves, the economy depressed, factories closing, parents killing children, children killing each other. She closed the paper again. It was all too much.

Clearing the remains of her meal, Ripley admonished herself for letting everything get to her the way it was. John needed her to be strong now, for both of them. She just wasn't sure where she was supposed to get that strength from.

She picked up her wine glass and headed to the sofa, feeling tired and achy. She had fallen asleep in front of a movie on that same sofa last night and had woken up stiff and disconcerted, watching a looping sequence telling her that the channel she had been watching was now off air. She promised herself she wouldn't do the same again tonight. A long bath and an early night would probably help. *Baby steps.*

She heard her phone vibrate on the kitchen counter. She hadn't turned it back off silent after leaving the hospital. She hauled herself up, unable to resist checking who it was. She didn't really want to speak to anyone, but what if the hospital was calling? What if something had happened to John? That underlying fear was with her constantly these days.

Looking at the screen, she smiled. It was her old friend Emma Drysdale.

"Emma," she said, happily. "Everything alright?"

"Hi Alex," Emma replied. "I'm very well. Sorry I haven't called earlier."

Theirs had never been a friendship which demanded regular contact to stay strong. They could go for months without speaking and pick up right where they left off, but Emma had been good recently about calling more regularly, especially since John had come home.

"God, don't worry," Ripley said. "I'm barely ever at home anyway."

Not strictly true.

"How are you?" Emma asked.

Ripley filled her in about John's progress. Emma was one of the few people that she could share all of her worries with without any fear of judgement. She knew Emma would understand.

"But he's getting the right kind of care there, do you think?"

"I think so," Ripley replied. "Sometimes I think he'd be better off somewhere private, you know, away from everything to do with the army. But then other times I think they owe it to him to make this better. It's going to be a long road."

"Are you still up for a weekend in the Lakes?"

The visit had been planned for weeks, and Ripley was really looking forward to it. Not just because she'd be seeing her friend again, but because she now wanted to drop in to this residential place Neil Wilcox was trying to get John into.

"Oh yes," Ripley replied. "I can't wait."

"Good, because there's something I want to pick your brain about while you're up here," said Emma.

Emma often called to ask her opinions about a case she was working on, and Ripley equally relied on her friend to access information she may not otherwise be able to get as a member of the public.

They had met at a conference on criminology where both had been guest speakers, and they had hit it off straight away, with Emma expressing her admiration of Ripley's careful negotiation of the complex lines between matters of faith and criminal behaviour – a role that had seen her dubbed The Miracle Detective by the press, and called in as a consultant any time a case had a religious angle to it.

The professional relationship had quickly turned to friendship, and both trusted each other's discretion and valued each other's trust.

"What's up?"

"I'm working on a case in Penrith," Emma said. "An assistant priest at the parish church was murdered, throat slit right open, earlier this week."

"Oh, that's terrible," Ripley said. "Inside the church?"

"Yes," Emma replied. "But that's not the worst of it. He was stripped naked, his clothes folded and placed on a bench and a note tucked into the top."

"What was on the note?" Ripley's interest was already piqued – stripping a victim's clothes suggested ritual, purpose, orchestration.

"A Latin phrase, *nulla est redemptio*, which the Vicar suggested may refer to the Last Judgement. We just can't figure out what the killer is trying to say with it."

"I've heard the phrase," Ripley said. "But it can have a number of interpretations. It's hard to say without more context."

"I guessed as much. Anyway, the police have just flagged two more cases that they think may be tied in to the same killer.

Different victim types, different MO, but just enough to make us think there might be a connection. Look, I know we were going to have a weekend of wine and walking, but I wondered if you'd mind having a quick shufty at what we've got so far? See if there might actually be a religious take on it or if we're barking up the wrong tree?"

"Sure," Ripley said, jumping at the chance of something to focus on. "Send me what you've got, and I'll take a look at it tonight."

"Really? That's great," Emma said. "Dan will be pleased to hear that."

"Dan?" Ripley asked.

"Yes, our young friend Daniel Cotter has left the clutches of Kirkdale and started the move up the greasy pole. He's a Detective Constable now, up in Penrith. This is his first big case with them."

"Poor kid," Ripley said, smiling. "He can't seem to shake us, can he?"

Ripley had a soft spot for the young policeman. She'd met Daniel Cotter on a case she'd helped him with in the Lake District last year. Come to think of it, Emma Drysdale had got her involved in that one too, sending her into the heart of a small, god-fearing community with a secret from the past that had locked them all in a self-destructive spiral of religious superstition.

Ripley smiled at the thought of working with him again. He was one of the good guys, and she was glad to hear he'd moved out of Kirkdale. Even though it had been his home all his life, that village had something toxic about it. A soft lad like Cotter would do better out of its grasp, somewhere he could learn and grow and see a bit of the world.

"Send me what you've got," Ripley said again. "I'll have a look, and we can talk about it when I get up there tomorrow."

She hung up feeling energised. It would be good to have something concrete to focus on.

5

FOLLOWING A HURRIED breakfast, Ripley loaded her overnight bag into the boot of her old Audi and slammed it shut, automatically pressing down on the centre of the boot to make sure the lock had properly engaged. Not least of the old car's problems was that the boot had a tendency to fly open while you were driving along.

The files that Emma Drysdale had sent across the night before had been fascinating, and Ripley was as sure as she could be that there was a connection between at least two of the deaths, if not all three. Despite the fact that they had been killed in different ways, there were certain clues the killer had left which had set off alarms in Ripley's mind.

Before she left, she'd called Neil Wilcox to tell him she'd be away for the weekend, and to get his view on whether she should drop in on the centre he had suggested.

"Great idea," he'd said. "Everything I've heard about them is good, if a little unorthodox. I'm not sure it will work for John, but he's willing to give it a go, and at least all the guys involved know exactly what it feels like to live with PTSD. It'll do him good to know he's not the only one. I'll let them know you're coming, if you like?"

"I don't want to seem like I'm interfering."

"Nonsense. I can't think of anyone better placed to check out whether they're a bunch of quacks and phonies."

He'd assured her he would be going in to see John over the weekend anyway to get him ready for the move, and he'd call her on her mobile if he needed her.

The cold engine was hesitant to start, but Ripley knew she just had to be patient with it. It hadn't let her down yet. Pulling out of her street, she wove through the back streets of Manchester, heading for the motorway. She had a few hours' drive ahead of her, with plenty of thinking time once she cleared the city.

The three separate murders Drysdale had sent her details of had occurred just about close enough together to be some kind of spree. The first had happened just before Christmas, some six months ago now, the second in March in a different part of the city, and now this third in the heart of the city, only this week.

The first had been a young boy, Dylan Parker, just twelve years old, and a chorister at St Michael's Church of England School in a suburb just to the north of Penrith. Dylan had been found in the school gardens, almost a full day after he had been reported missing.

He had been half-buried in some flower beds in a wooded area of the school grounds, stripped to the waist. The photographs Emma had sent showed his naked chest and shoulders emerging from the ground as though he was trying to climb out of his grave. The bizarre, deliberate placement of the body was a detail they'd fortunately managed to keep from the press for now.

There had been no evidence, thankfully, of sexual assault, and Dylan's trousers, shoes and socks were still on his body when they dug him up, though the rest of his clothes had never been recovered.

Despite Dylan's death clearly being a murder, there had been almost no other evidence for the police to go on. His bicycle had never been recovered, and his mobile phone had been switched off while still at school, and never turned back on again, meaning that the choir room was the last confirmed location anyone had for him.

He'd been the last boy to leave choir practice, having helped – as always – to put the song books away. Everyone else involved in the choir, including the choirmaster, had alibis which checked out.

The choirmaster had watched him cycle away from the building towards the gardens, never to return. The assumption was that his killer must have been lying in wait.

After the choirmaster and the other boys had all been eliminated from their enquiries, the police had turned the finger of suspicion on Dylan's step-brother, Hayden, who had a couple of charges for violent assault, and was in and out of trouble all the time. But his alibi was as good as watertight too – his girlfriend of the time confirming that they were together at her house on the other side of town at the time of his step-brother's murder.

The head teacher, Mr Hanson, had insisted that Dylan was well-loved and popular, a bright young thing on the scholars programme and destined for great things. None of them could understand why he had been attacked and left the way he had.

While the case was still open, and the police were doing what they could to come up with answers for Dylan's family, any tenuous leads they may have found had long since dried up. According to everyone they'd interviewed, Dylan was a charming, popular boy, who worked hard at school, shone in the choir, and was helpful and kind.

Despite his young age, he volunteered at the homeless shelter every Saturday, washing dishes and clearing tables in the soup kitchen. He'd even done a sponsored run and managed to raise several thousand pounds for the charity after his efforts bagged him a spot on the local news. It seemed he was a model child, and nobody who knew him could understand why anyone would want to hurt him.

The second victim had also been found outdoors, in a park in the middle of the town. An elderly nun, Sister Francis Burr, had been found kneeling beside a bench by the park warden when he opened up. She had been stabbed just once, just below the left breast, puncturing her lung. Her body had been propped up on her knees, head resting on clasped hands, leaning against the bench – arranged to look like she was praying.

When the police had finally moved her, they found that her habit had been sliced all the way up the front, exposing her completely as soon as she was moved.

She had been gripping a generic, dog-eared copy of the New Testament – the kind you'd get in Sunday Schools and small churches across the country. All the other residents of the convent swore blind they'd never seen it before. Sister Francis apparently had her own Bible, which she had inherited from her grandmother and kept safely in her rooms. The assumption was that the killer put the bible in her hand, but there were no clues as to why.

According to her report, Emma Drysdale had found no evidence of sexual assault despite the fact that her clothing had been cut open. And again, no other leads checked out. There was no evidence showing how Sister Francis had got into the park, though the old warden was certain no one had been there when he'd done his rounds before locking the gates the previous night.

No one at the convent could think of anyone with a grudge against her, or anyone that she may have wronged. Apart from, perhaps being a little persistent with her donations tin on the high street, there seemed to be no evidence that she'd upset anyone. Again, the assumption was that she had simply been in the wrong place at the wrong time.

Given the different nature of the two crimes, and the relative distance between them, the cases had been handled by different teams within Police Cumbria and, until yesterday, no connection had been made.

But this most recent murder had given the police cause to think that there may be a link. All three victims had been arranged post-mortem to send some kind of message. All three had been left naked or exposed. No motive had been established for any of the victims, though there was now a suspicion that they had been deliberately targeted because of some kind of religious affiliation, and that is why Emma had wanted her to look at the files.

Ripley didn't yet know how the other two murders tied in with the Reverend Tom Bainbridge's, and she was as stumped by the strange note – *Nulla est Redemptio* – as the others were. An interesting detail, but barely enough to build a theory on.

She had looked the phrase up online, discovering that Pope Paul III had used the quote when facing complaints about Michael Angelo's painting of the Last Judgement in the Sistine Chapel. It was also part of a phrase which appeared in medieval poetry, which in itself had come from a Catholic prayer cycle, so the potential meaning could be in any of those vast areas.

Without knowing what the note related to, the strongest suggestion the police had so far was that it pointed to some darker secret in the Reverend Tom Bainbridge's life. But Ripley wasn't so sure. There had been no notes left with the other bodies, but there had been other, similar clues. The precise way each of the bodies had been positioned, for example, had prompted a small theory in Ripley's mind, and she was keen to talk to Emma and get a look inside the church to find out if she was right.

After she had been through all the files Emma had sent, Ripley had spent some time looking into Reverend Tom online. He had a profile attached to the church's website, and he certainly seemed to be living a very generous, honest life – involved in most of the clubs, groups and societies that met at the church. He had a lovely, warm smile and eyes that danced, even in the flat photographs online.

The nature of his death, being so brutal and exposing, was as far removed from the world he had lived in as any Ripley could think of. Revenge killings were usually passionate, quick affairs, but this killer had known they would have time to position the body exactly how they wanted, constructing a tableau for the police to find.

Ripley had arranged to meet Emma Drysdale at a cafe near the church. They would go in together. She felt like she needed to see the scene for herself to make sense of it all, even though it would have all been cleaned away and re-opened to the public.

It felt strange to be back in the Lake District again, and Ripley was hoping that this time would be less dangerous than her last visit. She'd been helping Emma and Daniel Cotter to investigate a spate of teenage suicides which had been linked to some angel sightings in a small village near Windermere. She had almost lost her own life in one of the lakes up there, trying to solve a case which still haunted her now. Perhaps this visit would help to exorcise some of those ghosts.

She peeled off the motorway and was beginning to carve her way through the narrow lakeside lanes, flanked by low, neat grey stone walls which seemed to have become so much a part of the landscape that the trees actually grew out of them or through them – nature and man joining forces in the most unlikely way.

Ripley had deliberately taken the slightly longer detour off the motorway to enjoy the scenery here. Often bleak, even at this time of year, but always spectacular. Great mountainous ranges folded into flat farmland, edging on to huge, clear lakes. Sheep dotted the hillsides, clambering up impossible rock faces, or emerging from low verges onto the carriageway with the bullish confidence of the simple beast.

The now familiar moorland rose up to her right, lush green grass and moss, tinged with deep crimson reds from the low-lying bracken – burned by winter freeze and not yet regrowing for spring. On her left, just by the roadside, was Ullswater – one of the larger bodies of water in this area of the UK. The lake stretched away for miles, reflecting the pale blue sky, the clouds above heavy and full with the rain that had been forecast for the first part of the week. June already, and summer was still hiding its face.

Even now, despite the cool temperatures and the fact that the lake itself couldn't have been more than a few degrees, she spotted a group of teenagers at one of the many outdoor adventure centres along the water's edge, being led into the water by an instructor in his mid-twenties, bellowing enthusiastic encouragement at them all as squeals and screams of shock and delight rose from their throats.

At least they've gone in by choice, she thought, unlike those poor girls in her previous case up this way. A brief flash of the figure of an angel slipping beneath the roiling surface of the angry lake hit her, and she had to blink a couple of times to reset the image to the more simple, happy scene of teenage kids splashing into the water she was actually seeing.

She swerved as a branch at the roadside thwacked against the passenger side of the car. She needed to concentrate on the road and not let the ghosts of the past distract her like that.

She took the turning which would lead her through Pooley Bridge and on up to Penrith. It wouldn't be long now.

EMMA DRYSDALE WATCHED her old friend hurry across the road just as the pedestrian crossing light had changed back to red, eliciting frustrated hoots from the waiting car. She smiled at the withering look the driver got from Ripley for his trouble. She loved the fact that the esteemed and inimitable Dr Alex Ripley could give out such attitude with just a sideways glance.

Ripley didn't suffer fools gladly, could spot a snake oil merchant from a block away, and was quick to defend the vulnerable. Emma admired her more than most people she'd met. She was also an excellent drinking buddy and a great storyteller which counted for a lot in Emma's book.

The bell tinkled over the door as Ripley came into the tea room, smiling as she saw Emma.

"I got you a coffee," Emma said, hugging her friend. "It's great to see you."

"You too," Ripley said, shedding her coat and sitting down.

"Sorry to railroad our walking weekend," Emma said.

"Don't worry. I'm glad to have something to focus on, to be honest. I feel like I've been going a bit mad."

"Is it that bad?" Emma asked.

"Sometimes," Ripley replied, taking a grateful sip of her coffee. "It's wonderful that John is back home, and alive, but it's just so... hard. It's hard to see him like he is."

"I can't even begin to imagine," Emma said. "Is he getting better though?"

Ripley shrugged.

"Yes," she said. "On balance, I suppose there are little changes every time I see him. At least he's got rid of his beard now. It felt like he was keeping it to hold on to the memory of who he'd been forced to become out there."

"He just needs time," Emma said. "What he must have gone through..."

"I know," Ripley said. "It doesn't bear thinking about."

She smiled sadly. Emma hated seeing her like this, and genuinely couldn't imagine what she was going through. She had supported Ripley during the darker times while John had been missing and, if she was honest, she had always just imagined that he'd been killed in action. For him to turn up again, all these years later, having been held prisoner by the enemy, tortured and abused, was incredible. She didn't know how either of them were coping with it.

"He's in good hands though, right? The doctors know what they're doing?"

"Seems so," Ripley replied. "They're great, and he is definitely improving all the time, but he is just so far removed from the man I married, and I feel awful for saying that, because how is he supposed to ever be that man again?"

Emma took her hand across the table.

"I just want him back," Ripley said. "The real him. The man I go to visit each week is not my husband. I don't know who he is. And just when I feel like giving up on him, I see a glimpse of John, hidden in there, deep and lost, and I know I have to stick with him. But it's just so hard."

"I'm so sorry, Alex," Emma said.

"Me too."

They both drank in silence for a moment.

"Right then," Ripley said, stoically. "Enough of my misery. Let's talk about your case."

"Sure. What did you think of the possible connection?"

"It makes sense, I think," Ripley said. "I mean, there are enough similarities between the three that it's plausible you could have a serial killer on your hands."

Emma stiffened. Even though the cases had connections, they hadn't yet used the words *serial killer*. It was such an emotive label, and one that the press would jump on straight away, searching out the goriest, most gruesome details of each case, and probably fuelling the fire for the perpetrator to do more.

"But," Ripley continued. "Apart from the fact that all three victims had a religious connection of sorts, I can't quite see the motive yet."

Emma frowned, realising that she had been hoping that Ripley would turn up with some great theory about the phrase on that note, or the way the bodies had been found, which would explain everything. It was never that easy.

"Don't look so dejected," Ripley smiled at her. "It doesn't mean I can't help. I mean, there is still the religious connection, I just can't quite make all the pieces fit yet. But I do have a theory."

Emma smiled again, settling back in her chair, coffee in hand.

"Go on," she said.

"Well, something about this Last Judgement idea is troubling me," Ripley said, finishing her coffee and pushing the cup away. "You know? From the note?"

"How so?"

"I got to wondering if the killer had made reference to it in the other deaths but the people investigating hadn't spotted it at the time. The note was such an obvious clue, left very deliberately. Why only post it on the third murder? Why with this victim?"

"Because the killer wants us to know this particular victim was wicked?"

"But no one who knows him agrees with that," Ripley said. "Every witness statement for all three say what wonderful people they were. Even the kid was volunteering in his free time."

"Sure, but we know from experience that people are not always what they seem, don't we?"

"I know, but if the killer was trying to expose some big dirty secret, then the note is too obscure. One phrase, three words, in Latin. It feels like he's taunting you. Scattering breadcrumbs to see if you'll follow the trail."

"You think he has a God complex?" Emma asked. "Thinking he can stand in judgement?"

"Maybe," Ripley said. "But then why target these specific people? Maybe Reverend Tom had something to hide, and if he did, I'm sure Daniel and his colleagues will find that out. But what about Sister Francis? Who could she have wronged that also knew Reverend Tom? And the choirboy? I mean, surely he was too young to have enemies? So how did they all come into contact with the killer?"

"I don't know," Emma said, feeling frustrated. She had hoped for clarity from her friend. "But you *do* think they're linked?"

"Yes. If not the victims themselves, then certainly the way they were arranged. The killer is trying to tell you something, and I'm pretty sure it has something to do with the Last Judgement."

Emma pushed her own cup away, clinking it against Ripley's in the centre of the table.

"Go on," she said. "What's your theory?"

"It's based on very loose research."

"You mean Google?"

"More or less. You said we could go into the church, right? Take a look around?"

"Of course," Emma replied. "I mean, technically it's open to the public again – we can do whatever we like. The vicar has been very helpful, so far. She said she'd be happy to talk to anyone on the investigation team about Reverend Tom."

"Does she know either of the other two victims?"

"I don't think they've asked her yet," Emma said. "The possibility of any connection has only just come to light."

Ripley was already on her feet, shrugging on her coat.

"Right. Come on then. Let's go and have a look at the church and see if my theory pans out."

IT MAKES MY skin crawl just sitting here. Not because I'm within meters of the dark blood stain that has yet to be erased, and not because of the solid stream of visitors parading past my quiet vantage point. Oh, those mawkish spectators, trying to catch a glimpse of the horror that has so far been vividly, but incompletely, reported. I watch them stream past, getting their selfie before moving on.

No, my skin is crawling because everything about this place is testament to the great lie. From the gilded shrines to the stained-glass windows, the cloying smell of incense and the turgid drone of that bloody organ – it all feeds into the lie. And simply being in here fills me with rage.

Will they see my message this time? Will she come? I suppose I can only hope. It's taken her far too long already.

My eyes are drawn to the door as two women walk in purposefully, side by side. Aha! There you are, Dr Alex Ripley. At last. And about time.

The excitement of seeing her here, knowing why she has come, prickles the sides of my tongue. Delicious and salty, making my mouth water. The game is finally on. The truth will out. My truth.

I close my eyes in delight, savouring the thrill of a plan coming together, and just in time too – the big day draws ever closer.

RIPLEY LINGERED JUST inside the doorway of the church. She had been in more religious buildings in her time than she could count, though few made her stop and reflect any more. Few were as bright, as open, or as welcoming as this one. The stained-glass windows sparkled and shone – bright from the inside, though completely unremarkable from the outside.

The large flagstones of the central aisle were worn in soft hollows from years of footfall. Pews lined either side of the main body of the church, beneath the large wooden balconies above. More pews sat up there, too, on all four sides of the building. A huge pipe organ dominated the far right-hand side of the back wall, framed by two floor-to-ceiling murals, both depicting angels – one showing the angel announcing Christ's birth to the shepherds, and the other, the angel appearing to Jesus in Gethsemane. Ripley turned away from them, she'd had enough of angels in recent times.

She and Emma walked on up the central aisle, with Ripley's gaze casting about at the hidden treasures each new alcove presented. Colourful stained glass, tombstone markers embedded in the slate floor, paintings, ornaments, a fantastic wooden eagle formed the back of the lectern, temporarily decorated with a hand sewn banner depicting Christ's ascension into heaven.

Instead of the usual reverential silence with the odd awkward cough, there was a general murmur of conversation around the building too, visitors were welcome here. And though Ripley was sure some among them had come specifically to see the site of the recent murder, the majority were simply tourists, foreign and domestic, visiting one of the country's wonderful churches as they enjoyed their holidays in the Lake District.

Smartphone selfie-takers posed in front of columns, altars and paintings, grinning at the camera, ticking off another spot on the tourist trail. Meanwhile earnest worshippers, both local and foreign, quietly went about their prayers. Both were rituals of a sort, and strangely neither seemed to disturb the other, despite being at such close quarters.

Ripley found the place quite breathtaking. Imagine the toil of building it, the foresight required to make the whole building feel so open and impressive, and yet have so many private spaces throughout.

Emma stopped and looked back at her, enquiringly.

"You okay?"

"It's beautiful," Ripley said.

Emma looked up at the ceiling, nodding. *That'll do. Come on.* Ripley knew her friend had never been much of a fan of organised religion. She moved on with Ripley following behind, eyes drifting to and fro across each new discovery. She promised herself time to explore properly once they'd done what they needed to here.

"Ah, Dr Drysdale, you made it," a short, friendly faced woman in a casual clerical blouse with a white collar approached them, smiling, abandoning a pile of prayer books on a pew. She had dark hair, dark eyes, an easy, relaxed manner, and a smile that made you feel instantly welcome.

"Thanks for making time for us again," Emma said, shaking her hand. "Reverend Judith Clay, this is Dr Alex Ripley. She's one of our police consultants, here to help us understand a little more about what happened to Tom."

Ripley greeted her, feeling comforted by the vicar's warm handshake and genuine smile. Too often recently, Ripley had found herself in small, isolated communities whose fear of change and deep distrust of strangers made her work almost impossible. She didn't feel any of that here.

"I'm sorry for your loss," Ripley said.

"It's been a terrible shock," Judith said, and Ripley caught a glimpse of her genuine sadness. "We've reopened the building today, for the first time, but I have to say it does feel very strange knowing that Tom is no longer here. I just keep expecting him to come bustling in like he always did, juggling three things at once."

"I understand Reverend Tom played a huge role in the community here," Ripley said.

"That's right. Boys Brigade, Messy Church, Outdoor Church, Breakfast Club, Flower Arrangers, cake sales, coffee mornings, fundraisers, choir practice. You name it, Tom would have a hand in it somewhere. He was a force of nature."

Whenever she spoke of him, Judith's eyes flitted towards the side of the church. Ripley followed her gaze, recognising the small chapel she'd seen in the crime scene photographs. The place where Tom's body had been found.

"You'll obviously miss him," Ripley said.

Judith smiled at her, clearly remembering that they were here to talk.

"We certainly will," she sighed. "Right. How can I help you both?"

"I don't want to take up too much of your time," Ripley said. "I've already read your statement to the police, so we don't need to go over any of that. I wondered if I could see where the body was found. I feel there is more to the message the killer left than we are seeing."

Judith Clay cocked her head, intrigued.

"You think he was definitely the target then?" she asked.

"We don't really know anything for now," Emma said quickly. "That's why I asked Dr Ripley to take a look for us. She's got a better eye for these kinds of thing than I have."

Emma had already warned her that the suggestion of a connection between Reverend Tom's murder and the other two was not something they'd shared with anyone outside the team yet. Ripley didn't want to slip up and give anything away but, from what she'd read online about the church last night, she was sure there was one thing the police had missed that would help to inform the other cases.

"Of course," Judith said. "Sorry. We are just desperate for answers here. His poor wife is out of her mind. Her daughter's with her – obviously upset too – but she's a solid sort, mum of three herself. She'll be a comfort to Janet. Follow me."

Rather than holding things back or hiding secrets from strangers, Ripley got the sense that Reverend Judith was quite the over-sharer. Emma obviously felt the same, as the look they exchanged as they set off across the church suggested.

The walls up both sides were lined with small chapels, which all displayed some relic, statue or tomb of special interest. Ripley had read that they had once been rooms for private services for well-off families, but were now open to the public. Worshippers could enjoy a more private devotion before statues, tapestries or paintings of the good shepherd, or any number of historical saints, the apostles, even Christ himself.

Each chapel featured a different stained-glass window, and each had a space for worshippers to pray, separated from the public by rope cordons or, in some, the original wooden altar rails.

In one, Ripley noticed an elderly couple, on their knees in prayer. Heads bent, mouths moving around silent words. They were in perfect unison, she noticed, hands clasped gently in front of their chests, heads bowed.

As they finished their prayer, both wrestled their old bodies back onto the bench behind them. It was only as they sat down, the man taking his wife's hand and squeezing it gently, that Ripley saw her wipe the tears from her cheeks. *Who had they been praying for?*

At the same time, a group of three late-teenage girls hustled into position in the aisle in front of the same chapel, faces pressed cheek-to-cheek, grinning as one of them held a smartphone at arm's length to snatch a photograph of them all in front of the golden altar below the glimmering stained glass. Photograph taken, they moved on, talking excitedly, entirely oblivious to the elderly couple, and completely devoid of any reverence. Ripley chided herself for judging. *Each to their own.*

Almost halfway along the body of the church, Reverend Judith Clay stopped and turned to them, hands automatically clasped in front of her.

"This is it," she said, forcing a smile.

Ripley noticed she had stopped well clear of the dark stain on the floor where Tom Bainbridge's blood had seeped into the stone. No amount of cleaning would shift that for several months yet – this porous old stone would hold that reminder for a while to come.

Ripley stepped forward to the rope cordon protecting the chapel from the visiting public. A polite laminated sign hung from the rope on both sides – "Reserved for Prayer Only".

There was one man at the far end of the last pew, half-hidden in the shadows, head bent, hands resting on his lap. Ripley thought he looked more like he was sleeping than praying. He wore a dark, heavy woollen coat, collar popped up, and a green and blue striped scarf. He lifted his head slightly and smiled at her, standing up and gathering his coat around him. Ripley smiled back, worried that they had disturbed his prayer.

He eased past them as he left the chapel, and as he did, he nodded courteously. A handsome man, with striking hazel eyes and a solid jaw.

"I'll leave you to it," he said.

Ripley was sure she heard him humming gently as he left. He didn't seem to notice the dark stain on the floor, but she saw Reverend Judith wince as he stepped over it, frowning as he passed her.

As he left, the vicar lowered herself onto one of the pews in the main body of the church, staying a safe distance from the chapel. Ripley didn't blame her.

Stepping up to the now empty chapel, Ripley looked around the small room, at the statue of Christ on the cross. His face was carved from old wood in a benevolent smile, though the stains of dark red on his hands and feet, and the stab-wound in his side, all spoke of his pain and suffering.

The altar in front of the statue was also made of wood, painted in deep blue and crimson and burnished with gold leaf – a narrow, rectangular pedestal with a small bronze bowl placed centrally on top of it. The paintwork had faded a little in places, the gold rubbed away by countless hands.

The stained-glass window above was made up of a collection of small panes, forming a geometric pattern. No biblical scenes depicted here, but bright reds and blues again, just like on the altar. Ripley thought the window was beautiful, marvelling again at how the building had looked so plain from outside, designed entirely to give the righteous inside a sense of God and light, as though it was their secret.

Despite all this, the chapel was nothing out of the ordinary, but that wasn't what Ripley was here for. She was here to see what Tom Bainbridge had seen in his last moments. Why had he been brought to this chapel in particular? And why had he been left naked, arm outstretched, right here in front of this altar?

She crouched down behind the stain on the floor, looking up at the altar, and the statue. She saw nothing different from here. Nothing that stood out. A small inscription in Latin on the base of the altar, but it had no connection to the message on the note.

"Have you got the photos?" Ripley asked Emma.

Emma handed her a mobile phone with the crime scene images called up on it. Ripley scrolled through until she found the photograph she was looking for – Tom Bainbridge, lying naked on the ground, his right arm bent behind his back where the shoulder had been dislocated in the struggle. His left hand stretching outwards above his head, index finger straightened with the others folded, pointing at something behind him.

"You said in your report that all the fingers on his left hand were broken apart from the index finger?" Ripley asked as Emma came over to stand just behind her, looking at the image over her shoulder.

"Yes," Emma said. "It looks like he was tortured before they cut his throat."

They kept their voices low. Judith was far enough away not to have to hear the details, but churches were designed to carry sound perfectly, and Ripley didn't want this discussion overheard by either the vicar or any of the visitors.

Ripley looked behind her, following the line of sight from where Tom's outstretched hand would have been, all the way to the wall behind.

"I actually think his fingers may have been broken after death, and arranged to look like this."

"Why?"

"To point us in the right direction," Ripley said, standing up and motioning for Emma to follow her as she crossed the small room into the shadows at the back.

On the dimly lit back wall, protected beneath a clear perspex sheet, was the fading remains of an old religious painting. Ripley got up close to the perspex, studying the crumbling, faded image below.

"Come and take a look," she said.

"What am I looking at?" Emma asked, leaning in beside her.

"It's an example of a doom painting," Ripley said, crouching down on the left-hand side of the wall. "I read about it online. You find them in churches all over the world, usually dating back to a time before the masses could read and spiritual guidance had to be given in pictorial form."

"Right," Emma said. "Very interesting."

Ripley had grown used to Emma's indifference to all things overtly religious or historical.

"In this case, it actually is interesting," Ripley replied.

"Why? What does it mean?"

"Doom paintings depict the day of judgement. The second coming of Christ. Where the blessed are raised from the grave and taken to God's side, and the wicked are cast into the flames of hell."

"Charming," Emma said. "But why is *that* interesting?"

Ripley couldn't help the smile that crossed her lips. Emma always made her work hard.

"Well, I think this is your clue," Ripley said. "It was mentioned on the church's website, but there were no pictures of it, and I wasn't sure it meant what I thought it did."

"Which is what?" Emma asked, sounding interested now.

"You know the phrase on the note?"

"What about it?"

"It's an old phrase, often used in Medieval poetry, but it was also, very significantly, said by Pope Paul the third when he saw what Michel Angelo had created with his own Doom Painting in the Sistine Chapel. It doesn't really mean that there is no rest for the wicked, it means there is no escape from hell."

"You're going to have to enlighten me," Emma said, already shaking her head as though she wished she hadn't asked.

"Right, so Pope Paul had inherited the position while Michael Angelo was already painting the image. Anyway, I don't know if you've seen it, but almost everybody in the image is naked, lithe, fit, sexual. Naturally, many in the church were a little perturbed by that."

"Naturally."

"Anyway, one of the Pope's advisors, Biagio de Cesena, said that the figures were more suited to inns and brothels than the walls of the chapel. Michael Angelo was outraged with that comment, and so he painted a portrait of Biagio into the bottom corner of hell, depicting him as Minos, among a troop of devils."

"Cheeky," Emma said, but Ripley could tell she was growing impatient for the details.

"Biagio complained to the Pope, but the Pope just laughed, saying that Hell was outside his jurisdiction. *'Had Michael Angelo put you in Purgatory, there may be some remedy, but from hell, nulla est redemptio.'* he'd joked."

"What a card. And thanks for the art history lesson. But what has all of that got to do with this?"

"I think the note was a clue, telling us to look at the painting."

Emma frowned.

"Take a look at this guy," Ripley said, tapping the perspex. "Come here."

They both leaned in to look where Ripley's finger was. The image was faded and cracked, with bits of the painting completely missing, but what she was pointing out was clear enough.

"A man in a mitre hat," Ripley said.

"And he's as good as naked," Emma said.

"One of the few in this image who is," Ripley agreed. "Although often fabric or coverings were added at a later date as society became more prudish about nudity."

They both studied the image in silence for a moment before Emma stood up, standing back to take the whole scene in. Ripley did the same.

The figure of Christ in the centre of the image was the most damaged, obviously worn away where the hands of countless worshippers had touched the painting over the centuries. Ripley could still make out the trickle of blood from his chest, the crucifixion marks on his hands. He was flanked by angels on both sides.

A line of twelve apostles sat beneath his feet, in judgement – if Ripley remembered her scriptures correctly – of the twelve tribes of Israel.

In the lower part of the picture, faded and worn, were the human dead, resurrected and being led, either to heaven or to hell. Some embraced their demons, others fled from them. Meanwhile, a host of angels with trumpets called more from the ground.

"So, what's this then?" Emma asked. "Our killer is making a point about the judgement of the wicked?"

"No," Ripley said. "That's the strange part. The souls here on the left are the supposed to be the good ones. These are the blessed. They're the ones being lifted up to heaven by the angels, see?"

To Ripley's eye the delineation was clear between the souls on the left being heralded by trumpeting angels from their graves in a green field, and those on the right being chained and dragged downward by the demons of hell.

"And look here," she said, pointing to another part of the lower left of the painting – the good side – where souls of the blessed were being called out of their graves in a beautiful garden. She let her finger rest above another body – a young man, half in the ground, half out.

"Just like Dylan Parker was found," Emma said.

"Exactly," Ripley said, scanning the rest of the image for the equivalent representation of Sister Francis Burr.

Finally Emma pointed at a tiny figure, drawn near to those judging apostles, her knees bent in prayer.

"Of course," Ripley said. "Even the saints were not guaranteed their place in heaven. A few of these paintings often show them close to Christ, like this, but still forced to remind him of their good deeds on the day of judgement."

"Right," Emma said, standing up again, hands on hips, staring at the remains of the painting. "So, I think we can definitely say the three deaths are connected, but what the hell does this all mean?"

Ripley joined her in the centre of the chapel.

"I honestly don't know. I've seen a lot of religious vengeance in my time, but it doesn't make sense to be targeting only the good. I think we need to take another look at everything you and your colleagues have so far."

"Right. Well, let's get back to the hotel. I've booked you a room in the George, which is where I'm staying for the next few days too," Emma said. "The restaurant's not bad, and the wine list is great. We can pick through everything over dinner."

6

RIPLEY HADN'T REALISED how happy she would be to see Dan Cotter again. The time they had spent together on that case back in his small village had been fraught and terrifying, but she had enjoyed working with him.

A gentle man, whom both she and Emma had thought was too soft for the job of policeman, but actually whose compassion had allowed him to take control of a very difficult situation with people he'd known all his life, and proved that he was stronger than he appeared.

One look at him now as he strolled through the reception of the police station to meet them, told her that he was already benefiting from being out of Kirkdale. He stood taller, his shoulders seemed more relaxed. He'd even let his hair grow out a little from that neat, short back and sides he'd had previously. The soft curl of the slightly longer cut suited him.

He smiled broadly, embracing Ripley as he got to her, and then pulled back, realising the informality may not be appropriate.

"Dr Ripley," he grinned, blushing a little. "How are you?"

"Very well, thank you," she said, feeling genuinely warmed by his greeting. "Good to see you again."

"And I bet you're happy it's not back in Kirkdale," he said.

"You're not wrong there."

"Come on through," he said, cheerfully. "We've got an incident room set up out the back. You can meet my new partner."

Emma grinned at Ripley as they set off after him. He hadn't lost any of that enthusiasm for the job, which was great to see. Emma had given Ripley the lowdown on his new partner – saying she rated her as a good cop – and Ripley thought it was a good thing for Cotter to have a decent colleague for a change. His last one had been an old local boy, so mired in the village's history that he would do anything to protect its secret. Not exactly mentor material.

Cotter led them through the corridors of the station, greeting the odd passing colleague as they went, and pushed open the doors to a larger, open plan office, filled with pairs of desks facing each other. Everyone looked up as the trio made their way across the room, not stopping their work, just curious.

In a smaller room overlooking the street, they found DS Helen Dunn. She shook both of their hands solidly. No nonsense.

"Dr Drysdale," she said. "Nice to see you again."

"Emma, please."

By the way Dunn's cheeks flushed slightly, Ripley assumed that Emma had a new admirer. Emma, as usual, seemed oblivious to the young woman's blushes. She was definitely Emma's type though, so perhaps she was deliberately ignoring the detective's blushes.

The greetings over, they gathered around a whiteboard bearing images of the three victims, still smiling and alive. Beside each face were the images of their crime scenes and a few handwritten details – no more than their name, age, date and place of attack.

"So Emma tells me you agree with our theory about a connection," Dunn said, perching on the edge of the desk facing the whiteboard. "What do you think?"

As Ripley told them about the painting they had found in the church, and her theory about Tom Bainbridge's fingers being broken deliberately to make him look like he was pointing at it, Emma attached the photographs of the relevant parts of the painting to the whiteboard beneath each of the victims. Seeing the images from the painting beneath the actual crime scene photographs only confirmed Ripley's assertion.

"I can't believe we didn't see this when we were there," Cotter said.

"I only thought of it because of the phrase on the note," Ripley said.

Emma turned quickly.

"Dr Ripley has a *fascinating* lecture on art history and angry Catholics that she can share with you over a pint some time," she said, eyebrow raised, playfully cutting Ripley off before she started on the whole Sistine Chapel story again.

"So, you think our killer deliberately chose Tom Bainbridge because of the painting in that chapel?"

"I think all of them were chosen deliberately," Ripley said. "I don't think he's just picking random victims and arranging them post-mortem to replicate the painting. There must be more to it than that."

"Why so?"

"What do you understand the Last Judgement to be?" Ripley asked.

"It's the end of the world, right?" Dunn asked. "When we all have to meet our maker, and he gets to decide if we've been good enough to get through the pearly gates?"

Ripley chose to ignore the slight joking tone of her voice – if anything, she respected a healthy cynicism for religion.

"Okay," Ripley said. "So, say you've taken it into your own hands to pick victims to face the final judgement, why would you choose ones who were so obviously going to pass that test? Why not go for criminals, drug-dealers, despots, capitalists? Why not go for the people on the right-hand side of the painting?"

All three looked at her, no answers to give.

"It doesn't make sense, does it?"

"Unless," Dunn ventured, cautiously, still thinking it through. "Unless you're trying to prove it's all nonsense? I mean, if the good guys don't get in, what hope for the rest of us? Maybe it's a warning."

"Or, the killer's trying to preserve their righteousness so that they are guaranteed to be saved," Cotter suggested.

"Both good points," Ripley said. "But if you were preserving their righteousness, you wouldn't beat, maim or torture them, would you?"

"No," Cotter agreed, his theory gently dismissed.

"And if you were punishing people," Ripley continued. "Surely you would punish people who had pretended to be righteous, but were in fact sinning in some way."

"So we have no idea why, basically?" Dunn said, pushing herself off the desk and looking at the images from the painting that Emma had attached to the board.

"Not yet," Emma said. "But thanks to Alex, we can confirm a solid connection between the three cases, which means you two are on to something big, and you should be able to get the brass to throw some money at a few more bodies to help out."

Cotter looked excited, Dunn doubtful. The passage of experience summed up in two expressions.

"Dr Ripley?" Dunn began. "Would you have time to stay and help? Even for a few days. I feel like we're out of our depth here with all this bible stuff."

"Of course," Ripley said. "I think there's more to the message than I've figured out yet. I'd like to talk to the people who knew the other victims, if you could set that up for me?"

"Of course."

"And then I might spend the rest of the afternoon in the library, looking at the history of doom paintings. Especially this one."

"What are you both doing later?" Cotter asked, and Dunn looked up at him, surprised.

"Dinner, I'd imagine. Wine. Incessant conversation about religion and crime," said Emma.

"How about I cook for us all?" Cotter said, quickly. "I make a mean stew, as Dr Ripley knows. And we can catch up on everything then."

Ripley remembered the rich stew that Cotter had cooked for her on the last case. Simple but absolutely delicious. She wasn't going to refuse a rematch.

"Sounds perfect," she said.

"Count me in," Emma said.

Dunn gathered some papers on the desk.

"Will you join us, DS Dunn?" Emma asked, nodding at Cotter behind Dunn's back. He shrugged an agreement.

"Uh... I..." Dunn stuttered.

"You can't turn down an offer of home cooked stew now, can you?" Ripley asked.

Dunn glanced at her quizzically.

"And you can vouch for his cooking skills, can you?" she asked, grinning. "Only, he's not much cop as a detective, so I had been wondering where his real talent lies."

"You won't regret it," Ripley replied.

RIPLEY HAD MADE an appointment to visit the Mother Superior at the convent where Sister Francis had lived, but with a few hours to kill, she'd decided to stop in at the residential group house that John would hopefully be moving to.

It was only twenty minutes out of town and Ripley, perhaps selfishly, had figured that if he did move up here, that she could perhaps rent somewhere in Penrith, keeping her closer to Emma, and even Dan Cotter, who she realised could become a good friend. Having their support and distraction would be a godsend.

Pulling up to the address Neil Wilcox had given her, she realised that she had been expecting the place to look similar to the military hospital where John was currently staying. She couldn't have been more wrong.

The house was not visible from the road, shielded by a thick coppice of trees, with a heavy gate covering the drive. Even the access spoke of isolation, silence and privacy. Exactly what these men needed, she guessed.

She pulled up to the gate and checked for an intercom. There was nothing. She was about to kill the engine and get out, when the gates clunked and began to open. Engaging gear, she drove through, following the winding drive through the trees to emerge in front of what looked like an old school.

It wasn't a big building, red brick with peeling paint on the window frames. Four large bay windows make up the ground floor, two on either side of the door, and upstairs is a row of five smaller windows, all identical in shape and size.

Ripley eased the Audi to a stop and killed the engine, gathering her phone from the passenger seat and climbing out. As she turned from locking the car, she found a man standing in the doorway, ready to greet her.

"You must be Dr Ripley," he said, smiling. He stayed in the doorway as she approached, leaning against the frame with a practiced nonchalance.

"That's me," she said, reaching out a hand to shake his as she reached him.

"Adam," he said, not giving a surname, but shaking her hand warmly, if for slightly too long. "I run the place. Captain Wilcox warned me you would be dropping in."

She felt his gaze linger on her face, her eyes, and when she withdrew her hand, he smiled again as though he had understood something about her in that moment of contact.

Ripley had met his type before, confident, charismatic and convinced of their own abilities. Funny how they often ended up as therapists.

"I was in the area," Ripley said. "I hope you don't mind."

"Not at all," he said, stepping back and waving his hand expansively. "Come in."

She closed the door behind herself and followed him down the corridor, which was relatively bare, but clean and tidy. No pictures adorned the walls, no carpet on the old, wooden floorboards. He looked back as though reading her mind.

"We like to keep things stripped down. Tidy house is a tidy mind, and all that."

He led her through into an equally sparse, large sitting room where eight individual armchairs were neatly spaced out, all facing the windows.

"Take a seat," he said. "I would offer you a drink, but I've got a session starting in a few minutes, and I can't be late."

Ripley sat as instructed, noticing that Adam didn't. Instead he leaned against the wall between the two bay windows. He seemed to think better of it straight away, and stood up straight again.

He looked familiar, she thought, but perhaps it because he had one of those generically handsome faces. Dark wavy hair, left a little long, framed his square jaw, pale blue eyes danced beneath dark brows. His skin had a honeyed tan to it. He looked healthy. Alive.

"What can I do for you, Dr Ripley?" he asked. And then, before she could answer: "We don't usually allow visitors, but Captain Wilcox told me of your... area of expertise... and I have to admit to being rather fascinated."

He perched on the arm of one of the chairs nearest her and leaned in, looking at her with a strange expression. Instead of finding it disconcerting, she found his scrutiny strangely childlike. He seemed excited.

"Why so?" she asked, preparing herself, yet again, to defend her work.

"Because I looked you up," he smiled. "After the captain called, and I think you and I agree on a lot of things when it comes to religion and miracles."

He had a way of speaking that was both soothing and compelling. She could see why he would make a good counsellor – you couldn't help but be drawn to his words.

"Really?" she said. "What makes you say that?"

A door slammed outside, and he looked up with a hint of annoyance, returning his glance quickly to her with another smile.

"Now *that* I really don't have time to discuss but, perhaps if you wanted to, you could sit in on our next session and you may see what I mean. Besides, it will give you the best idea of the kind of work we do here, and the ways we help our residents find their way again."

"I'd like that," she said. "Unless you think it would be too distracting?"

"No, not at all," he said. "This is a drop-in session for former residents. We never leave anyone out in the cold."

He stood up, clapped his hands quietly and nodded, seeming unduly pleased that she was going to join them.

"Okay then," she said, smiling tightly.

"Great. Stay there, and I'll bring them in."

Ripley watched him hurry away and stood up, crossing to the window, feeling suddenly self-conscious that she was already in the room, on display, before the normal group participants were brought in. Had he been planning this all along, or was there genuinely a group planned? Too late to back out now.

She peered out of the window into the woods, realising that there was no sign of anything but nature from here. No pylons, no buildings, no cars, even though the road was less than a hundred meters away. *Very clever.*

The sound of a throat being cleared made her turn, and she saw a tall, thin man in a navy overcoat take a seat in one of the armchairs. His head was clean-shaven, and he kept his coat wrapped tight around his thin frame, despite the relative warmth in here.

When he looked up at her, with the faintest of nods, she saw a haunted, almost angry look in his eyes. Mistrust of the stranger, or perhaps he didn't like the fact that there was a woman in the meeting room. She smiled and he looked away immediately.

She reminded herself that, if he was a former resident here, he would have been suffering from the same condition that John was. Why should he welcome her into his safe space?

Adam wandered back in, with two other men flanking him, followed by a third only a moment behind. They all took their seats and Adam, this time, sat too, but angled his chair around to face them all. He looked at Ripley, raised an eyebrow, and she sat immediately.

"Welcome, all," Adam said, to a chorus of mumbles. "We have a friend with us today, you'll see. Don't be afraid. She's one of us."

Ripley smiled, but only one of the men looked up at her. He was in his late thirties – strong-looking, with broad shoulders and a thick neck. Unlike his compatriot in the overcoat, he wore a simple grey T-shirt, which strained across his broad chest. His eyes, she noticed, had that same anxious, haunted look, though.

It was a look that John had, but his was more pronounced. She wondered, looking around the room at these men who had, in theory, left the care of this institution, whether John would ever shake it off. Possibly not.

As Adam continued to describe her as a friend of the organisation, she couldn't help feel like she could finally relax about John's condition. She *was* a friend. She knew, more than most, what these men had been through, and she could see how far they each must have come, just to be here and be getting on with their lives in the outside world.

When Adam spoke, their eyes fixed on him, and she could see that he had their trust. Perhaps one of the few people in the world that they did trust, but she saw them visibly relax as he spoke. She, too, let his words wash over her, relaxing into her chair and watching his eyes dance as he talked of their place in the world, the strength they had, the family they were part of. Every word seemed to shore them up.

She had been expecting a little more to and fro, a little more talking from the men, but that didn't seem to be the purpose here today. Perhaps they had talked enough, and now they just needed a weekly dose of reassurance that everything was going to be okay.

Adam spoke of a big day approaching, which they would all need to prepare for, and as he did, he looked across at her and narrowed his eyes slightly, as though checking she was listening. She wondered what they had planned. He also spoke of welcoming new brothers into the fold, and she guessed he meant John.

She wondered what John would make of this when he got here. He had mentioned that it was a religious group of sorts, but Ripley didn't think he would have any problem with the kind of words being used here. There was no preaching in this room.

By the time the session was over, Ripley realised she was already cutting it fine to get back to the convent in time for her appointment with the Mother Superior.

"I'm sorry to dash off," she said, after the men had moved away to the kitchen for refreshments and left her and Adam alone in the corridor heading towards the door.

"I wonder if I might come into town and meet you, while you're up?" Adam said, and he looked so sincere, she felt obliged to agree. Besides, she wanted to find out more about this intriguing man who would be looking after her husband.

"That would be great," she said. "I'm here for the next couple of days, I think."

"Where are you staying? The George, isn't it?"

He laughed at the surprised look that crossed her face.

"Captain Wilcox mentioned it," he said. "I'll send a message via reception when I'm coming into town. I'm afraid I don't use mobile phones."

Ripley noticed that he waited in the door, watching her as she got into the car and drove away, only closing the door when she was out of sight. Strange, perhaps, or maybe just cautious. She quite liked him, anyhow. John would be safe here.

THE COMMUNITY OF Saint Mary was housed in an old manor house on the outskirts of the town, tucked away up a long drive, isolated from the noise and disruption of daily life.

The old house was not large, but had been beautifully maintained, with white plantation shutters at the windows and a wide front door sitting at the top of a short flight of steps. The house had been bequeathed to the Order of Saint Mary at the turn of the last century after the sisters had tended the ailing Lord of the manor in his final years.

Set in several acres of private land, the sweeping driveway had led Ripley away from the busy roads out of Penrith and through an avenue of well-established trees, into a forecourt with a well-tended Victorian knot garden full of box and lavender.

Off to the side of the manor, a red brick wall guarded what she assumed would be a kitchen garden. The sisters were mostly self-sufficient up here, she had been told. Several identical, sit-up-and-beg style bicycles were parked in a rack to the side of the house, and as Ripley pulled her old Audi to a rattling halt outside, she watched a young novice sweep gracefully up the drive on another identical bicycle, dismounting and coasting on one pedal as she sailed into the open space in the rack – a practiced movement, timeless and efficient.

As Ripley stepped from the car, the same novice greeted her cheerfully.

"Hello there," she beamed.

"Good afternoon," Ripley said, locking the driver's door.

"Can I help you with anything?" the young woman asked, looking eager. "I'm Sister Anne."

She was quite short and, though her habit did much to conceal it, was also softly plump. She had bright eyes, behind dark-rimmed glasses, and an infectious, innocent smile.

"Dr Alex Ripley," she said, unable to stop herself smiling back at the young woman. "I have an appointment with the Reverend Mother."

"Oh, wonderful," Sister Anne said. "Shall I take you to her?"

"Sure," Ripley said. "That would be very kind."

Ripley followed her up the steps and through the wide, heavy-looking door. Inside, the hallway floor was made up of small black-and-white tiles, set in a central strip about a meter wide, surrounded by a dark wood parquet floor. The smell of wax polish and floral disinfectant was strong, but pleasant.

Neat sconces lit the walls at regular intervals, lifting the eye from the wood panelling that lined the lower part of the wall. A broad stairway led up from the hall, with a banister of the same dark wood, set on black metal railings. Ripley felt like she had stepped back in time. The old manor could easily be used as a location for a period drama without needing much set dressing.

Sister Anne smiled at Ripley's expression.

"It's beautiful, isn't it?" she asked.

"Incredible," Ripley replied, following her up the stairs.

"We're very lucky," Sister Anne said enthusiastically. "The house is wonderful, but you really should see the gardens. You can walk for hours. There's even a lake, with swans. Last year Sister Claire said she saw otters down there, but I've never been lucky enough to see anything like that. I probably make too much noise."

She giggled. Ripley guessed Sister Anne might be correct in that assumption.

"Are you going to be joining the order?" Sister Anne asked.

"Oh, no," Ripley said, quickly. Too quickly.

The girl looked crestfallen.

"I'm afraid my vocation lies elsewhere," Ripley said.

"I see," Sister Anne said.

"Have you been here long?"

"No. Not really. This is my second year. I'm still a novice, you see?"

She lifted her habit in her fingers, showing it to Ripley. Ripley had to admit not knowing enough about the different stages of becoming a religious sister.

"We novices wear grey," Sister Anne explained. "It will be a while until I get my penguin suit."

She laughed at her own cheek. Ripley had to laugh too. Such an innocent joke, but it seemed to give the girl so much pleasure.

"Well, here we are," Sister Anne said proudly, knocking gently on a solid-looking door.

Ripley looked up and down a corridor lined with similar doors. At some point these would all have been bedrooms, or drawing rooms. She wondered what the place had been like in its former days, as a family home.

"Come," a strong voice called from within.

Sister Anne pushed the door open and walked in.

"A guest for you, Reverend Mother," she said. "A Dr... uh... I'm so sorry, I've completely forgotten."

"Alex Ripley," she said, stepping into the office.

The elderly woman stood up and swept around the old oak desk, taking Ripley's extended hand in both of hers.

"Ah, Dr Ripley," she said, her voice low. Quiet and gentle. Nothing would rush this woman. "A pleasure to meet you. That will be all thank you, Sister Anne."

Sister Anne nodded, retreating.

"Sweet girl," Ripley said as she closed the door behind her.

"She lacks focus, but she has a good heart. And she bakes an excellent cheese scone."

The Reverend Mother was a slender woman, slightly hunched at the shoulders, her face lined with wisdom and kindness, eyes creased as though in a permanent smile. She looked kind, but firm. She reminded Ripley a little of her old school headmistress. A formidable woman until you had her on side, and then one of the most empowering, supportive advocates Ripley had ever had. The Reverend Mother had that same air about her.

"Do sit down," she said. "Can I offer you a cup of tea? Some water?"

Ripley agreed to tea, looking around the room while the Reverend Mother poured them both a cup from an old-fashioned tea set arranged on an ornate trolley beside her desk.

The room was neat, organised, and sparsely furnished. Aside from the desk, and the chairs surrounding it, a bookcase lined one wall, and the others remained bare. An old rug covered the centre of the room, softening the floorboards. A crucifix of wood and bronze hung on the wall behind the desk, between two windows which overlooked the extensive gardens that Sister Anne had mentioned.

"So, what can I do for you, Dr Ripley?" The Reverend Mother asked, delivering the tea with a slight wobble in her hand. "I understand you're looking to learn more about poor Sister Francis."

"That's right," Ripley said. "I'm so sorry for your loss."

"God calls us all as he sees fit," the Reverend Mother said. "I only regret that the poor girl was made to suffer so before she was released. Still, she has her place now."

An interesting choice of words, Ripley thought, given the context of the painting.

"Can I ask what your particular interest is?" the Reverend Mother asked. "You mentioned that you were helping the police with their investigation, but I'd been led to believe the case had stalled a few months ago."

"Some new information has come to light," Ripley explained. "I act as a consultant at times, for a number of police forces, usually when the crime they're investigating has some kind of religious angle. It helps, apparently, to have someone who understands the vernacular."

"I see. Very wise." She slurped slightly as she sipped her tea. "What is it you would like to know, that the police haven't already heard?"

Ripley sensed a hint of resistance there, but she couldn't quite place it. Protectiveness, perhaps. She already knew the basics of Sister Francis's life here – when she'd joined, how long she'd been here, how old she was, the kind of work she did for the order, all of her various community works. That wasn't really what Ripley was here for.

She had discussed with Cotter and Dunn the option of revealing their thoughts about a link between the deaths, and they had agreed that they would mention it to those most closely related to the victims, but insist that they keep the information to themselves until the case became clearer. It would be impossible, otherwise, to ask the right questions.

"We are working on a theory," Ripley said. "That Sister Francis's death may be linked to another two recent murders in the area."

It was best to just say these things straight and deal with whatever shock it provoked. Certainly, the Reverend Mother took her cup away from her lips before her next sip, and clattered it back onto the saucer, her hand shaking noticeably.

"Please explain," she said.

"It's only a theory, and we would like to keep this information as far away from the public as possible, especially if we are correct. If I tell you, will you promise to keep it to yourself for now?"

"You don't need to lecture a religious sister on the virtues of silence, Dr Ripley. You have my word."

"Thank you," Ripley said. "Police Cumbria have been investigating three deaths which until a few days ago they thought were completely unrelated. The first was Sister Francis, who as you know was found in a position of prayer, arranged that way by her killer."

The Reverend Mother nodded, her lips quivering slightly. She would have been given all the details of Sister Francis's murder, and Ripley saw no need to rehash them for her now.

"The second was a young boy, a chorister at St Michael's School in the centre of Penrith."

"I read the story in the papers," the Reverend Mother said. "Awful. They said he'd been found in the school grounds. But I thought they'd arrested someone for that?"

"No," Ripley said. "They questioned a few suspects, but they couldn't press any charges against any of them."

"Terrible. And so young. His family must be distraught."

"There were a few details of the boy's murder which have been kept from the press, deliberately," Ripley said. "His body was also arranged post-mortem, similar to the way Sister Francis was. But this time, the victim was actually half-buried in a rock garden. He'd been stripped to the waist and arranged to appear as though he was climbing from the grave."

"How despicable. Why must we bring such violence to bear on one another?"

It was a question Ripley pondered often.

"Finally," she continued. "The Assistant Vicar of the Parish Church was murdered earlier this week."

"Goodness," she said, looking rocked by the flow of revelations. "We don't really have any dealings with the Parish Church. I hadn't heard anything about this. To be honest, I try to avoid reading any of the news at the moment. It's all so negative and it makes me too sad for the future of the world."

"I know," Ripley agreed. "The thing is, Reverend Tom was found in a small chapel within the church, little more than an alcove, really. He, too, had been stripped naked, a ceremonial mitre placed on his head. A note bearing the phrase 'nulla est redemptio' was left on top of a pile of his clothes."

"Well, that is certainly true," the Reverend Mother said. "Poor man."

"His hand had been rearranged after his death to point the way to a painting on the wall of the chapel he was found in. The remains of a doom painting."

The Reverend Mother frowned, shaking her head.

"I'm afraid my theological expertise is more limited than your own, Dr Ripley. You'll have to enlighten me."

As Ripley explained the purpose of the paintings, the Reverend Mother nodded gently, taking it all in. Ripley reached into her satchel and took out the three printouts of the photographs they had taken of the painting, presenting them one after the other to the elderly sister. First the man in the mitre hat, second the body climbing from the grave, and finally the saintly woman, bent in prayer at the feet of the Apostles.

"I see," the Reverend Mother said, staring at them all in turn. "And now I understand why you think the crimes are linked. But what on earth is the meaning behind all this?"

"That's what we're trying to understand," Ripley said. "We believe that the victims are specifically chosen, but we don't know how. I wondered if you could tell me a little about the last few months of Sister Francis's life?"

"Of course. She was a very active member of the order, always out working in the community, but fortunately she had quite a set routine. I will call Sister Margaret to join us too. She has a far better understanding of the day-to-day routines of all the sisters."

Ripley smiled, hoping that Sister Margaret enough to give them a stronger connection between Sister Francis and the other two victims.

THE LIFE OF a prophet – a messiah, if you will – is never easy. Even with the truth behind you, and God – the real God – at your side, there are constant tests sent to shake you from your path. I've learned, by now, that planning is the key to success. And I have to admit that my plan is proceeding well so far. Years I've spent, quietly spreading the good word, and if it hadn't been for a chance glimpse of that interview on the television, I would never have known that I had such a powerful ally. And with her help, soon, everybody will hear the truth and understand it.

Dr Alex Ripley – the Miracle Detective – has seen my message. She understands. And she will help me convince the rest. She's travelled the world, proving to these people – these devout believers – that their God is a liar. And yet nobody calls her mad, do they? Nobody tries to silence her, or lock her away, or feed her drugs to numb her brain. No.

Instead, they give her airtime on popular TV shows; they publish her words in books with glossy covers; they make her into a celebrity. A doctor of theology, no less. But now she's heard my call, it's as though we're already connected. And, soon, we will be, forever.

EMMA DRYSDALE SMILED as DS Helen Dunn walked into the lab. She had invited both Dunn and Cotter down to go through findings on all the bodies so far, in light of their new theory, but only Dunn had shown up.

"You drew the short straw then?" Emma asked.

"Oh, I wouldn't say that," Dunn said, hanging her coat up at the entrance and smiling back at Emma.

Her eyes were such a pale green that they were almost grey under the harsh fluorescent lights in the lab. Even so, they glinted when she smiled, lighting up her whole face with a genuine excitement.

"I'm a bit of a geek for forensics to tell the truth," Dunn continued.

"You should think about switching sides," Emma said. "We could always do with more talent."

"Ha," Dunn laughed. "Tell that to my high school science teacher. I barely scraped through. I'm afraid my skills lie elsewhere, but I don't let that dampen my enthusiasm. Now, where do you want me?"

Emma got the distinct sense that Dunn was flirting with her. Perhaps it was just her way of ingratiating herself with strangers.

"We'll start with the most recent," Emma said, leading the way over to a bank of computers on a large desk. "And we can work back from there."

"Great. Sounds like a plan. I've brought the witness statements we gathered too. I haven't had a chance to read everything from the Reverend's case. Uniform only just finished filing the door-to-doors, and all the interviews with kids and parents from the scout group thingy. I'll go through them properly later."

"So are you new in the area then?" Emma asked. "I don't remember seeing you around on crime scenes before."

"Me? No. I've been with Cumbria for years, but I was in the armed response before. When the post came up for DS, I jumped at the chance of changing units. ARU is a bit macho, even for a tough bird like me. I was getting a bit tired of having to be one of the lads, you know?"

Dunn laughed, but Emma had a feeling that she would have given as good as she got, seeing how she behaved around Dan Cotter. Besides, a career in the armed response unit took a lot of skill, not to mention a healthy portion of bravery, so she doubted a few macho lads would intimidate DS Dunn.

"Anyway," Dunn continued. "Strangely, I'm more at home among the MIT lot. We've all got the same sense of humour, for one."

Emma had to admit that she enjoyed working with most of the detectives in the Major Incident Team in Police Cumbria. Dunn was right though, there was quite a specific sense of humour among the team – gallows.

"They're a good bunch," Emma agreed, tapping in her password and unlocking the screensaver. "Right, pull up a chair."

Dunn sat down, close enough that their knees touched, smiled briefly and moved back slightly. Again, Emma couldn't tell if she'd done it deliberately, or whether she was just naturally tactile.

Emma loaded the results from her examination of Reverend Tom Bainbridge onto the screen, briefly recapping the main details of name, age, date and time of death.

"Despite evidence of a struggle," she said, "We are confident that he died from a cardiac arrest brought about by extreme and rapid blood loss."

"After his throat was slit from ear to ear," Dunn said, flatly.

"Exactly. If it's any kind of blessing, we think he would have bled out quite quickly."

"But it would have taken long enough that he would have known he was dying?"

"Yes, certainly."

"I hope he got to meet his maker in the end," Dunn said.

Emma looked across at her, trying to assess the comment.

"Do you believe?" she asked.

"What? In God? I don't think so. I don't know."

She shrugged, smiling almost cheekily. Emma had noticed that, at times, she seemed quite young, shrugging like a teenager who'd been asked where her homework was. But when Emma looked at her closer, she realised DS Dunn wasn't as young as she'd assumed. She had thin lines around her eyes, which crinkled when she smiled, a slight loosening of the skin on her neck and few barely noticeable strands of grey on the sides of her temples. All of which made her all the more attractive.

Concentrate, Emma.

"I mean, I went to Sunday School as a kid, but not because I wanted to, just because that's what we did. We never really went to church as a family, apart from the carol service at Christmas."

Emma let her talk, enjoying the soft Scottish lilt that crept into her accent as she reminisced.

"My granddad was a vicar, though, and I think my poor dad had been forced to go to every church function imaginable, so I guess he was rebelling. We did the bare minimum. I'd like to believe there is something a little more meaningful than just the beginning and the end of life. But I'm not sure God is it. You know what I mean?"

"Only too well," Emma said.

"Your friend, Dr Ripley. Where does she stand on all this? Because I can't make head or tail of her job title."

"Oh, well, now that *is* complicated," Emma said. "She seems to have spent most of her adult life looking for actual, physical proof that God exists, but thanks to science, rationality, or straight-forward common sense, she just keeps proving to herself that He doesn't. But it doesn't stop her trying. She's quite an amazing woman, you know? You should hear some of the stories she's got to tell."

"But what does she do?"

"She understands religion, or at least the power of it, and how people can use it to hurt others, or help themselves. She basically goes around trying to stop innocent people getting duped, defrauded or hurt in the name of God."

"Wow, I bet she's put some backs up in her time, then," Dunn said.

"Oh yes. Especially because another huge part of what she does is to debunk miracles."

"What, Jesus's face in my tortilla kind of stuff?"

Emma laughed. There were some odd claims like that which Ripley had investigated in her time, but usually it was a little more serious.

"She has just published a book about faith healing, and how people can use it to make millions. And off the back of it, got caught up in this crazy scene in Wales where some woman was wheeling her poor daughter – who was in a coma, no less – out in front of groups of worshippers, all believing she had the power to cure them."

"Sounds nuts," Dunn said.

"What was nuts was that there were some people there willing to kill to keep the little miracle business going, and poor old Alex got herself into trouble with them too. I swear she's going to get herself killed by some religious psychopath one of these days."

"Who'd have thought believing in God could be so dangerous?"

"Hmm," Emma smiled. "And with only a couple of millennia of bloodshed, murder and torture as evidence?"

"Fair point," Dunn said, nodding her concession.

"I mean, just ask this guy," Emma said, pointing at the image on her screen of the late Reverend Tom Bainbridge.

"True. Right, let's see what else he's got to tell us then."

Dunn leaned in again, looking at the screen.

"Okay, well, I wanted to look at the way his body had been positioned."

"To point to the painting. It's a bit crass, isn't it?"

"Sure," Emma said. "But if our killer had left us clues before and we weren't seeing the connection, perhaps he was getting frustrated."

"Why? Because he wants us to figure it out?" Dunn asked.

"Maybe because he wants us to know that this is a mission. A cause."

"He *wants* us to chase him?"

"Many serial killers like the whole game of outsmarting the police. Often, that becomes a bigger driver than the killing itself."

"Yeah, well, nobody likes a smart arse," Dunn said.

Emma liked her – she had a way of saying things that was both impertinent yet to the point. It was a rare talent among the officers Emma had dealt with.

"So, what else have we got?" Dunn asked.

"Okay, look at the way he's lying," Emma said, pulling up a couple of angles on the crime scene. "We know that his throat was slit from behind, right?"

"Right."

"So, there was tissue damage to the hair follicles on the top of his head, consistent with his head being pulled back by the hair."

Her hands unwittingly mimed the action as she spoke.

"So, what? The killer likes violent control?" Dunn suggested.

"God knows. More than likely," Emma said. "But what I mean is, unless he is unnaturally tall, the killer must have forced Tom Bainbridge to his knees before slitting his throat. Now, bear in mind that we found scuff marks up by the storeroom which we know came from Tom's shoes. So we can assume he was dragged over here to this altar, where he was forced to onto his knees, presumably to pray. Now why would you do that?"

"To give your victim a chance at redemption?" Dunn suggested. "It would make sense with the whole 'no escape for the wicked' thing too wouldn't it? Maybe he was making him confess his sins and beg for forgiveness."

"Maybe," Emma said. "It fits, I guess."

"Do you think he's been leaving us clues all along, and he was getting frustrated that we hadn't seen them, so he arranged Tom to point to the painting?" Dunn asked, thinking out loud.

"But why go to all that trouble to show us the painting, if we still don't know what it means?"

Dunn turned back to the computer screens, lifting a printed image of the saint praying to the apostles at the same time, and holding it beside the photograph of Sister Francis. Then she did the same for Dylan Parker, and then for Tom Bainbridge.

"What is it?" Emma asked, sensing that the detective was on to something.

"Sister Francis had a bible in her hand, right? Do we still have it?" Dunn asked.

"Yes, it's in the evidence files. We processed it already."

"Was there anything odd about it? Any underlined passages, markings, anything?"

"Not that I found. Though it wasn't a huge priority in the case at the time. The only thing odd about it was that the other sisters swore blind that it wasn't Sister Francis's."

"So the killer put it there deliberately for us to find? There must be a clue in it."

"I'll dig it out and take another look," Emma said. "I could get Alex to have a look and see if there is anything special about it."

"Good idea. If there's something in the text, Dr Ripley will figure it out, I'm sure," said Dunn.

RIPLEY HAD SPENT almost an hour taking down notes while Sister Margaret had gone through the diary, detailing most of

Sister Francis's movements for the last few months. She was certainly active in the community and had clearly been well-loved by her peers. Sister Margaret had proudly showed Ripley a cutting from the papers a few months previously where Sister Francis had been featured holding a cheque for just over ten thousand pounds which she had almost single-handedly raised for a childhood cancer charity.

Her *Nuns On The Run* event had been quite the media sensation. They admitted that Sister Francis was one of a small handful of the religious sisters who actually took part in the sponsored park run that she'd organised, but it had been well attended by the public and the theme had really taken off – everyone had come dressed the part, and the whole thing had drummed up a lot of support and enthusiasm locally.

Nothing about the nun's reported movements in the past months had immediately struck Ripley as showing a connection between her and Reverend Tom Bainbridge, and according to her colleagues, they knew of no link to either the church or the school that Dylan Parker had attended.

Ripley was sure the connection was there somewhere, she just hadn't seen it yet. The doom painting in the church was a hint as to the motive, which she would need more time to figure out, but she didn't believe the painting was the way this particular killer was selecting his victims. She had no doubt that he *was* selecting them, but she believed he was arranging them to match elements of the painting, rather than selecting them because they have a connection to it already. So she still had to work out why that particular choirboy? Why this specific nun? Why Reverend Tom and not the vicar?

After leaving the convent, Ripley had made the short drive back into Penrith town centre, parked in the supermarket multi-storey car park near the new square, feeling slightly lost as she walked out to face a bunch of modern looking shop fronts, all seemingly closed, with signs in the windows to say where in the old town they had now moved to. Obviously, something had happened to the rents in this more modern part of town to make them shed their tenants so universally.

Ripley had been to Penrith a couple of times before, but only as a child. Somehow her recollection of the town was more romantic than the reality. The shops up and down the main streets were the same chain stores as most other high streets across the country, though there were still some independent relics.

She cut through Market Square, past an old department store with an almost illegible sign over the doors which she knew to be Arnison and Sons. The side walls of the building had old-fashioned billboards painted onto the walls advertising the shop's wares. Millinery, hosiery and gloves on one; carpets, curtains and linoleum on the next. What filled the window displays between each billboard was a more modern collection of products – now mostly electrical – but the spirit of the place lived on.

The other buildings in the square had mostly been occupied by banks. Why would one town need five different banks in the same square mile? But at least they were all still open, and the square wasn't yet reduced to a series of empty storefronts with fading signs, and only charity shops and pop-up eateries able to fill the void.

She left the square and headed up to the church, striding through the doors beneath the clock tower, through the entrance hall, past the medieval tombstones displayed and preserved there, and through into the body of the church.

She had called from the Covent to warn Reverend Judith that she was coming over, and sure enough she found the woman at a desk in the vestry, head down over a laptop.

"Ah, Dr Ripley," she said, sounding pleased to see her.

"Am I interrupting?" Ripley asked.

"I'm grateful of it," Judith said. "I'm trying to fill in the events calendar for the Parish newsletter and I'm afraid I can't seem to get it right. Tom always used to…"

She trailed off, Tom's absence hanging between them again.

"I'm sure people will understand if you miss one," Ripley said, trying to reassure her.

"Oh, God forbid," Judith said. "No, the Parish newsletter is a gem. It's a real highlight for many of our parishioners and the only way we can share news locally, really. Take a look."

Reverend Judith closed the laptop with a click and picked up a thick paper booklet, which she handed to Ripley.

"That's last month's," she said. "But it'll give you an idea of what I mean. If there's something going on in the area, it'll be in there. It's a proper community thing. Tea?"

Ripley took the booklet and followed her out to the kitchen, leafing through the pages as she went. Articles about the girl guides bake sale, a fun run, a pair of students due to do a talk on their missionary work abroad, as well, Ripley noticed, as a number of advertisements for local stores and businesses. Judith had been right. It was a real shop window for the community.

"You didn't get accosted on the way in then?" Judith asked as she popped tea bags into two waiting mugs and flicked the kettle on.

"No, by who?" Ripley asked.

"Oh, we had a man outside earlier trying to shove leaflets into people's hands. Martin. He's often here, but Tom usually managed to persuade him to leave. I'm afraid I'm not as effective. He's a bit of a pain to be honest, but I suppose handing out leaflets is harmless enough. I just wish they weren't quite so offensive. It upsets some of the older parishioners."

"What are the leaflets about?" Ripley asked.

"Oh, you know, your usual end-of-the-world stuff," Judith replied, rolling her eyes. "How everything from the Internet to Donald Trump is a sign that the apocalypse is on its way."

"I have to admit to thinking that myself sometimes too," Ripley laughed.

"Yes," Judith replied. "It *is* all a little relentless, isn't it? I tend to take one of his leaflets when I see him, just to shut him up, and pop it in the bin later. Each to their own, and all that. Anyway, I'm glad he's gone now. Right, are you hungry? I've got some cracking cookies that one of the flower-arrangers made to keep my spirits up."

Ripley liked her. She clearly had a strong faith, and there was no doubt that she believed in the power of Christ, but she didn't take herself too seriously. She was almost human enough to encourage Ripley to attend one of her services. To see if it helped pull her out of her current funk. She knew she and John just needed time, but she couldn't see any light at the end of this particular tunnel for now, and it was slowly eating away at her resilience. Having this distraction was definitely helping, though.

BY THE TIME she left the church, nearly an hour later, Ripley was awash with reading material. Reverend Judith had been an enormous help, and had pulled out all sorts of old documents relating to the painting, and the history of the church. She had also spoken more of Reverend Tom Bainbridge, acknowledging that nobody can ever truly know someone else's heart but, as far as she was concerned, he was an honest Christian man with a heart of gold, a loving husband and a caring father, kind to a fault and with a baritone that could sink ships.

She'd sent Ripley away in the end with a handful of leaflets about the church and its activities, fundraisers and groups – most of which Tom had played a part in – as well as several old copies of the newsletter, and a printed page about the history of the church, which included everything they currently knew about the doom painting in the chapel.

As Ripley walked back through the central doors, intending to go back to her hotel and change before heading to Dan Cotter's flat for dinner, she was approached on the path through the graveyard by a tall, gangly man in a thick, black duffel coat. His scraggly beard was laced with grey and, coupled with the wildness in his eyes, he reminded her a little of John.

When he thrust a leaflet into her hand, wordlessly, and walked on she realised he must be the man Judith had mentioned. The leaflet bore the headline: It's The End Of The World. Where Is Your God Now?

Ripley looked back over her shoulder at the man but he was already approaching two elderly ladies in full waterproof hiking gear, cameras around their necks and walking poles in their hands.

She looked at the leaflet again, tucked it into the pile of other papers, booklets and flyers in her hand, and headed back to the hotel without a backward glance.

BUSY, BUSY, LITTLE bee. Buzz Buzz Buzz. I'm watching you. But you don't see me.

I see her tuck the leaflet away as I follow her out of the church grounds, keeping a safe enough distance. I needn't bother though; she's obviously distracted. She doesn't so much as glance back and, though I don't want to be seen, I can't help feeling disappointed that she doesn't seem to feel me near her. We're so similar, after all, I was sure she would sense a kindred spirit.

I follow her all the way to her hotel and wait outside, peering through the window, watching as she approaches the reception desk and asks a question. The young man behind the desk looks at his computer and shakes his head.

She shrugs, says something which makes the young man smile, and heads for the elevators.

I move closer to the window, to make sure I can see the display above the lift doors. It stops at floor three. I smile. I like to know where people are. It reminds me of my omnipotence beyond this weak human form.

Still, much as I would have enjoyed following her for the rest of the evening, I can't hang around here all night – I've got work to do. No rest for the wicked.

HAVING SHOWERED AND changed, Ripley stepped out of the hotel onto the main square, tucking her chin into her collar and hunching her shoulders to keep out as much of the persistent drizzle as possible. She walked quickly up Middlegate, past the old department store, past a delicious smelling Indian takeaway, and on up the road.

She was grateful that Dan Cotter's rented flat was only a short walk, since she'd stupidly forgotten to bring either a waterproof jacket or an umbrella. It was June, after all. It shouldn't be raining like this.

She dashed across the road beyond the Tourist Information Office, without waiting for the pedestrian crossing to change – traffic was light anyway, and she wasn't going to hang around in this weather.

She passed an old church that had been converted into a series of flats, and turned left at the brightly-coloured children's centre as instructed. Dan Cotter's flat was on the second floor of a two-storey converted terrace house just off Brunswick Square.

Ripley pressed the buzzer and hurried in when the door clicked open. Shaking off her coat and running her fingers through her damp hair, she headed upstairs, following the delicious smell of one of Cotter's legendary stews. He was at the door to his flat to greet her, smiling.

"You found it alright then? Bit grim out, isn't it?"

"Just a bit."

She shivered as the warmth of the room fought with the chill in her bones.

"Come on in," Cotter said. "You're the first here, the others got a bit held up at the lab, apparently."

She hung up her coat and followed him into the kitchen.

"Smells delicious," she said.

"There's some wine on the table," Cotter said. "Help yourself. I hope I remembered it right?"

Ripley smiled. The last time Cotter had cooked her supper, she'd turned up with exactly the same bottle and ended up drinking most of it herself. Cotter was more of a beer man.

"You star," she said. "Sorry, I've come empty handed this time."

"It's been noted," he smiled, pretending to be offended.

"It's really good to see you again, Dan," Ripley said, as he turned back to the stove and stirred his stew. "How are you enjoying life in the metropolis?"

"It's a bit busier than Kirkdale," Cotter said. "The noise takes a bit of getting used to, but I think I'm getting the hang of the job. It's good to be out of the village, anyway."

"You must miss your cottage."

Ripley remembered the cosy little two-storey cottage Cotter had inherited from his parents.

"Yes and no," Cotter said. "I'm renting it out anyway, so I can always go back. I'm quite happy here for now. New start."

"How are you enjoying the job?"

"I feel a bit out of my depth half the time," he admitted. "There's a lot to learn. But the team's good. Everyone's pretty friendly."

"DS Dunn seems nice," Ripley said.

"Yep," Cotter replied. "She's a good laugh. She's a bit of a rising star in the force, apparently. The boss likes her anyway. So I'm sticking with her if I can."

The doorbell buzzed.

"Speak of the Devil," Cotter said, dashing enthusiastically over to the intercom.

Dunn and Emma arrived in a flurry of damp greetings and vociferous complaints about the weather, Emma carrying a big satchel over her shoulder, Dunn gripping two more bottles of wine.

"These are for you," she said, handing them to Cotter.

"Does nobody ever bring beer to dinner parties," Cotter joked.

"Only students," Dunn retorted. "You need to learn a bit of class, son."

"Charming," Cotter said. "Help yourselves while I finish the supper off."

"Productive day?" Emma asked, sitting down beside Ripley, pouring two glasses out for her and Dunn.

"Very interesting indeed," Ripley replied. "You?"

"I think so," Emma said. "We've been going back over the case files, but I think we've come up with more questions than answers."

"One inevitably leads to the other," Ripley said.

"I reckon our killer had been laying clues out for us from the beginning. We just didn't see them," Dunn said.

"How so?" Ripley asked, watching Cotter dollop large portions of thick stew on top of small hills of mashed potato.

"Aside from the way the bodies were arranged, like you spotted," Emma said. "DS Dunn noticed that something else had been added to each scene. Dylan Parker was clutching a handful of mustard seeds. Sister Francis had been holding a bible that wasn't hers. And Tom Bainbridge had been covered in that swathe of red material. All subtle enough that we didn't really see any significance in them, but it means that each scene was deliberately different to what was in the painting, and that must mean something. Don't you think?"

"Yes, but what?" Ripley asked.

"We were hoping you might know," Dunn said. "We're pulling that bible back out of evidence, thought you could take a look."

"Right," Cotter said, delivering the first pair of plates to the table prompting exclamations of delight from his guests. "Dig in."

"I'm impressed, Farm," Dunn said. "This actually looks edible."

Cotter sighed exaggeratedly, smiling as he brought over the last two plates and sat down. He was obviously getting used to her banter.

They talked as they ate, Ripley filling them in on her chats at St Andrew's Church and at the convent.

"I even got harassed by an angry evangelist," Ripley laughed.

"Wouldn't be the first time for you," Emma replied, smiling. "What was he angry about?"

"Something to do with Trump, the Internet and the End of the World."

"Sounds about right," Dunn said, laughing. "You must deal with that kind of stuff all the time in your work, Dr Ripley."

"Alex," she corrected, to an acknowledging smile from Dunn. "I do, I suppose. Look, everyone has an opinion on the God question, don't they?"

The comment led to a long, wide-ranging discussion about the presence of God, and the people who still believe, despite all the advances in science, evolution, and, as Dunn called it 'All that normal, scientifically provable stuff.'

Ripley could see Emma warming more to the detective with every word the woman uttered. It was like listening to a young Emma Drysdale herself, back in the early days when Ripley had first met her, before Emma had learned not to challenge Ripley too hard on religion for fear of an hour-long lecture on the subtleties of true faith without proof. Most people assumed, as soon as they learned what she did for a living, that Ripley was an atheist. She had always enjoyed disavowing them of that notion.

Cotter did his fair share to defend those with strong faith. His upbringing had entrenched certain beliefs in him, and though he'd taken himself out of the toxic environment of his old village, he still understood what it meant to people to have a belief in God.

As he stood up to replenish plates for those who agreed to seconds, Emma got up and opened another bottle of wine, refreshing all of their glasses. While they tucked in to both, Ripley filled them all in on her earlier chat with the Reverend Mother, and all the good work Sister Francis had done for the community.

"Apparently, she was quite the local celebrity," Ripley said.

"Which may explain why she was targeted," Cotter said.

"Quite possibly," Ripley said. "But the kind of work she was doing also meant that she came into contact with a number of troubled people, any of whom could be our killer."

"Any connection with Tom Bainbridge that they knew of? Other than him being another pillar of the community," Emma asked.

"Not really," Ripley said. "Although obviously Reverend Tom also ran most of the groups associated with the church, and

Penrith isn't a huge town, so there's every likelihood that there was a crossover somewhere, we just haven't found it yet."

"I can get the lads to draw up lists of all people involved with any of the activities either of them organised and see if there are any matches," Dunn said.

"I know that Dylan Parker's family were regular visitors at St Andrew's," Cotter said. "The whole family would be there most weekends, although they didn't tend to engage in any of the group activities. Dylan used to be a member of the Boys Brigade, but hadn't been for a few years. His parents said he was too busy with his fundraising activities when he wasn't in school. Apparently, the kid had raised thousands for a childhood cancer charity after one of his school friends had been diagnosed. He'd been in all the papers. They showed me. Quite the young hero."

Ripley swallowed her mouthful, suddenly reminded of something the vicar had shown her. She went back out to the hallway and collected her bag, digging out the selection of parish newsletters that she'd taken from the church. She'd flicked through some of them back at the hotel, trying to get a sense of Reverend Tom's activities. She brought them back to the table and sat down, fork in hand, still eating as she waded through the pages.

"There was a thing in one of these newsletters about a boy raising money for a cancer charity. Hang on," she said, through a mouthful of stew.

The others ate in silence as she leafed through the pages. Each newsletter was a small booklet, numbering a good forty pages, full of stories, news, poems and pictures – a celebration of community. Ripley didn't stop eating as she skimmed them, looking for what she'd seen earlier. Finally, she found it. An article advertising a fundraising event in the local park to raise money for the Bloodwise charity.

"Here," she said. "Look at this."

She turned the pages round to face Cotter.

"That's Dylan Parker," he said, looking at the black-and-white image. "Local boy raises hopes and hearts."

"Let's see," Dunn said, holding out her hand.

Cotter handed her the paper, as Ripley opened another and handed a third newsletter to Emma. They all knew what they were looking for.

"What section's it in?" Emma asked.

"Area news," Dunn said.

"Here, look," Ripley said, spreading the page of her own copy on an article about Sister Francis doing a talk and slideshow about her missionary work in South Sudan, and how all the donations received had been spent.

"God," Dunn said, taking Ripley's newsletter and scanning the headline. "Two for two. I'm guessing Reverend Tom is featured in one of these too, then."

"He's targeting his victims through the parish newsletter?" Cotter asked.

"Could well be. They're all in it," Dunn said. "When was Tom Bainbridge mentioned? Do we know?"

"Here," said Emma, spreading the pages open with her hand. "Same section as the other two, look. Area news."

They all looked, it was true. All three victims had appeared in the same section of the newsletter.

"Not only that," Cotter said. "All of them were events for the Monday Night Club."

"What the hell is the Monday Night Club?" Dunn asked.

"Reverend Judith told me about it," Ripley said. "It's some community get-together thing that Tom Bainbridge ran."

"I thought Sister Francis and Dylan weren't part of the church?" Emma said.

"I think it's open to anyone, it's just about good works in the wider community. Like a talking billboard for everything that's going on around Penrith."

"And the perfect place to pick your next victim, by all accounts," Dunn said.

Ripley looked up, a thought suddenly striking her.

"Do you think the killer randomly chooses the victims from what's written in the newsletter?" she asked. "Or does he go along to the events?"

They all looked at each other for a moment, the cogs whirring.

"Well, it would make sense, wouldn't it, for him to have been there each time," Dunn said. "If we reckon he's spending some time planning these murders – following the victims, learning their patterns, choosing where they should die and how they should be presented. The way each of them was staged, I'm sure nothing was left to chance."

"How long after their event did each of them die? Is there a pattern there?" Cotter asked.

"No," Emma said, "Sister Francis did hers back in the summer last year, Dylan did his in October, yet Dylan was killed first, just a few months after he attended the group."

"And Reverend Tom?" Cotter asked.

"Well, he was there every week. He ran the thing."

Cotter sighed. Dunn patted his arm.

"Don't worry newbie," she joked. "The answers don't always just leap out at you. Let it all stew for a while. Speaking of which, that was bloody delicious."

She pushed her plate away, scraped clean and smiled at them all.

"What if we go along to the next group meeting," Cotter said. "See if we can spot him?"

Dunn snorted a small laugh.

"Yeah, and if we're lucky, he'll be wearing a name badge – Psycho Killer."

"It's not a bad idea, actually," Emma said, and Dunn's smile dropped immediately. "We could at least scope the group out, and ask around if there was someone who'd joined around the time that Sister Francis did her talk. See what people know? If he is targeting his victims through this event somehow, it feels like a small crack that we can poke at."

7

STANDING CLOSE TO the fence, I watch the children run and skip through their last few moments of freedom before the school bell rings. Faces bright, squeals high, no cares in the world. Yet even they aren't innocent – not truly. How can they be? Having been raised under a false God?

The God their parents worship is a demon God – a sadist. People have been blindly following the wrong one all along. For thousands of years. And look what He has done to them: Greed, corruption, narcissism, slaughter, destruction. Everything that was predicted, and so much more.

Of course, these little ones here haven't made the decision for themselves yet, but they've been brought up believing His lies, raised to follow teachings that will see them end up just like all the others, selfish, unkind, corrupt and cheating. Suffer the children.

Take that kid – a young boy running in circles around an even younger girl, taunting her with a silly rhyme, trying to tug at her pigtails as he dances around her, and she, growing more upset with each taunt, tries to spin fast enough in the middle to avoid his nasty grasp. It already there, despite his youth. The poison is in his veins. That cruel behaviour, innate in his being.

I feel my fists clench, watching the little lad, and realise I am only slightly mollified when the girl has finally had enough and snaps, lunging at him in a frenzy of scrabbling fingers and scratching nails. The boy cries out. A whistle blows from across the yard, harsh and shrill, and a short, squat woman in a floral dress strides across the playground towards the fighting pair.

"Charlotte Dean. You stop that right away!" she calls, blowing her whistle again.

The girl slows her attack, finally stepping away from the boy, face curled into a nasty little scowl. The boy looks up, red track marks from her vicious little claws standing proud on his cheek. The teacher bears down on them both. And on cue, the nasty little boy saves his own bacon by bursting into a howl of childish crocodile tears, ensuring that his victim will take the full blame.

"She said she was going to scratch my eyes out," his thin, reedy voice wails.

The girl begins to protest, trying to fight her own corner, but the teacher is in no mood to listen – the boy's performance has done its job. Mind made up, the teacher grabs the young girl by the wrist and marches her across the playground, her pleas for clemency falling on deaf ears.

"How many times do I have to tell you that we don't solve our problems with our fists," she admonishes the protesting child.

"But Miss, he was pulling my hair."

"I don't care what he was doing, or who started it. You do not attack the other children."

And there it was, the perfect tableau to prove my point. The poison is already in their systems. The rot slowly crawling through their veins. Innocence is not to be found here.

"Can I help you, mate?" a male voice calls, defensive and angry, pulling me out of my reflections.

I look up to see a young man standing inside the fence. Pale shirt and dark trousers, hands on hips, staring aggressively at me.

I'm in no mood to engage with him, so I turn away with a sneer, walking deliberately slowly, running my finger along the criss-crossed metal links of the fence all the way to the end. The pressure of my finger on the wire makes the most gentle, pleasing little rattle.

I can feel the teacher's eyes on my back all the way to the corner of the block. But I refuse to be rushed. I stop and turn for one last look at the young man, just to be sure. Yes. I'll see you later.

Turning the corner, the grand gates of the main school stand proudly before me. I haven't been back here for months. There's been no need. But the *delightful Dr Ripley has drawn me here today, and it feels strangely comforting to be back, to see my message again. Of course, the police still haven't seen all of it, not the full details. That's what's been so disappointing. But now that Dr Ripley is here, she will show them.*

I am desperate to talk to her about it, but it's not time yet – I have to make sure she is ready to listen. Meanwhile, I'm enjoying walking in her footsteps. I slip into the shadows on the far side of the road, under the great big oak tree that gave him cover before. It's the perfect vantage point to see all the way down the wide path, through the ornate gardens, all the way to the broad main entrance.

And there she is, walking purposefully along the path, head facing front, not distracted by the perfectly sculpted box balls lining the drive, or the neat and precise planting in the borders and beds. She's on a mission.

A bell rings, loud and solid, and she is enveloped in a sudden wave of youngsters piling through the doors to begin their indoctrination all over again. I settle against the low wall, the slightly rounded stone pressing into my back, familiar and comforting, reminding me of the hours spent planning my first test. It had been colder back then, Christmas time – the worst possible time of the year, when their ignorance hurts me the most.

As the bell's sound fades into the sky, I check my watch. Delicious as it is to keep tabs on my new friend, I need to get a move on. There's so much to do today. My delicate, deliberate planning is all coming to fruition now, exactly on schedule, but there's no time to dally. I have to get it just right.

RIPLEY STOOD IN the small hallway of St Michael's Church of England School, wondering if she'd ever get over that feeling of being in trouble when outside a Headmaster's office. She'd never been that naughty at school; a little too talkative, perhaps. Especially in Religious Studies, where her often vociferous disagreements with her teacher had seen her reprimanded a handful of times. Her Headmistress had, in the end, just told her to try to listen as much as she talked. Sound advice from a wise woman.

The hallway walls were lined with black-and-white year group photographs dating back to the late 19th Century, and Ripley spent a little time studying each of the line-ups, wondering what had happened to those young men. The school had been a male only environment until the 1980s, if the photographs were anything to go by. Hosts of cheeky faces, grinning for the camera, who would have gone on to fight in the wars, serve their country, die on battlefields, or live on with the strange afflictions that the survivors had brought back with them.

Shell shock, they'd called it back then. PTSD now. Her John was just another young boy who had grown up and gone to a hostile foreign land to serve his country and lost part of his mind in the process. She wondered if she should try to call him. Would he speak to her on the phone? He hadn't managed it yet. She would call Neil Wilcox later, when she had a moment, and see how he was doing.

She was quite enjoying being distracted from her own life for a moment. Especially among friends. Dinner at Dan Cotter's last night had been one of the first times she'd felt like a normal woman having a normal night out for ages.

She was brought back to reality as the door to the Head's office opened and a round-faced man with a neat bowl haircut beamed at her, red-cheeked and watery eyed. He looked like he could play a perfect Toad of Toad Hall in the local theatre.

"Dr Ripley?" he asked. "Morris Hanson. I'm the Head here at St Michael's. Do come in. Sorry to have kept you waiting."

"No problem at all. I was just admiring the old school photos."

"Ah yes, we've a long legacy of fine students here. Some scoundrels among them too no doubt. Though no Prime Ministers, yet, thank God. Come in, come in."

He ushered her into a large, old-fashioned office. Like the rest of the school it was all dark wood and deep blue carpets. The school crest, two fighting lions around a shield, gold on a deep green background with the motto Super Omnia Veritas displayed beneath. *The Truth Above All Things.* A nice sentiment, Ripley thought, and one which resonated with her.

"Please, have a seat. Maureen has popped off to make us some coffee. She'll be along in a minute. I would suggest we have tea on the balcony, but the weather's not really on our side is it?"

He was a blustery man with a strange, nervous energy about him. A fusspot. The word popped into her head unprompted, in her mother's voice. Absolutely accurate.

"It's a lovely view," she said. Looking out of the French doors over a quadrangle framed by the perfectly landscaped gardens of the school. Off to the right were the ruins of the castle. To the left, the reaches of the park, high over to rest of the town.

"Ruined by that bloody glass, if you ask me," he muttered. "Bulletproof, you know? Installed for a visit from the Prince of Wales. Takes more cleaning that my whole bloody house."

Ripley turned from the window and took her seat, smiling as he lumbered into his chair opposite her, puffing his cheeks as he adjusted himself. Finally settled, he looked at her properly for the first time.

"Maureen tells me you're with the police," Hanson said, by way of a question.

"I'm a consultant," Ripley clarified. "They often call on me to assist with cases, especially where there is an element of faith or religion involved."

"Huh," he exclaimed, as though delighted with the concept. "There's an expert for everything these days, isn't there?"

Ripley didn't quite know how to respond to that, so she said nothing. He obviously realised it may not have been the politest response.

"I'm terribly sorry, I have an awful habit of blurting things out. Maureen usually tells me to shut up. I meant nothing by it, it's simply that I am impressed that the police would take enough interest in matters of faith to have their own expert."

"I'm freelance," she said, realising that he genuinely did just speak his thoughts out loud without a filter. "But I think the police know enough to recognise that a little specialist knowledge goes a long way. Especially when it comes to murder investigations."

That shut him up. He sat forward, red cheeks flushing just a little more.

"Of course. Terrible business," he muttered. "Lovely man, too, the Reverend Tom."

Ripley frowned. She'd come here to find out more about Dylan.

"You knew Reverend Bainbridge?" she asked.

"Of course," Mr Hanson replied. "I'd even go so far as to say he was a friend."

His jowls quivered as he swallowed hard, seeming a little nervous.

"If only he'd come for that drink with me," he continued. "This might never have happened."

"You saw him," Ripley asked. "On the night he was murdered?"

He looked at her quizzically, confused.

"Well, yes," he said. "I assumed that was why you wanted to see me."

Ripley's mind caught up. Was this man the connection between the three deaths? Was he the killer? She couldn't let him think, even for a second, that she suspected him, though he didn't seem the type. Still, she had long since learned never to make judgements about what a person was capable of simply from their appearance.

"No," she said, quickly. "I actually came here to talk to you about Dylan Parker."

He frowned now, a flicker of something crossing his face. What was that? Anger? Annoyance? Guilt? He shuffled in his seat, the leather and wood groaning quietly under his bulk.

"Hmm," he said. "Such a good boy. So polite. Promising future. Voice of an angel, he had, especially as a young lad, but even as he got older. I know people say it all the time of the dead, but he really could have gone on to such great things."

He shook his head, jowls wobbling, lips pursed.

"It's just terrible," he continued, "that such a wonderful young man could be taken from us so soon. But the nature of his death. *That's* been the hardest thing to understand. What evil must live in a man to do that? What hate?"

What evil, indeed, Ripley thought, watching him for any tell-tale ticks.

"I know the police have already asked you a lot of questions, and I've read those reports," Ripley said. "But I wonder if I may ask a few more?"

"Of course," he said, leaning back. The chair creaked ominously.

A timid knock at the door, and a short, broad woman came in carrying a tray of coffee, milk and biscuits.

"Sorry to interrupt," she said. "I've brought coffee."

"Thank you, Maureen. Why don't you join us? Dr Ripley has some more questions about young Dylan Parker."

He turned to Ripley, as though to check it was okay, but Ripley could sense his relief at the interruption.

"Maureen is the eyes and ears of the school, as I told your colleagues," he said. "If there is anything happening with our pupils, she'll know all about it."

Maureen smiled sadly, a long slow blink, as she made herself comfortable, settling down with her own cup of coffee, and looking at Ripley with interest.

"Fire away, Dr Ripley," Maureen said, authoritatively. "Mr Hanson needs to be free by first break. We're running through preparations for the Whitsun Walk on Sunday. The whole school takes part, you know? Parents and friends too. This year, we're hoping to make it our biggest celeb…"

"Thank you, Maureen," Mr Hanson cut her off. He was obviously used to her waffling, but she still looked put out.

"I understand Dylan was in the choir?" Ripley asked, filling the gap.

"That's correct," Maureen said. "He has been a chorister since primary. Year six he joined. Beautiful voice."

"And who runs the choir?"

"The music department," Mr Hanson said. "Mr Richards and Miss Bevan."

"And it was Mr Richards who was running the rehearsal that night?"

"That's correct," Maureen said. "He feels terrible about it all. If Dylan hadn't stayed behind to help pack away the song books and stack the chairs, perhaps he wouldn't have been in the park exactly when—" she faltered.

"It's hard not to ponder the what ifs," Ripley said. "I do understand. But we believe that Dylan Parker may have been deliberately targeted by his killer."

"Really?" Mr Hanson spluttered. "The officers who came to talk to us said he had been a victim of a random killing."

"Some new evidence has come to light," Ripley said. "And it leads us to believe that Dylan's murder is connected to at least two more deaths in the area."

"No!" Maureen said. A drawn-out exclamation of disbelief.

A paroxysm of coughing seized Mr Hanson, bringing a halt to the questioning until he had recovered himself enough for Ripley to explain some of their theory.

Deciding to test what he knew, she showed them the images from the painting in the church. She kept the actual photographs of the other scenes to herself for now, not wanting to distress Maureen any further.

"Well. This is very peculiar," Mr Hanson said. "I mean, what on earth could possess a man to do something this barbaric, based on the scriptures which are supposed to teach us right from wrong, to help people understand how to behave in this life. Why?"

Ripley felt a small pulse of excitement. There was something in that question which was absolutely pertinent and she had overlooked it. The doom paintings had been intended to teach the illiterate masses about the scriptures, to warn them against doing wrong lest they end their days with the damned, in hell. The paintings were designed to shape behaviour and that seemed to be exactly what this killer was trying to do with the scenes he was recreating. She couldn't quite make the pieces fit yet, but there was definitely something there.

"Can you tell me a little about the charity work Dylan had been doing? I understand he had raised a lot of money for a blood cancer charity," Ripley asked.

The question of how the victims were selected still bothered her. They had found a link between the three victims in the parish newsletter, but it wasn't quite enough to satisfy Ripley of the pattern yet.

The Monday Club ran weekly throughout the year, and it had started two years previously. So there would have been over a hundred of them to date, all of them celebrating another facet of community support and life. Yet he'd only chosen three victims to date. So the question still remained: Why those particular victims? There had to be something more to the selection process, but Ripley couldn't put her finger on it.

"One of his classmates, Joseph Goldman, had been diagnosed with a rare form of leukaemia in their last year of junior school. Dylan took at as a personal challenge to help him beat it. He turned every moment of spare time he had to raising funds," Maureen said, smiling fondly at the memory.

"Fun runs, bake sales, dressing up days, raffles, auctions, you name it, Dylan organised it," Mr Hanson added. "And he got the whole community behind him. You'd even find him packing bags in the local supermarket in the evenings after school, waiting for his mother to finish work. He was an incredible young man. So selfless, so kind."

Maureen nodded, lips trembling slightly as she was reminded that he wasn't here anymore. Ripley got the feeling that Mr Hanson was making sure only to accentuate the positives, whereas Maureen's reaction spoke of real grief.

"I just don't know how anyone could do that to him, when he did everything, everything for others," she muttered.

"I'm trying to understand how Dylan came to his killer's attention," Ripley said.

"Well, he was always in the papers," Maureen said. "He was very good at getting the local press to cover all of his fundraising antics. He'd been on the radio a few times, talking about his new targets, how much they'd raised, and how it would help children like Joseph in the future. Our local BBC news had him on a couple of times. And you know, he never let a chance go by to thank

God for giving him the strength and passion to help. He was such a good boy."

"So he was pretty well known locally, then?"

"You think the killer targeted him because he was doing such good work?" Mr Hanson asked, sitting forward.

"Perhaps because he was doing it so publicly," Ripley said. The idea was forming in her mind as she said it. Sister Francis had also done a lot of work for the community, as had Reverend Tom. Was the killer targeting those who did the most good? Why?

"One more thing, Mr Hanson," Ripley said, about to test a theory. "Did you know Sister Francis at all? The second victim."

She watched his brow crease into a frown. Was he thinking about it or had she caught him out? It was hard to tell under all that skin.

"We don't have anything to do with the convent," Maureen butted in, firmly.

Mr Hanson leaned back again, question answered.

"Now, Dr Ripley, I'm afraid we really do have to get on. Break is almost upon us, and Mr Hanson does need to run this parade rehearsal with a clear head."

Ripley left the office, with Maureen hurrying to take her across to meet the choir master, who had only added to the picture of Dylan's incredibly kind nature. Ripley was used to people speaking well of the dead, but even she found the lengths to which the young boy had gone to help others quite impressive.

It hadn't just been the charity fundraising either. He would regularly visit local care homes to read to or talk to the pensioners there, he would help out cleaning tables and washing dishes at the homeless shelter, talking and laughing with the people who came in for a hearty meal and a bit of relief from a life on the streets. Across the whole community, he'd found things to do that would make the world a better place, and he seemed to have done a great job of getting others galvanised behind him, too, using the media to shout about his causes from the highest rooftops. The more she heard, the more Ripley was convinced that this was why he'd found himself in the crosshairs – because he'd been so vocal about his good work.

After her chat with the choir master, the head gardener had been roped in to guide her to the site in the gardens where Dylan' body had been found. He seemed reluctant to take her, though, and ambled along slowly, in silence, grunting monosyllabic responses to her compliments about the grounds.

He led her to a copse of old trees, with a series of small rockeries gathered in the dappled shade beneath their broad canopies. A temporary metal barrier had been erected around the site, every inch of the railing covered in bunches of flowers, cards, notes, drawings – a memorial to a friend lost. They still hadn't opened that section of the gardens back up, and the gardener wasn't sure they ever would.

Ripley noticed that he hung back from the site, allowing her to walk the perimeter alone, reading the notes and cards. She peered over the fence at the rockery itself. The small succulents and alpines tucked in among the rocks providing little cushions of colour in the shade, and making the site where Dylan's body had been buried stand out even more. The plants had been cleared when the body was buried which would have taken time. *How had no one seen these preparations taking place?*

Now, she noticed, the bare ground was littered with tall leafy weeds with bright yellow flowers.

"Bloody mustard plants," the gardener said. "I need to get in there and root them out, or they'll take over, but I just…"

His voice tailed off, and Ripley understood. The seeds that had been found with Dylan's body were mustard seeds. The gardener was hesitating to touch that final reminder of what had happened here.

Ripley was reminded of the parable of the seeds, sown on rock, path and fertile ground. That particular story had been all about how people heard the word of God, but it wasn't the only time the mustard seed was mentioned in the Bible. It was used regularly as a metaphor for faith.

Emma was right, there had been clues in the scenes all along, they had just been too opaque. Only someone with Ripley's experience would see the hidden meaning. The thought that perhaps she had been destined to come here to help – summoned even – chilled her.

She'd promised Dunn she'd go into the station and look at that Bible too, and now she felt like she had an idea what its significance might be. She was circling closer to the truth. She could feel it.

As they walked back towards the school building, the gardener looked sideways at here.

"I blame myself for not noticing earlier," he said, quietly.

"Not noticing?" Ripley asked.

"The rockery," he replied. "Someone had moved all the stones, dug out the space. I built that rockery, and I know it would have taken time to move all those stones. They hadn't just been moved, either, they had been removed. I've found some of them since, hidden all over the grounds, in different places. Someone had been moving them, slowly, and covering his tracks, and I didn't notice, because it's a part of the gardens that never needs tending. There is no grass to mow – it won't grow in the shade – and the plants in the rockery don't need pruning or watering. But I should have noticed."

"You can't blame yourself," Ripley said.

She left the school with her mind racing. If nothing else, she had discovered another connection between the three victims – Mr Hanson, the Head of the school. She was sure from his reaction that he knew Sister Francis somehow, too. Could he have spent the time clearing the grounds? Would anyone in the school have thought it odd, the Head helping out with the grounds. Would anyone even have noticed?

The gardener had confirmed that the school grounds were open to the public and, in fact, a public footpath ran right through the middle of the gardens, flanking the rugby pitches, and cutting up past the junior school playground. He told her he'd petitioned for the path to be moved to keep it outside the school grounds, but Mr Hanson had admonished his lack of faith in human nature. He'd sneered when he said that, clearly believing he'd been proved right.

As she hit the street, heading back to her car, she called Emma and arranged to meet her for lunch, so she'd run her new theories past her friend, and see if they couldn't get a step ahead of their killer before he struck again.

MY NEXT HAS shown himself to be a good choice, after all. Better than the one I had originally planned. I mean, they're all part of the same corrupt, demonic chain, but there are some who wear their righteousness a little too boldly. And they're the perfect ones to choose. Through their suffering, the rest of the little sheep will begin to see that the louder you proclaim your love for the Demon God, the more delight he takes in seeing you suffer.

That's why I always force them to pray to their God, one last time, before I free them. To prove his lies. I have returned to show them all the error of their ways, and I will get it right this time.

A loud bang makes me jump and I press myself against the fence, heart thumping. It was nothing – a motorbike backfiring. But it reminds me how much I hate the weakness of this human flesh, this feeble mind that holds me.

I slide through the section of metal fencing, careful to lift it so it leaves no trace that I've been here, and cross the clearing towards the ramshackle building on the far side – an old church. Perfect for my needs – small, remote, long abandoned, part-dilapidated, and due to be destroyed.

Inside, I allow myself a moment to admire my choice of venue. It sets the scene so perfectly. The old, fire-ravaged beams, blackened and cracked. The roof open to the sky, with tatters of an old tarpaulin which had long since given up serving any purpose, fluttering in the breeze like ghosts. The stained glass that hadn't been destroyed in the fire had been smashed by kids throwing stones at the wire-covered windows. Now only small shards of coloured glass cling to the old stone frames.

The skeletons of burned pews litter the floor, rotting into a ground covered in soot and grime, with weeds sprouting optimistically among the detritus. My seeds. My message.

The remains of the cross loom over the space, one arm blackened and halved where the flames had licked up its side. The figure attached to the cross is equally charred, his face smashed in by vandals. It makes me sad. He doesn't deserve your hate. He tried to tell you, but you wouldn't listen.

Working quickly, I finish preparing the scene. There are other things to attend to this afternoon. It won't do to let anything slip at this stage. Not now that I have the end in sight.

RIPLEY WAVED AT Emma as she came into the pub. They'd agreed to meet somewhere central, and Ripley had got here early. Emma shook off her damp jacket, and sat down, running her hand through her short hair.

"God, it's grim out there," she said, sitting down. "How're you doing?"

"I'm good," Ripley replied. "Busy morning."

They ordered their food, and Ripley filled Emma in on her discussions at the school. Both warmed by the homemade pies they'd ordered, and the cheeky glass of red they'd washed them down with, they settled into trying to unpick what they knew so far.

"So he's preparing his scenes way in advance of the murders?" Emma said.

"Yes, looks that way. Although the gardener couldn't say for sure how long before. All he knew was that he would never have been able to clear that rockery in one night, without being seen or heard. So he must have been moving one rock at a time for a few days at least."

"That's pretty ballsy, isn't it?"

"Yes. I mean, the gardens are open to the public, and there is a footpath running right through the middle of the grounds, but still, you'd think someone would notice a guy carrying rocks about the place," Ripley said.

"Unless they thought he worked there," Emma replied.

"Do you remember the scene, when his body was found?" Ripley asked. "Did it look like there'd been a lot of recent excavation work?"

"It wasn't my scene," Emma replied. "But I've studied the notes. Nothing was mentioned about recent clearance work in the garden. The only thing was a statement from the gardener saying he never had much call to go into that part of the grounds."

"Yeah, that's what he told me too. He blames himself for not noticing the changes earlier."

"I wonder if the killer did that at the church, too?" Emma asked. "Judith didn't mention anything about any changes there, but perhaps it just didn't need as much preparation. I mean, burying Dylan, even up to the waist, would have required a lot of time. The CSOs just assumed he'd been disturbed half way through the act of burying him when they examined the scene, but of course we know different now."

Emma reached into her satchel and pulled out an evidence bag which she slid across the table towards Ripley.

"What's this?" Ripley asked.

"The bible that Sister Francis was holding when her body was found. DS Dunn asked me to give it straight to you, see what you can find."

Ripley hesitated, holding the top of the sealed bag.

"Am I alright to open it?"

"Yeah, of course," Emma said. "I've put your name on the evidence chain. It's already been processed for prints and trace. Turned up nothing, so I figure the clue has to be something to do with the book itself. The killer obviously placed it in her hands deliberately, but why?"

Ripley took the book and opened it carefully. The New Testament, English Standard.

"It's a fairly generic copy," she said. "You can pick these up almost anywhere, so you'll have a job tracing where it came from. Most churches order them in bulk."

Ripley fell quiet, leafing through the pages, while Emma poured them both a glass of water from the jug on the table. The bible was a cheap one, thin paper pages with a small typeface, the verses packed close together to save on printing costs, the cover plain.. There was nothing special about the version, no alternative translations which might make this copy stand out – it was kind used in churches and Sunday Schools up and down the country.

Ripley turned page after page, knowing that the needle she was looking for may not be at all obvious. Finally, she found it.

"Huh," Ripley said, and Emma leaned forward.

Ripley flicked back a few pages and then forward a few more. She pushed the spine of the book open further, peering into the crack, flipping the pages back and forth again.

"What is it?" Emma asked.

"There are pages missing," Ripley replied.

"What?"

"Look," Ripley turned the bible round to face her, and Emma picked it up to study it closer. "There are at least two pages removed."

Emma confirmed her assessment and handed the bible back.

"Do you know what was on them?"

"It's the gospel of Mark," Ripley replied. "But I'll have to look up the verses. I've got an idea though."

She lifted her phone from the table, opening a browser window and, cross-referencing the last verse on the page that remained in the book, she typed in a search for Mark 4:1-20.

"Aha," she said, as the page refreshed.

"What?"

"It's the parable of the sower," Ripley said.

"The one about the seeds on the rocks," Emma asked, and Ripley could hear the excitement prick her voice. She felt it herself. They were closing in on something.

"Yes, among other places."

"What does it mean?"

"Well, the whole parable is about how God's word is heard and listened to. Each place where the seeds are scattered have a different significance for how the scriptures are heard and how they are interpreted."

"Dylan Parker was found with a handful of seeds," Emma said.

"Exactly," said Ripley, frowning and falling silent as she read and re-read the missing verses on her phone.

"The deaths have all got something to do with hearing the word of God, but I'm just not *getting it* yet," she mused, not looking up.

There was something here, a deeper message in this missing parable, and it was knocking on the back of her mind. The killer had obviously cut this page out to point their attention back to what they'd missed on Dylan's crime scene – the significance of the seeds.

In the vague recesses of her memory, Ripley remembered that there had been something significant about the parable of the sower that she couldn't quite put her finger on now. The page she was looking at on her phone gave the basic interpretation. She laid the phone down and flicked forward in the bible, checking the books of Matthew and Luke, knowing that the same parable was written there too. Both of those versions were still intact. So there must be something specific about the way the parable was told in Mark's version that was significant.

She searched through another few pages from the web, looking for an alternative meaning and found nothing. With each page she read, that sense of an answer just out of her reach grew stronger. Perhaps she was being too literal. *Think, Alex.*

These parables, all of them, were written to share Christ's teachings in a way that the masses would find less radical at the time. When asked why he spoke in parables, Jesus had told his disciples that it was because people would hear the teaching but think they were just listening to a story. They would be more likely to hear and understand it, if they enjoyed it.

The parable of the sower, in particular, was about hearing and understanding the teachings of Christ. But Ripley remembered, too, that the parable was interpreted differently in each of the gospels it featured in. In Mark – the one that was missing here – the parable came directly after a section describing the developing anger and hostility about the way Jesus was spreading his message. He was seen as a maverick – offering miracle cures, and not observing the Sabbath. Slowly, but surely, he was making enemies among the Pharisees. Some of the scribes had even gone as far as to suggest that Jesus's power came from demonic sources.

Ripley snapped the bible shut and looked at Emma.

"What?"

"I think I understand," she said. "Come on."

She got up quickly, grabbed her coat and phone, threw enough cash on the table to cover their meals, and hurried out of the pub with Emma in tow.

RIPLEY DASHED THROUGH the quiet streets, heading back towards the St Andrew's Church. Finally, the penny had dropped. The idea of Christ being demonic had been one of the statements she'd read in the strange leaflet that had been thrust into her hand as she'd left the church last time.

Reverend Judith had said the guy was often there, handing out leaflets. Ripley wanted to see if the message in the leaflet *was* the same as she'd just read on the internet. Because if it was, it might make some sense of why the victims so far had been those doing Christ's work most publicly.

"What is it, Alex?" Emma asked, just about keeping up with her.

"Do you remember I told you about that guy giving out leaflets about how God had deserted us?" Ripley asked, not breaking stride.

"Yeah?" Emma sounded unsure.

"Well, part of the leaflet went on about how God was a demon, and was enjoying watching people hurt each other, and how everyone needed to hear the truth and stop listening to His lies if we were to survive as a species without killing each other."

"And what's it got to do with the missing pages of the bible?"

"It's a long story but, basically, in Mark's Gospel – the missing one – the leaders were angry with Jesus because his teachings were leading people astray. Some of them said he was getting his powers from a demonic source. And that people shouldn't follow him."

"Right," Emma said, still not quite understanding.

"Which might be what our killer is trying to say with all of his clues," Ripley said, exasperated. "That we shouldn't be following Christ's teachings, and we should be listening to him instead. Whatever message is in those leaflets."

Emma almost stopped running as the reality hit her.

"He has a Christ complex?"

"Even worse," Ripley said, not slowing down. "A God complex."

"We have to call Daniel," she said. "You can't just go running in if your crazy leaflet guy is the killer. What are you thinking?"

"I just want to check," Ripley said. "I'm hardly going to try to take him down myself. You call Dan, and I'll see you at the church."

"Alex…"

"Don't worry, I won't do anything stupid. I just want to see that leaflet again," Ripley said, leaving Emma in the main square, already pulling her phone out of her pocket.

Entering the church ground at the bottom of the old graveyard, the side of the big red brick building loomed in front of her. She hurried up the curved path to find that, apart from a couple of tourists bending to examine one of the medieval tombstones, the churchyard was empty.

She did a quick, full circuit of the church, just in case, glancing out of each of the three gates which gave out onto the pedestrian streets beyond. There was no sign of the leaflet guy.

Ripley huffed to herself, regretting chucking her own copy in her hotel bin yesterday. She just wanted to check the wording he'd used to see if her hunch was right. Was this the message these awful deaths were supposed to convey? That the Christian God was a Demon God, and he revelled in the deaths of his followers?

Struck by another idea, she strode into the church. Reverend Judith had told her she often took a leaflet from the guy, just to keep him quiet. Perhaps she'd still have one, and if not, at least Ripley could talk to someone who might understand his odd viewpoint.

The church was quieter today than when she'd last been in – already the morbid fascination with the murder had faded. A couple of worshippers sat in one of the front pews, heads bent in prayer. A young couple walked, hand in hand, around the side of the building, admiring the stained-glass windows in each chapel. Ripley hurried quietly down the centre aisle, heading towards the vestry where she hoped she would find Reverend Judith.

The door was closed, so she knocked and waited.

"Hello?" a voice called from inside.

Ripley pushed the door open and found Judith on her hands and knees, head deep inside a cupboard. She looked up as Ripley greeted her.

"Ah, Dr Ripley," she said. "How lovely to see you again. Excuse the position, but I'm trying to find our altar cloth for the Pentecost celebration. It seems to have vanished into thin air. What can I do for you?"

"I was wondering," Ripley said, "if you had one of those leaflets we spoke about the other day? The one that doomsday chap hands out outside."

Judith stood up, groaning at her sore knees and dusting her clothes down, a strange smile on her face.

"I'm not sure," she said, looking quizzical. "I usually just throw them out as soon as I come indoors. Let's have a look."

The pile of papers on her desk was random and messy, leaflets for church events, a couple of gossip magazines, a few clerical publications. A large blotter with lots of scribbles all over it in big, blousy handwriting. Flicking through the pile, Judith came up blank.

"Hmm, she said," turning back to Ripley. "It's looks like my filing system remains as efficient as ever."

She cocked her head to one side, suddenly struck by a thought.

"Oh now hang on," she said. "Come to think of it, he was here yesterday. Hmm…"

She turned her attention to another pile of books and papers on the chair beside her own, finally looking up triumphantly.

"Ta dah!" she exclaimed. "Is this what you were looking for?"

"Thank you," Ripley said, taking the leaflet eagerly.

She opened it to read the words she'd half-remembered. Sure enough, the majority of the inside-spread listed examples from modern life to prove that the God Christians followed was, in fact, a demon. Most of the examples were of people who claimed to be good Christians who were less than such in their actions – His ambassadors, they were described as. It read as a who's who of the corrupt, adulterous, lecherous, murderous men and women of our time. Ripley raised an eyebrow. Reading this list, one could almost believe he had a point.

In the final paragraph, she found the line she'd remembered: "*From as far back in time as the days of Christ himself, people knew that*

God's powers were demonic. But those who stood against him were destroyed, including Christ himself, until only those who followed His word remained, and His indoctrination of the innocent was complete. "

Ripley closed the leaflet. There was definitely something in this theory.

"What is it?" Judith asked, seeing the look on Ripley's face.

"How much do you know about him?" she asked. "The guy who gives these out?"

"Martin?" Judith asked. "Not much. He's always around. I think people have got used to him now. He's fairly harmless. Not too aggressive about getting people to take his leaflets. He can sometimes be a little too loud in his pronouncements, but that isn't surprising, with his condition, is it?"

"His condition?" Ripley asked.

"Well, he can't be completely right in the head, can he?" Judith said. "Sorry to say it, but with views like that. I mean. He must have – you know – mental problems."

Ripley wasn't so sure. Just because his conviction went against common teaching didn't mean he was mentally unstable.

"When did he start coming here?" Ripley asked.

Judith frowned.

"I don't know, about six months ago, maybe," she said. "Wait, do you think this has something to do with Tom…?"

Her voice trailed off, the frown deepening on her brow.

"I'm working on a theory," Ripley said, realising that she probably shouldn't share too much with the vicar before she'd spoken to Dan Cotter and his colleagues. "It may be nothing."

Reverend Judith was still looking concerned when Ripley took her leave, hurrying from the room with thanks and a promise to be in touch soon.

"Oh, Dr Ripley?" Judith called after her, suddenly remembering. "We've decided to go ahead with the Monday Club event tonight. I know you and your colleagues wanted to come. I have to say I'm not happy about it, but if it helps you catch Tom's killer, we can't not, can we?"

Ripley knew that Cotter and Dunn had been pressuring the church to hold the event as normal, and that Judith had initially refused, saying she felt it was too soon after Tom's death. Obviously Cotter had found a way to get through to her.

"Great," Ripley said. "We'll all be here."

"Starts at seven," Judith said. "DC Cotter promised they would send plain clothes officers to be part of the gathering."

"He'll make sure everyone is safe," Ripley said. She could see that the vicar was still wrestling with the idea of putting any more of her community in danger. "You're doing the right thing, Reverend."

Judith smiled softly, appreciating the support.

"I'll see you tonight, then."

Ripley hurried back through the body of the church, and out into the pale sunshine. Her heart was thudding a little harder than usual, the smallest flutter of excitement that she often felt when pieces of the puzzle were starting to come together. She found Emma waiting for her at the gates.

"Any luck?" Emma asked.

"No sign of the guy, but I got a name, and another copy of his leaflet."

"Dan's tied up over at the school, apparently they've reported some guy hanging around the playground, teachers thought they'd seen him before too. Anyway, they're taking that kind of thing more seriously after what happened to Dylan. Dan says to tell you not to get yourself into any trouble."

"As if," Ripley smiled. "So, the vicar's going ahead with the Monday Club event tonight."

Emma raised an appreciative eyebrow. "Who's presenting?"

"A pair of students who have been doing mission work on their gap year," Ripley said.

"Great, let's hope he shows."

As they left the church grounds, Ripley tucked the leaflet into her pocket. She knew the message it contained was a big link to what had happened to their three victims, and she wanted time to lay everything out and piece it all together.

IT WAS ALREADY dark when Ripley walked back into the church grounds, the bells striking the half hour as she passed through the lower gate. Six-thirty – plenty of time to chat to the others before taking her seat in the small meeting room.

Reverend Judith was waiting at the doors and smiled when she saw Ripley. She looked nervous.

"How are you feeling?" Ripley asked.

"Anxious," Judith admitted. "The others are all inside already, and I've encouraged a few of the regulars to come early too. They've been setting up the refreshments and raffle stand."

"Good," Ripley said, patting the vicar's arm gently. "I'm going to see what they need me to do."

"What am I looking for?" Judith asked, betraying the real source of her anxiety. "I mean, is it Martin we're waiting for, or..."

"Not necessarily," Ripley replied. "Anyone who looks suspicious really."

"I've never run one of these events. I don't know who is a familiar face and who isn't. Tom would have known..."

"Don't worry," Ripley said, calmly. "We don't even know if they're going to come, let alone be stupid enough to make themselves known. You have good instincts, Reverend. All you have to do is trust them."

"If I trusted my instincts, I'd have cancelled this evening."

"I'm sure Tom would have wanted the club to go on, and if there's a chance that his killer is using the events as a way of picking targets, then we owe it to him to catch them before they strike again."

Judith sighed and nodded. She didn't have to like it, but it had to happen.

Ripley walked into the room to find Emma and Dunn in close conversation near a long trestle table, loaded up with plastic cups, jugs of watery looking cordial, and two silver catering urns for tea and coffee. Plates of Family Mix biscuits sat either side of the table.

"Where do you need me?" Ripley asked, sidling up to Dunn and noticing how they both jumped apart slightly.

"Ah, Dr Ripley," Dunn said. "Nice to see you."

She was blushing slightly. Ripley raised a questioning eyebrow at Emma, who winked almost imperceptibly, confirming Ripley's suspicion – they were up to something.

"Good afternoon?" Emma asked her, before she could say anything about it.

"I think so," Ripley said, keeping her voice low and quiet. "I'm pretty convinced that the killer is trying to prove that God is, in fact, the source of all evil."

"You think the leaflet guy is the killer?" Dunn asked, looking around as though he might show up at any point.

They were too close to the strangers in the refreshments queue for Ripley's liking – too many inquisitive eavesdroppers.

"I think the message in the leaflets is the clue to why those three people were killed the way they were," Ripley said. "I'll fill you in properly after this though. Too many eyes and ears here."

"But you saw him, before, right?" Dunn said. "What are we looking for?"

"I didn't really look at him," Ripley admitted. "I'm sorry. I just took the leaflet. I remember he had grey hair, a bit scruffy. But that's it, really."

"Would you recognise him again?"

"Possibly," Ripley said, but she wasn't so sure she would. She had been wracking her brain for any detail of the man who'd thrust the leaflet into her hand outside the church, but all she could remember was his hand, pushing the leaflet into hers. Thin and sinewy. She hadn't really had the chance to look at him properly.

Cotter arrived beside them, looking busy and efficient.

"Alright?" he asked. "Everyone's in place. About a third of the people here are ours."

"Good stuff," Ripley said. "That'll reassure the vicar. She's pretty nervous."

"We've got it covered," Cotter said.

"I'm going to mingle," Ripley said. "And find myself a good seat."

No more than twenty chairs had been arranged in rows, five each either side of a small aisle, facing a projector screen. The two students who would be presenting their adventures were both smiling and greeting people as they came in. Unaware that their presentation was little more than a front for a police investigation.

Ripley wondered again if this was such a good idea. She had felt they should stage the whole thing, and not involve the public at all, but Cotter had reminded her that the session had already been advertised in the newsletter, and a change to the line up now would seem even more suspicious than the full bench of new faces in the shape of their undercover team.

Looking around the crowd as the room began to fill up, Ripley was struck by how friendly everyone seemed. A few couples sat together, old friends chatting happily to each other, the odd peel of laughter at a shared story. In the front row, a stylishly dressed woman sat with her three children ranked in height order beside her. Their hair – identical shades of fiery red – marked them out as the siblings of one of the student presenters.

Ripley sidled into a seat at the far end of the back row, offering her the best view of the whole room, behind a reasonably tall man with dark tousled hair and an expensive looking dark wool coat. Ripley caught a waft of his aftershave as she adjusted her position and was instantly transported. It was the same one John used to wear – Armani.

Without turning around, he removed the dark blue and green scarf he was wearing and folded it with purposeful precision, placing it on the chair beside him. It was the same scarf as she'd seen the boys at St Andrews school wearing. An old boy, perhaps, or one of the teachers there? They all seemed to keep wearing the colours. Either way, he provided good cover for her to hide behind. He settled back into his chair and Ripley continued her scan of the room.

Surely none of these people could be their killer? They all looked too *normal*. Even the pinched-faced man with a sour expression, who sat alone in the second row, hands fidgeting in his lap. Dunn caught Ripley staring at him and subtly guided one of the plain clothes over to sit near him. Just as the officer sat beside him though, Ripley saw the man give a double thumbs up to the other student present for the night, his face briefly transforming into the picture of paternal pride. *Too normal*.

A couple of women – strong-shouldered, broad-hipped, red-lipped – chatted away to each other, catching up on the week's gossip. Their close familiarity was clear; years of repeated conversations, exchanges and laughter shaping their ease in each other's company. They both looked up as they were joined by another three similar women. Pleasant greetings exchanged and boiled sweets passed around the group, they were ready to hear from the students.

With almost every seat now full, Ripley felt a slight sinking feeling that no one there looked anything like the vague sense she had of Martin, the leaflet man. In fact, no one in the room looked anything other than interested parishioners here to learn about the wonderful work these two bouncy, energetic young adults had been doing all the way over in Africa.

Ripley continued to scan the room with decreasing frequency as their presentation rolled on, only vaguely listening to their slightly self-congratulatory duologue. The images they showed were everything you would expect of young missionaries in Africa – the pale red-haired boy surrounded by beaming African children, or the two of them painting a brightly coloured school building, or standing in front of a class, educating them in the word of God. Ripley had seen it all a hundred times. At least they were trying to give something to society, she chided herself for her cynical thoughts.

By the time the presentation had ended, the gathered community had been encouraged to part with a little more of their cash for the good cause and, amid much back-slapping for the two young missionaries.

As they all filtered out of the room, Ripley felt quite deflated. Perhaps Dunn's original cynicism had been well placed. They'd been silly to think he would turn up. If he was using the Monday club at all to choose his victims, it was probably only through picking them out of the newsletter, rather than actually coming to sit through their presentations.

Cotter and Dunn were coordinating their team to head home, and Emma was talking to Reverend Judith at the door. The two young missionaries, accompanied by their families stopped at the door. Much handshaking and broad-smiling congratulations saw them on their way.

Ripley stood up and pulled on her own coat, accidentally brushing it against the man in front, who was knotting his scarf around his neck. He half-turned to apologise and it was only then that Ripley recognised him.

"Adam?" she asked. "What are you doing here?"

Somehow, away from the residential clinic, he seemed even more handsome. He smiled warmly.

"Dr Ripley," he said, a small laugh tickling his throat. "Are you following me?"

"Not at all," Ripley said, suddenly stuck by a thought. "Do you come to these events often?"

"And other chat-up lines..." he winked, nudging her elbow playfully as they stepped into the aisle at the same time.

She could feel the blush hitting her cheeks.

"I'm teasing," he said. "Sorry. I do come quite often, as it happens. If I can make it. It's nice to hear some positives every week, you know?"

Ripley knew what he meant. Especially if he spent his days working with men in a similar condition to John.

"I wouldn't have had you down as a church-goer, though," he continued. "What brings you here? I'd have thought you'd be out on the town."

"Oh, just something I'm working on," she said, noncommittally.

He raised an eyebrow, as though expecting more, but she wasn't really prepared to share any of those details with a member of the public.

"Listen," she said. "Have you got time for that drink now? I really enjoyed the session today, and I think John will be in great hands with you, but I still have so many questions."

He stopped and looked at his watch, sucking air through his teeth and shaking his head.

"I'm sorry," he said, wincing. "I've got to run. Raincheck?"

"Okay," Ripley said.

"You'll still be here tomorrow, right?"

"I guess so," Ripley said. After all, they were no closer to solving the case.

"Great," he said. "What say I swing by your hotel tomorrow evening, say seven? I'll buy the drinks, if you promise to tell me all about your work."

There was something so charming about the way he smiled at her that Ripley wondered for a second if he was flirting with her. Before the thought could take hold, he turned tail, glancing at his watch again.

"Gotta run," he said, patting her elbow. "See you tomorrow."

"Who's your friend?" Emma asked, as Ripley reached her. The teasing tone in her voice made Ripley uncomfortable.

"He's the guy who's going to be looking after John," she said, shutting down any thoughts Emma might have of ribbing her. "I'll wait for you outside."

She shouldn't have snapped, but she was suddenly feeling like they'd been wasting their time here tonight, and she wanted to get back to the hotel and get some time to think.

Stepping out into the cool air, she saw Adam step into the pool of dim yellow light from the streetlamp on his way to the gates. He was approached by another man – shambling and unsteady-looking, hand outstretched. Adam shook his head angrily, and Ripley heard him say a gruff: "Not now, just go away."

It was only after he shouldered his way past the other man and out of the gate, that she realised the man he'd rejected was Martin, the leaflet guy, trying to hand out more of his missives. He clutched his canvas shopping bag tightly to his chest, and walked with a slow determination, muttering quietly to himself, looking left and right, presumably for people to hand his papers to.

Ripley turned quickly back to the door, calling out in a low, urgent voice.

"Emma, he's here. Get Dan."

Ripley turned back to the approaching figure, her heart beating hard. She positioned herself on the path in front of him, effectively blocking his passage. He stopped just short of walking into her. When he looked up into her eyes, she was struck by how hollow his face looked. Eyes sunken deep in dark sockets, cheekbones high and sharp, skin sallow even beneath the scraggly beard and ingrained layer of dirt that covered his face. It hadn't crossed her mind that he might be a rough sleeper, but that's exactly how he looked now.

"Martin?" she asked.

He blinked slowly, confused by her proximity, confused that she knew his name. He tried to step aside, but Ripley put out a hand. Not quite touching, but enough to stop him. She noticed how he recoiled slightly, as though afraid of human contact. It reminded her, in a flash, of how John responded to her sometimes, before he caught himself and remembered who she was.

"I'm sorry," Ripley said softly. "I just want to talk to you." *Where was Cotter?*

Martin said nothing, head tilted to one side like a curious dog, wondering whether it was about to receive a treat or a beating.

"You gave me one of your leaflets the other day," Ripley said, pointing to the one he was clutching in his hand. "I wanted to talk to you about it. About your message."

She saw the man's shoulders relax – the faintest trace of a smile flickered across his lips, fading quickly. Ripley wondered whether she was the first person who had ever engaged him on the subject. Her heart was still racing. Could this man, this nervous-wreck of a man, really be their killer?

A movement over his shoulder caught Ripley's attention. Adam had turned back and was approaching fast, looking concerned.

"Hey," he called, and Martin spun round.

"It's okay," Ripley called, trying to warn him to stay back, she didn't want Martin to make a run for it before Cotter got out here. She glanced back over her shoulder to see both Emma and Dan Cotter hurrying up the path towards her, with Dunn making up the ground quickly behind them.

Martin spun back towards Ripley looking frightened by the sudden rush of people towards him.

"Hey, you leave her alone," Adam shouted.

Ripley wished he would listen to his own advice. Martin's eyes locked with hers, fleetingly. The look of panicked betrayal clear in his watery gaze. He shoved the canvas shopping bag at her, pushing her roughly.

"Martin, wait," she called, but it was too late. He barged her to the ground and set off at a surprisingly quick sprint.

Cotter tore past her in pursuit, with Dunn hot on his heels. Emma stopped to help Ripley back to her feet.

"You alright?" Emma asked.

"I'm fine," Ripley said, grumpily brushing herself down. "I nearly had him, but Adam spooked him by coming back."

"Who?" Emma asked.

Ripley looked around. There was no sign of Adam anywhere. Perhaps he chased after Martin too.

"He was right here," Ripley said. "The guy I was talking to. He must have gone after Martin."

"Great," Emma said. "All we need is a have-a-go-hero getting involved."

"Well, hopefully Dan will catch him, and we can talk to him properly," Ripley said.

"Or we've dropped the ball and lost him," Emma huffed.

"We've got *this*, though," Ripley said, holding out the bag Martin had thrust at her as he'd sprinted off. "I'm sure your team will be able to get all sorts from this lot."

"Silver linings," Emma nodded, as they both turned and walked off in the direction of the chase. As they passed the front entrance of the church, Cotter came back through the gate, looking flushed and frustrated, breathing hard.

"He got away," Cotter said. "He just vanished."

"Probably knows all the shortcuts," Emma said. "Never mind, we'll track him down."

"Did you see the way he took off though?" Cotter said. "I would never have thought a guy his age could run that fast."

"I don't actually think he's that old," Ripley said.

Sure, his hair and beard were greying but, if they were cut shorter, he would look ten years younger. Just as John had when she'd gone in to see him the other day. Up close, Martin's eyes had been bright, and his skin, though dirty and pale, was not deeply lined. Given the speed he'd taken off at, he was both younger and fitter than he'd appeared. And accustomed to running from the police. He might well have had the strength to kill Reverend Tom the way he had.

Dunn finally reappeared too, equally empty handed.

"Slippery bugger that one. I thought I had him cut off, and he just vanished. Still, we'll get the lads out looking for him. At least we know what he looks like now."

As Cotter and Dunn rushed off to issue the warrant for his arrest and get his description and name circulating, Emma looked at Ripley.

"Back to the hotel for a drink?" she asked.

"Damn right," Ripley said.

As they said goodbye to Reverend Judith, asking her to call the police if Martin showed his face again, Ripley looked back over her shoulder. She couldn't help feeling that they were still being watched. Had Martin circled round to check what they were doing now? She wished she'd been able to talk to him, even for a moment. She was intrigued by the message he was trying to send but, until he'd sprinted off like that, she wouldn't have said he was strong enough to have carried out any of the murders they were investigating. Perhaps she was wrong. At least they had an actual suspect now, though.

I PULL MY cap low over my eyes, and slip out of the driver's seat, making my way to the back of the van. A quick check to make sure I'm not being watched, and I open the doors to climb inside.

It doesn't smell good in here. Fear does that to a man. He's still unconscious, which is a blessing. I can't risk him struggling or crying out before I get him into the church. I check his pulse. All good, nice and strong. Excellent.

Hopping back out of the van, I close the doors gently. Nightfall came a few hours ago, but I'm still grateful I'd disabled the streetlight closest to the gates a few nights before. Darkness is a friend. I allow myself a small smile as I lift the clanking metal gate and swing it open enough to back the truck in.

With the gate closed behind me, I reverse right up to the open end of the church building. Killing the engine and lights, I sit in silence for a moment, listening to the slow ticking of the engine as it cools, gathering my thoughts.

I could feel that familiar doubt threatening to creep in. Have I rushed this? Have I chosen the right one? I push the thought aside, getting out of the van. Of course he's the right one — he presented himself so perfectly at exactly the right time.

He's almost the same height and weight as my original target, so I hope the dose I gave him wasn't too strong — I don't want to have to wait too long for him to wake up before I can start. And he has to be awake, because otherwise, how will he pray? If he can't pray, he'll never know why he was chosen — he'll never know he's been wrong all along.

As I lift him from the back of the van, I hear the faintest of murmurs. It won't be long now. The last dance has begun.

8

EMMA WAS ALREADY in the breakfast room at the hotel when Ripley came down, nursing a hangover from their impromptu drinking session the night before. Cotter and Dunn had both joined them after their shift had ended, with no sign of Martin having been caught yet.

They had all been too hyped to go to bed, so they'd sat up in the hotel bar, quietly discussing Ripley's theory about the murders being messages to prove that God was evil. They tried every angle using their own cod-psychology to figure out why someone would go to such lengths to spread *that* message, but kept coming back to the fact that they just needed to find Martin to understand what was really going on in his mind.

By the time they had gone their separate ways, they were all pretty tipsy, though Ripley had been observant enough to notice that Emma hung back to speak to Dunn, and by the grin on Emma's tired face this morning, Ripley guessed that Dunn had stayed the night.

"Late one?" Ripley asked, eyebrow raised.

"No comment," Emma smiled with a small wink. "Coffee's just arrived. And it looks like your need is even greater than mine. Help yourself."

Ripley poured herself a cup from the small cafetière and breathed it in deeply before taking a sip.

"Didn't sleep much myself," Ripley said.

She had spent the night chasing thoughts around her head, circling answers that weren't forming properly, only to leave her with more questions.

Something about Martin had reminded her so much of John. That crazed look in his eye when he'd thought she was going to touch him. That visceral panic, which told her that he, too, was tormented by things he had seen. *What was his history?*

"Dan called," Emma said. "Looks like they've got something on your doomsday leaflet guy. I said we'd drop by the station after breakfast. That okay?"

"Great," Ripley said.

Her sleep had been so troubled with thoughts of John, and what his life would become when he was eventually allowed home. What would he do? Would he end up wandering the world, haunted by his own demons, like that poor Martin so obviously was.

She wondered if Martin had served in the forces, too? It made some sense. Being in the theatre of war would surely be enough to convince many that God either didn't care, or actually took pleasure in the destruction of his followers. If you left home a staunch believer, how on earth could you reconcile your beliefs with the devastation you both saw and caused?

"I'm going to head into the lab too, to see if the guys have been able to get anything from the leaflets," Emma continued.

Emma had dropped the abandoned bag of leaflets into the forensics lab after the incident at the church, in the hope that either the bag or the leaflets themselves would yield some clues. Fingerprints, DNA, anything that might help them get an accurate ID on the guy. Cotter and Ripley had worked with a police artist to create a photofit image of Martin, which they were now running through their many databases. Cotter had insisted that the way Martin had run off as soon as he saw them approaching, meant that he'd had a brush with the law in his past. But Ripley wasn't so sure.

Just as breakfast arrived at their table, Ripley's phone rang. Neil Wilcox, John's friend, returning her call.

"Start without me," she said to Emma. "I have to take this."

Emma didn't need to be invited twice, tucking in to her Full English with a contented smile. Ripley got up and walked out to the foyer, answering the phone as soon as she was out of the hubbub of the breakfast room.

"Coxy," she said. "Is everything okay?"

The same rising panic she felt every time she got a call from someone to do with John's care.

"Everything's good," Coxy said. "John's asking after you."

The panic faded as quickly as it had risen. John was alright.

"I told him you were working," Coxy continued. "But he's got something he wants to tell you, so he insisted I call."

Ripley was dumbstruck. This would be the first time she'd spoken to John on the phone since he'd got back. Was this a good thing? What was so important that it could persuade him to use a phone, when he'd been so against the idea?

"Great," she said, trying to sound positive.

"Wait there," Coxy said. "I'm going to switch you to video."

Another first. Ripley held the phone away from her ear, clicking to accept the request to switch. The pixels cleared quickly, but at first she didn't recognise what she was seeing. It was only when the figure sitting casually in a chair near a low window waved, that she realised it was John.

"Hey Lexi," he said. Even through the slightly tinny crackle of the video stream, his voice made her heart skip. He hadn't called her Lexi since he'd come home. It was what he'd called her from the first time they'd met, having joked that Alex sounded too butch, and point blank refusing to call her Ripley as many of their friends did.

"Hey you," she replied. "You look different."

She realised it was because it was also the first time she'd seen him not in his hospital bed. She knew that Coxy had been getting John up and moving, but he hadn't wanted to do that with her – he was too embarrassed to lean on her for the support he needed. Just the fact that he was in a normal chair made him look ten times more human again.

"I feel different," he said, happily.

"Where are you?" she asked. She didn't recognise the room either.

"They've agreed to move me," John said. "That's what I wanted to tell you. I didn't want you turning up to visit and finding my bed empty."

"What?" Ripley's heart skipped a beat. "They're sending you home?"

Was he ready for that? Was she?

"Hold your horses," John said, his voice breaking a little. "A place came up in that residential group I told you about. I'm going to give it a go. Coxy says you've given it the thumbs up, too?"

Ripley tried not to let her relief show. It was only when faced with the idea of John coming home that she'd understood she definitely wasn't ready for that. Even with help on hand, they had far too much to work through before they could cope alone. The realisation made her feel guilty and selfish, but there it was – the ugly truth.

"I just thought I'd drop in since I'm up here," she said, feeling a little defensive.

She'd asked Coxy not to tell John that she was checking the place out. She didn't want him to think she was controlling his recovery.

"The guy running it seems nice," she continued, breezily, trying to hide her annoyance. "He's on the level. You'll like him."

"I'm so glad you approve," he said, with a small laugh that turned into a cough. A sound like crunching gravel. Laughing naturally would still be a long time coming.

"It looks like a good place," she said, more confidently now. "You'll be safe there."

John smiled, though he didn't look convinced. Coxy took the phone back out of his hands, as another cough rattled his chest.

"Right. I think that's enough for now, mister," Coxy said. "Alex, we're just waiting for transport. I'll be coming up to help him settle in. Perhaps we could meet up too, if you're still up there?"

"Great. Sure," Ripley said.

She saw that Coxy had moved away from John, and he brought the phone's camera close to his face now.

"Listen, Alex," he said in a half-whisper. "I don't know what you said to the guy up there, but thanks. He said that your visit had made him see how much John had to live for. John wouldn't have got the place so quickly if it hadn't been for you."

As she hung up, she wondered exactly what it was that had persuaded Adam to take John in now, rather than after his parade event. She'd deliberately not talked about him too much, for fear of jinxing it. She would have to thank him when she saw him.

It was such a relief to see John smiling and looking almost happy for once. She walked back to her breakfast feeling happier than she had since she'd heard he was coming home. She'd already been looking forward to meeting up with Adam tonight, but now she found she was actually excited.

THE CALL HAD come just after Dan Cotter had sat down at his desk, his first coffee of the morning still untouched. Demolition workers had turned up to begin work stripping down a condemned church out on the edge of town, only to find a dead body laid out on the altar inside.

Another dead body. Another religious link, and the suspicion was that it was the same killer. He'd called Dunn immediately, only to find she was already on her way, along with Emma Drysdale. So obviously his instinct about the two of them had been correct.

The drizzle had turned to full rain by the time Cotter stepped out of the car and greeted the uniformed officer covering the entrance of the construction site, now cordoned off with police tape.

Dunn was already at the door of the church, talking to Emma Drysdale. Both looking tired and concerned, sheltering as much as they could under the old entrance arch.

"What have we got?" Cotter asked.

"A young man, no ID yet," Emma replied. "He's been laid out on the altar. Looks like his blood was drained out slowly."

"Not one of the kids from the Monday club?" Cotter asked, hoping that they hadn't put those two youngsters at unnecessary risk. They had made sure that both the students and their families were being watched by plain-clothes officers from the time they left the Monday Club venue, just in case the killer was targeting them. They'd felt it was a safe enough risk, given that the other three victims had all died a reasonable period after their own presentations.

"No," Dunn said. "I've got a couple of guys going through all the newsletters now with a picture of the victim's face, trying to figure out who he is."

"Is Dr Ripley inside?" Cotter asked.

"No," said Emma. "She's driving over now, she had a couple of things to do before she left the hotel and she's got to go on somewhere after. She won't be long."

"But you think it's the same killer?" Cotter asked.

"You'll understand when you see him," Emma said, handing Cotter a set of shoe covers.

The inside of the old church was burned black, with scars of scorched plaster gaping between the skeleton of ancient beams. The majority of the roof had been burned away, leaving a charred framework of rafters, some of which had also collapsed and lay broken on the floor below.

"Is it safe to go in?" Cotter asked.

"It's been cleared, go on," Dunn said, impatiently.

Cotter picked his way through the burned-out aisle, stepping over beams and broken furniture. At the very far end of the small building, still protected by a small part of the roof, was the altar. An old stone plinth, decorated with carved figures of Christ and the Apostles, with a clutch of weeds threatening to overtake the stone, finding enough light and protection to thrive here. The rain was running in small rivulets from the edge of the broken roof, splattering on the edge of the altar, and creating a pinkish wash over the stone where it diluted the pool of blood surrounding the body there.

The body itself lay on a bright red altar cloth. Blood had seeped into the fabric to darken it. As he stepped into the covered area, Cotter peered at the young man lying on the slab. Despite the paleness of his skin, the deep cuts on his wrists where the blood had been drained from him, and the lifeless staring eyes, Cotter recognised him immediately.

"I know him," he said, feeling his stomach hitch. "I spoke to him yesterday. Mr. Sampson. James Sampson. He's a teacher over at the junior prep for St Andrew's School. He called us yesterday about some guy hanging around the playground. He thought he'd seen him before. I went over to get the details."

"Oh God," Dunn said. "That's not good."

"You get a description?" Emma asked.

"Yes," Cotter replied. "But it's pretty vague. Male, about my height, long coat, woolly hat. Nothing particularly outstanding or unusual. Mr Sampson said he'd seen the guy hanging around before, but not for a few months. The staff are on high alert to strangers lingering, even though the path goes right through the school grounds. He said there were always two members of staff on playground duty."

"Right," Dunn said, decisively. "I'll get back to the office and confirm the ID and see if we can find a connection with our Monday Club or any of the other victims. You go back and talk to the other teacher who was out there yesterday. See if she, or any of the others, can give us a better description. But keep what's happened to Mr Sampson under your hat for now, until I've told next of kin. Okay?"

"I'll come by the station after Alex has had a look at the scene," Emma said, as the two detectives headed off with purpose.

Before he got in his car, Cotter looked at Dunn.

"Dr Ripley mentioned that the Headmaster had a connection to all three previous victims," he said. "This would make a fourth that he's linked to."

"Have we spoken to him yet?" Dunn asked.

"He made a statement after Dylan Parker's death, but the other links only came to light when Dr Ripley was talking to him the other day."

"I say we bring him in, too," Dunn said. "See if he'll come voluntarily, but if not, him knowing all four victims gives us a reason to bring him in for questioning under caution, I'd say. Think you can handle it?"

"Of course," Cotter said.

RIPLEY'S SAT NAV beeped a triumphant declaration that she had reached her destination and she shut it off, pulling to a stop at the kerb in front of the construction site surrounding the old, burned out church.

She'd left the hotel only about ten minutes after Emma, having waited behind to leave a note on reception for Adam, telling him she may be a little late for their drinks, but asking him to wait for her.

She had a feeling today was going to be a busy day, but now that she knew John was coming up and that Adam had gone out of his way to make that happen quickly, she really felt she owed it to him to answer some of his questions.

First though, she had to face another murder scene, and on today's hangover, she wasn't really feeling strong enough for it.

Taking a deep breath, she steeled herself for what she was about to see, and headed in.

COTTER STOOD BY the school gates, watching the morning activity. The bell for the end of break had rung just as he was approaching the gates, and he'd hung back, watching a flustered teacher – her greying hair piled in a scruffy bun on top of her head – herding the children out of the enclosed play area and back into the school building. She chivvied them along by name, skirting the perimeter of the fenced off playground and moving any stragglers along.

Another teacher stood on the steps of the main entrance to the junior school, arms folded over his broad chest, using his higher vantage point to monitor the whole playground, barking occasional warnings and instructions to slow down or be careful, always with a smile. Cotter recognised him as the Headmaster he'd spoken to briefly yesterday when Mr Sampson had called about the stranger at the gates – Mr Morris Hanson. He hoped the man would agree to come in voluntarily, he didn't fancy his chances wrestling him into the car.

Cotter decided to wait until the post-break excitement had settled down and the kids were all safely back in their classrooms before approaching. Besides, he was still waiting for a message from Dunn to say that next of kin had been informed. He didn't want to be the one breaking the news out of turn and he didn't think he'd be able to keep it from any of them.

Turning away from the gates, he walked slowly down the long avenue, through the perfectly kept gardens towards the senior school. He hadn't attended Dylan Parker's crime scene – it was before his time. Since he was here with time to spare, he thought it would be a good idea to see the site in person.

It struck him that this was the exact path the killer would have walked along, following Dylan, watching James Sampson. How long had he spent planning their deaths?

Dunn had headed back to the station to see if they could get a name from the description James Sampson had given them yesterday. Cotter wished he'd made the young teacher go through the description with the police sketch artist now. Still, there may be a chance that one of the other staff members saw him too.

The area where Dylan had been found was dark and damp, overshadowed by the heavy canopies of the ancient trees. He recognised the scene immediately, helped by the temporary fencing around the multi-levelled rockery he'd seen in the crime scene photographs. The hole had been filled in, so the area no longer had the feel of an open grave, and weeds had sprung up in the freshly moved earth.

It was the only part of the garden that Cotter had seen any weeds in, and it struck him as both sad and poignant. The same feeling he'd had in the old, burned out church where they'd just found poor Mr Sampson – the weeds were quick to take over, nature wasting no time reclaiming what has once been hers. And then it struck him properly. These weeds were particularly noticeable, not because they were out of place here, but because they were the same weed he'd seen in the church. Mustard plants.

Cotter turned away from the former crime scene, pulling his phone from his pocket and dialling Dunn's number.

"I was just about to call you," she said. "What's up?"

"I'm just here at the school, I haven't been in yet," Cotter said. "But I was looking at the spot where Dylan Parker's body was found, and it's covered in mustard plants."

"Right, and…?"

"Well, they're the same ones as are in the old church," Cotter said.

"Thanks for the update, Monty Don," Dunn replied. "Any chance you could explain why I need to know this?"

"Dylan had mustard seeds clenched in his fist when they found him, didn't he?"

"Uh-huh?"

"So, I may be wrong, but if they've grown here since Dylan's death, then they must have been dropped in the church around the same time, because they're at exactly the same stage of growth. I think the killer has been preparing the sites for each of his scenes months in advance of using them."

There was a moment's silence on the line, before Dunn replied.

"You beauty," she said. "I'll pull up any CCTV we can get from each of the sites for the last few months. All those empty buildings around that church have security cameras on them. Good work, Farm."

"Thanks," Cotter said. "I'm going to go and see the other teachers now, have you got hold of the family yet?"

"That's what I was about to call you for," she said. "We've informed his mother, and she's confirmed his identity, so you can share the bad news with his colleagues. Call me back when you're done there."

Cotter hung up, tucked the phone away and walked through the now quiet playground, over brightly painted hopscotch grids, to go and deliver the bad news, and hopefully catch a break.

RIPLEY STOOD AT the back of the blackened church, looking at the scene from yet another angle, trying to see the message that the killer had left. She'd examined the scene both near and far, with Emma at her side, and hadn't yet been able to see the same kind of significance with the doom painting that she had with the others.

There were obvious biblical overtones – the body on the altar, the red altar cloth, the destroyed place of worship. Perhaps the message had been something to do with the fire in the first place. Did that fit with the Demon God message? His houses consumed by the flames of Hell? Or was she grasping at straws?

Looking at the whole scene now from the back of the church, with Emma bent over the body, lifting his arm to examine something she'd found there, Ripley finally saw what she'd been looking for. It was another reference to the same doom painting, but this one actually incorporated Emma as part of the scene. The image in the painting had been of a woman, bent over the body of a man on a slab of rock, holding his hand up, trying to help him towards the angels. But the angels had already turned away. It was in a more damaged part of the painting, and the slab of rock could well have been an altar. She could check the detail back in the police station later.

"Emma, come and see," she called. "And bring the camera."

She positioned Drysdale where she had been standing.

"Wait there," she said, heading back through the overgrown aisle towards the body.

She stood where Emma had, and lifted James Sampson's hand just as Emma had been doing.

"Right," she said. "Take a picture of this scene, from there."

Emma did what she was told, only questioning her when she lowered the camera again.

"Is that from the painting too?" she asked.

"Absolutely," Ripley said, as Emma joined her beside James's body. "I didn't see it until you lifted his arm."

"He's playing with us," Emma muttered.

"I'm not sure it's a game," Ripley replied.

By the time they left the church, the rain had stopped and Emma had a handful of evidence bags and a memory card full of photographs of the scene. Ripley said she was going to drop by the library and collect some photocopies she'd had sent from the University library in Manchester.

"I'll meet you at the station in a couple of hours," she told Emma as she climbed into her old Audi.

As Emma got into her own car and pulled away, Ripley stood for a moment looking at the ruined skeleton of the church. She reminded herself to look up when the fire had happened, when she got a chance. She wasn't sure if he had chosen the site because it had burned down, or whether he'd burned it down previously himself as part of the scene setting.

Certainly, the part of the painting the crime scene was mirroring showed the young man on the stone slab dangerously close to the fires of hell at the bottom of the painting. Perhaps she was reading too much into it, but at this stage, every thought was worth checking.

COTTER SAT IN Mr Hanson's office, waiting for the headmaster to finish briefing his PA, Maureen. He could hear their voices, low and urgent, outside the door, but he couldn't make out what they were saying.

"So sorry," Mr Hanson said, stepping back in and shutting the door. "We're a little stretched over at the junior prep. One of our teachers is off rather unexpectedly, and I'll have to fill in for him if Maureen can't find a replacement."

Cotter watched the big man ease himself into his chair. *Was he talking about Mr Sampson?* If so, was this a great piece of acting or did he genuinely not know what had happened. Cotter decided to play his cards close to his chest and say nothing for now.

"So, what can I do for you?" Mr Hanson asked, brusque and official, looking at his watch again as though to emphasise his lack of time.

"I came in yesterday to talk to one of your members of staff, a Mr James Sampson," Cotter began, in no hurry.

"Yes, I saw you," Mr Hanson said, sounding cautious. "I'm afraid if you're here to talk to him again, you're out of luck. He's not in today."

Cotter watched his face for any tell-tale expressions, but he got nothing. *Was this guy that cold?*

"I actually wondered if you had seen the man in question," Cotter said. "I was after a more detailed description."

Mr Hanson puffed out his cheeks.

"I'm afraid not," he said. "I can get Mrs Tew to talk to you though. She was the other member of staff in the playground, although it'll have to wait until the lunchbreak now."

"How close would you say you are to Mr Sampson?" Cotter asked.

"Close?" Mr Hanson spluttered. "He's a member of staff."

He sounded exasperated enough for Cotter to push a little further.

"But you get on with him, would you say?"

"Of course," Mr Hanson said, looking confused. "Look, what is this? Is he in some kind of trouble?"

"You could say that," Cotter said. "When did you last see Mr Sampson?"

A frown flickered across the Head's face.

"Yesterday evening," he said. "There was a staff meeting for the junior department heads."

"And what time did that finish?"

"Six, or thereabouts. Listen, what's all this about."

"I'm afraid to tell you that Mr Sampson's body was found this morning," Cotter said, still watching for a reaction.

What he saw was a flicker of something, quickly masked by a look of confusion. *What was that?*

"His body?"

"I'm afraid he's dead," Cotter said. "Murdered."

Hanson stood up, too quickly for Cotter to read his expression, and crossed to the window, pacing.

"Oh, that's terrible," he said. "What? I mean, how?"

"I'm afraid I can't go into details right now," Cotter said. "I wonder if you wouldn't mind accompanying me to the station to answer a few more questions?"

Hanson turned to him, an exasperated look on his face.

"What? Me?"

"Ideally, yes," Cotter said.

"Why? Am I…?"

"I just want to ask you some questions about Mr Sampson, and about Dylan Parker, and the Reverend Tom Bainbridge. I think it would be better if we did that down at the station. On the record."

"Am I under arrest? You can't possibly think I had anything to do with any of their deaths."

That's exactly what I think, Cotter thought, but he said nothing.

"You're not under arrest," he replied instead. "Although, the fact that you are associated with each of the victims would give me grounds to bring you in if necessary. It's better all round if you come voluntarily. I have a couple of officers waiting to give you a lift."

He'd called for a squad car to be on hand as soon as Dunn had told him he should bring the guy in. He still wanted to get a better description from the other teacher of the guy who'd been hanging around yesterday, but he definitely wanted more out of Mr Hanson.

"I'll get my coat," Hanson said, sounding a little panicked.

9

DAN COTTER LOOKED up and smiled as Ripley and Emma were shown into the office. His smile got broader when he realised they'd come armed with coffee and cakes. Dunn followed them in, with an armful of folders which she dumped on the desk in front of Cotter.

The small space in the corner of the open plan office they had commandeered to create an incident room looked busier now. More notes had sprung up on the board since Ripley had last seen it, including comments about Martin Gibbs and his potential motives for harming the three victims.

Ripley put the cardboard tray of coffees down on the desk, well away from Dunn's teetering pile of paperwork, and took one for herself, stepping up to the board to read their notes.

"We managed to track down this Martin Gibbs guy," Dunn said, lifting one of the folders from the top of her pile and straightening the others beneath to stop them sliding off the desk. "He's got some recent records locally. Nothing big – nuisance, disturbing the peace, verbal abuse. The last two times he was picked up, he said he was of no fixed abode."

Emma took the report from her and studied it.

"We've spoken to the homeless shelters in town, and he is known to all of them, but hasn't stayed in any of them for a while, so he's either sleeping rough, or he's found somewhere to doss down that's outside the system."

"It's a bit cold for sleeping rough," Emma said.

"My money would be on him squatting somewhere," Dunn said.

"Who is he though?" Ripley asked. "Where is he from?"

"Scotland, originally," Cotter said, referring to his own notes. "Born in Aberdeen, family moved to Kendal when he was a kid. You were right, by the way Alex, he's only in his late twenties."

Even younger than Ripley had assessed, and certainly much younger than he looked. What had happened to him to make him appear so haunted?

"He must have had a hard life," Ripley mused.

"Doesn't excuse what he's done to his victims," Dunn said, flat and cold.

"If it *is* him," Ripley said. She didn't know why she was defending him, but something about his panicked reaction at the church had made her doubt his ability to kill anything. "What else do we know about him?"

"As far as we can tell, he was fine until about twenty-four. We've pulled his school and university records and he was strictly middle of the class. Studied English at University in Cumbria, passed with a 2:2. No disciplinary issues on any of his records. We haven't been able to track what he did for work, but he was admitted to St John's with clinical depression in 2014. Just before his twenty-fourth birthday. He seems to have slipped off the path ever since."

"What happened to him in 2014? Do we know?"

"We're still waiting for a warrant to get his file from the hospital, they're reluctant to give up the details of his case, though the overall diagnosis was made available," said Cotter.

"We did manage to find out that both of his parents were killed in an RTA the year before, so I'm assuming that was part of the trigger," Dunn said. "I've just pulled the accident report."

Ripley, Cotter and Emma all gathered around Dunn, peering over her shoulder as she opened the folder. A standard traffic incident report made the first page, and she pushed it to one side, to reveal the first of a series of still photographs from the scene.

A small, blue Ford Sierra, the bonnet pushed back like a concertina, wedged under the front cab of an articulated lorry. The lorry had half-mounted the car, crushing the passenger side completely. The driver's side was mostly intact, though all of the windows had smashed.

"Jesus," Emma said. "You're not walking away from that without some kind of miracle, are you?"

In the next image, closer up, Ripley could see the blood stain on the airbag which had clearly inflated on impact, doing nothing to protect the passenger from the weight of the lorry crushing them from above. In the following image, they could see that the rear passenger door had been cut away, revealing a blood-stained seat there too.

"Oh God," Dunn said, lifting up the typed report for Cotter to see. "Well, that explains the depression."

She handed the page to him and Cotter read in silence for a moment.

"Martin was driving?" he asked.

"Yep," Dunn confirmed. "And read on, because while his mother was killed outright, his father – Reverend Michael Gibbs – died later in hospital."

"His father was a vicar?" Ripley muttered the question, more to herself than any of the others.

"And, by the look of things, Martin was the one at fault in the accident," Cotter said, reading on. "In the end, he was charged with causing death by dangerous driving."

"According to the report, it took over an hour to cut his father from the car. He died shortly after arriving at the hospital."

Ripley shuddered. Martin would have been witness to all of that pain. Even if he hadn't been charged, he still would have blamed himself for his parents' deaths. Any driver would. Had that been enough to trigger his psychosis? Or had he already been suffering?

"Did he serve time for it?"

"Three years in a secure hospital. He was moved to St John's half way through. We're still waiting for release details, but the manager at St John's did confirm it was around six months ago, which ties in with when all this started.

"You have been busy," Emma said.

"So what now?" Ripley asked.

"We find him, somehow, and bring him in," Dunn said. "He can't be that hard to find, can he? He's quite distinctive looking, and I doubt he's got the means to get too far out of the town."

"We've got his description out to all units, just in case. We'll find him."

Ripley looked through the pages of the report, sipping idly from her coffee cup. Did this explain the haunted look she had seen in his eyes, and the fear she'd seen when she'd reached for his arm? She had learned enough about PTSD in the last few months to know that the triggers could be any stressful event, and there was no doubting that killing your own parents, however accidentally, would be a stressful enough trigger.

His father – a religious figure – had suffered for over an hour before finally dying. Ripley could imagine the air in the car filled with prayer, beseeching God to help him, to let him live. Had they prayed together? Had Martin's prayers, like his father's gone unanswered. Was that the moment when he'd made up his mind that God had left him. Was that the beginning of this new understanding?

It made a kind of sense, when you mapped his life from that tragic incident, through a number of institutions, both punitive and restorative, to what they were now beginning to understand of their killer.

And yet, Ripley still questioned whether it could be true. She had looked into his eyes and seen fear and confusion, not hatred and vindication. God knows she'd stared down enough people filled with their own sense of religious justification to know what true conviction looked like, and Martin hadn't seemed like he'd had it.

And yet, the first time she'd seen him, when he'd handed her the leaflet himself, he had seemed different. More confident, more convinced of his truth. Had his reaction the second time simply been because she'd caught him off guard?

"Sarge," a young uniformed officer called to Dunn. "We've got your fella in Interview One. He's getting restless about how long it's been."

"Right," Dunn said. "I'm on my way."

She turned back to Cotter.

"Farm, you fancy helping me interview this Headmaster chap, then?"

"Sure," Cotter said.

"Well, I'm going to head across to the lab and see what, if anything, we got from the leaflets and bag you grabbed," Emma confirmed.

They all turned to look at Ripley. What was she going to do? She looked at the pile of folders, the notes on the board and the uneaten cakes.

"Do you mind if I stay here a while and go through everything you've found on him so far?" she asked.

"Be our guest," Dunn replied. "You can use my desk."

As they left Ripley sitting at Dunn's desk, she pulled the folders closer to her. On the surface, everything they'd discovered so far about Martin Gibbs made him seem like the most likely suspect. But Ripley had a niggling feeling that she was missing something, and she wanted space to go through everything herself. She hated jumping to conclusions, even if they turned out to be right.

She pulled her copy of the leaflet out of her bag and opened it, spreading it out on top of the other documents. Part of what was troubling her was the extent to which Martin would have had to study the scriptures and the different interpretations of them to come to the conclusions that were presented here. Reading the text again, she was struck once more by how eloquently the argument was presented.

It wasn't your standard end-of-the-world, tin-foil-hat propaganda. This was a balanced, well presented argument that had been carefully prepared. The leaflets, too, were glossy and well-designed. None of it struck Ripley as the workings of a madman. Had she set them all off down the wrong trail, with her interpretation of the clues?

If Martin had been at best an average student, when did he suddenly become so learned in the ancient scriptures and the interpretations of them? Whoever wrote that leaflet, whoever had put together that argument, had a much better grasp of academic study than an *average* student, no matter how hard he'd worked. Although, she knew that certain psychoses could unlock hitherto unknown intellect or ability. Was this how Martin's pain had been channelled?

She wished she could talk to him herself, but until they found him and brought him in, she would have to satisfy her curiosity with what details she could glean from his various dealings with the authorities over the years. She laid the leaflet to one side and made a start on the first folder.

COTTER FOLLOWED DUNN into the interview room where Morris Hanson was already sitting. His shirt was pulled tight across his large belly, and sweat marked dark patches in his arms pits and below his chest. He straightened up as they took their seats opposite him, mopping his brow with a stained handkerchief.

"Thanks for waiting, Mr Hanson," Cotter said, shuffling his paperwork in front of him and smiling.

"Did I have any choice?" he asked, sounding surly.

They had agreed that Cotter would lead the questioning. Dunn was good at giving him the chance to learn. She sat down in silence, leaning back in her chair with a creak of plastic against metal, arms crossed, head to one side. Cotter sat beside her, taking his time to place a card folder on the table in front of him, letting the silence linger between them.

"Do I need a solicitor?" Hanson asked.

Leaving him to stew for a little while had been a good idea – he was nervous, anxious, more likely to trip himself up.

"This is just an informal chat, Mr Hanson," Cotter said, his voice soft and friendly. "Why would you think you need a solicitor?"

"It's just…" Hanson began, but faltered. "Well I…"

He shut up, mopping his brow again. Obviously, there was no answer to that question that didn't incriminate him before they'd even begun.

"Now," Cotter said, opening the folder in front of him to reveal a plain sheet of A4 paper. "Do you know why we wanted to talk to you, Mr Hanson?"

Hanson looked at the blank piece of paper, and then at Cotter, only able to hold his eyes for a second before he looked down at his hands. He was certainly acting like a man with something to hide.

"Because you think I had something to do with what happened to poor James?"

Cotter noticed the way the man swallowed hard before he said his colleague's name.

"Mr James Sampson," Dunn said.

Hanson couldn't even bring himself to look at her. His hands were shaking.

"Nobody's accusing you of anything, Mr Hanson. I'm sorry if I gave that impression."

Hanson looked at him, a flicker of relief masked by confusion.

"It's just that – and I'm sure you'll understand why we're keen to resolve this – It's come to our attention that you are one of the few people we've spoken to who has some connection to all four victims in this recent spate of horrific murders."

Hanson's mouth opened and closed again quickly. How was he supposed to respond to that?

"So, you can see why we want to talk to you?"

"I…" he stammered.

"Where were you last night, Mr Hanson?"

"I was at home," he said, his frown deepening. "This is ridiculous."

"And can anyone vouch for that?"

"I live alone."

"Any phone calls? Takeaway deliveries? Chats with neighbours?"

"No…" he paused, thinking. "I don't know."

"So, you were at home, alone, all night?" Cotter made a point of writing this down at the top of the blank sheet of paper. *Home. Alone.*

"I am most nights." There was a hint of defiance in his tone there.

"How about Thursday the 30th May?" Cotter asked.

"The day Reverend Tom died?" Hanson asked quietly.

Cotter nodded, pen poised.

"I stopped in at the church around the time the Boys Brigade finished."

"Why?" Dunn asked.

"I often do," Hanson said, this time looking at her briefly. "I like to make sure the boys have behaved themselves. Often Tom and I would go for a drink together."

"But not that night?" Cotter asked.

"No."

"Why not?" Dunn wasn't wasting any words.

"He wanted to get home."

"And how did that make you feel?"

This time he fixed her with a glare.

"It didn't make me feel anything," he said, tersely. "He was a friend. I can't tell you how much I regret leaving him in that church. I will never stop regretting it as long as I live, but the insinuation that I had anything at all to do with what happened to him is completely abhorrent."

His face had flushed red as he spoke, and he finished his outburst with no breath left in his lungs, his voice strained. Taking a deep breath, he leaned back in the chair, causing another ominous creak of straining plastic.

Cotter moved the blank sheet of paper aside, revealing a photograph of Dylan Parker's crime scene. He turned the picture to face Hanson, and pushed it gently across the desk towards him. Beneath that was an image of Sister Francis, which Cotter positioned beside Dylan, followed by an image of Reverend Tom Bainbridge."

Hanson shook his head and closed his eyes, refusing to look at the images.

"Dylan Parker was a pupil at your school. Sister Francis was a volunteer supervisor in the after-school reading group. Reverend Tom Bainbridge was a friend of yours. And James Sampson a member of your staff," Cotter said, laying a picture of James Sampson's murder scene beside the others.

Hanson kept his gaze averted.

"Four innocent people, all brutally murdered. And you had a close connection with all of them," Cotter said. "Can you explain that to us, Mr Hanson?"

"No," he said angrily. "No, I cannot explain that. And neither do I need to. I don't like the tone of your questions."

"Why those four, in particular?" Dunn asked, ignoring his complaints. "I mean, when we interviewed you before, you seemed to only have good things to say about Dylan Parker."

"That's because he was a lovely boy."

"So why did he have to die?"

"You have no right to treat me like this," Hanson said quietly. With a big sigh, he stood up.

"Sit down, Mr Hanson,' Dunn said. "We're not finished here."

"Well, I am," he snapped. "If you want to pursue this line of questioning, you'll have to arrest me. And you'd better have something more concrete than just the fact that I knew all four victims. Because I also know your boss, and his boss, and I won't hesitate to tell them how you've treated me."

"We're only doing our jobs, Mr Hanson."

"Wasting my time with this nonsense is not doing your jobs."

Hanson lifted his jacket from the chair and shrugged it on. Cotter stood, as though he was about to stop him leaving, but Dunn shot him a warning look.

"Well?" Hanson said, showing true headmaster sternness. "Do you have anything more to ask?"

Dunn smiled a thin smile, standing up herself.

"Plenty. But thanks for your time, Mr Hanson. We'll be in touch."

Cotter gathered up the photographs as Hanson let the door slam behind him.

"We should have arrested him," he muttered.

"On what grounds, Sherlock," Dunn replied, patting his shoulder. "Apart from knowing the four of them, there's nothing to say he killed them. And, to be honest, he doesn't look in much of a fit state to have done any of them. Tom Bainbridge wouldn't have been easy to overpower, neither would James Sampson."

"Unless he caught them off guard. If they knew him, they may not have been expecting him to attack them. I still like him for it."

"I'm not sure I agree with your detective work there, Farm," Dunn said. She stood up and stretched. "Come on, let's go and see if they've found this doomsday guy."

RIPLEY RAISED HER head from the pages she'd been lost in. There was a sudden vibrant energy around the office. She'd been on her own for the majority of the afternoon, slowly piecing together a picture of a fairly average young man called Martin, who had been raised as a vicar's son, and not pushed hard at school, in sport, or in life – neither an underachiever nor a star.

The traffic report had been clear about the crash. The car was seen swerving out-of-control moments before the impact. Witness statements said it was speeding, but not excessively. One witness claimed to have seen the passenger lunging for the wheel further down the road. Whatever had happened in that car in the moments before the crash, the fact that Martin had been exceeding the speed limit, and had been seen driving erratically, and there were no other factors that could have caused the crash meant that a conviction was inevitable.

Fortunately, his very average life up to that point encouraged leniency from the judge. Ripley had read through the transcript of his short trial. He hadn't refuted any part of the report the police had made, nor deny that he had killed his parents, but he did say that he had not been alone. He had gone into a rant about how it was God that had killed them, ultimately, and he, Martin, should not be the one to be punished for it. His lawyers had tried to use that part of his testimony as evidence of Martin's unfitness to stand trial, but the police psychologist had dismissed that.

In the end, Martin had been sentenced to four years. And had moved to a secure wing at St John's – a psychiatric unit on the outskirts of Penrith – halfway through that sentence.

Apart from the couple of minor charges that Cotter had mentioned earlier, there was no evidence in any of Martin's files of the violent, calculating killer that they were searching for now. Had something else happened recently that had triggered this violent spree?

"Dr Ripley?" Dunn called, peering round the door into the office. "Can we borrow you for a moment?"

Ripley closed the folders and joined Dunn and Cotter in the corridor.

"We got him," Cotter said. "One of our units found Martin out distributing more leaflets in the new square. Bold as brass. They're bringing him in now."

"Would you mind listening in while we talk to him? I'm totally out of my depth on this whole Demon God business."

Ripley smiled at her honesty.

"Of course," she replied. "Whatever I can do to help."

MARTIN GIBBS SAT at the small, plain table, fingers drumming, knees jittering. Beside him, a duty solicitor fiddled with her pen, clicking the nib in and out, which Ripley could see was beginning to make Martin even more fidgety.

Ripley stood behind Cotter and Dunn in the small office beyond the interview rooms. A bank of monitors showed views from cameras covering each of the interview rooms. Currently, Martin was the only occupant in any of them.

"He looks nervous," Cotter said.

"Good. I think he's stewed enough, don't you?" Dunn asked.

Ripley had briefed them as well as she could on the theory Martin was presenting in his leaflets, but she figured it would probably help draw him in if he thought they didn't really understand. In her experience, evangelists loved to explain their theories at length to anyone who would listen. If Martin was passionate enough about his belief to be killing for it, then he would be only too happy to explain himself to them now.

"Don't try to pick too many holes in his message, though," she had warned. "If he thinks you are dismissing it, he won't open up and you need to keep him on side if you're going to find out how far he'd go to prove his beliefs. It's one thing mistrusting his message, another entirely to accuse him of multiple homicide."

Cotter had looked at her questioningly. "So, you don't think he *is* our killer?"

"I'm not saying that," she'd said. "I'm just warning you not to dismiss his thoughts as mad ramblings. If he is our killer, and you want a chance of proving he knew what he was doing when he killed those people, you're going to need to give his theory the credence he thinks it deserves."

"Got it," Cotter said.

They both nodded grimly, and left Ripley to observe from the privacy of the small room. As the two detectives took their seats opposite Martin, Ripley was struck again by how frail and frightened he looked. That same wildness she had seen in his eyes outside the church was there again now. A similar wildness to the look she had seen in John's eyes on those occasions when the past overtook him. She had seen how that fear could change her husband. It wasn't unfeasible that this nervous-looking man could turn violent and murderous under similar mental pressures. But she had to keep reminding herself that those murder scenes had been the work of a calculating mind, not a wild one. That's what was bothering Ripley the most about Martin's arrest.

She watched Martin's responses carefully as Dunn ran through the initial formalities at the start of the interview. He nodded to each question, only speaking to confirm his name, and that he was of no fixed abode. To everything else he answered "no comment".

He wouldn't be drawn into conversation about his leaflets, or about his beliefs. He answered "no comment" to questions about his whereabouts on the dates of each of the murders, and the same to questions of whether he knew any of the victims. His solicitor nodded each time, as though daring Dunn and Cotter to challenge his rights.

Ripley could sense Dunn's mounting frustration with him. She'd obviously prepared herself to let him rant about his religious beliefs in the hope that he would expose some justification for the murders, but she was hitting nothing but a brick wall here. Ripley was equally confused by his reluctance to speak.

She had been sure that Martin would want to share his beliefs with any audience. Why start this violent killing spree if not to draw attention to the message? Not for the first time, she wondered whether she had put two and two together and made five. Perhaps there was no connection between Martin's leaflets and the murders, after all.

Dunn leaned over to Cotter and muttered something to him, and then announced, for the benefit of the recording, that Detective Cotter was leaving the room. She then sat silently staring at Martin, out of options. Cotter stuck his head round the door to the viewing gallery.

"Would you mind stepping in?" he asked.

Ripley followed Cotter into the interview room, immediately feeling the tension as she sat. Nervous energy was radiating from Martin almost as strongly as the musty, old smell coming from his clothes. His solicitor looked at her watch and sighed. She couldn't be less interested. With the introductions concluded, Ripley looked at Martin for a moment before beginning.

"Martin," she said, her voice low and calm, "I wonder if you would be happy to talk to me about this." She slid her leaflet across the table towards him. "You remember giving this to me, the other day? Outside the church?"

He nodded, but made no movement to reach for the leaflet.

"It's very interesting," Ripley said, leaning forward, despite the strong, stale smell floating across the table. "But I'm confused. I wondered whether you could help explain it to me a little."

Martin studied her with calculating eyes. He reached out a dirty, shaking hand, and slid the leaflet back towards her, tapping it with his forefinger.

"It's all in there. Perfectly clear," he said.

His voice was low, a deep, resonant rumble that didn't seem to fit his current demeanour. Ripley remembered being struck by the same thing outside the church. In another life, he would have made a great TV evangelist. Perhaps not with this particular theory, though.

"I've read it," she said. "I just thought you might like to discuss your thoughts."

"Not really," he said. It was more disinterested than aggressive.

Again, Ripley found it strange that he wouldn't jump at the chance to expound on his theory.

"I know you," he said, quietly. "You're not police."

"No, that's right. I am a consultant," Ripley said. "This is my specialist subject."

"So you don't need me to explain it to you then," Martin said, leaning back in his chair. "What do you want from me?"

Ripley sensed Dunn shifting in her seat. She wasn't going to put up with his blanking for much longer.

"I want to understand," Ripley said quickly. "Properly. If you do know me, you'll know I need proof."

Martin laughed – a horrible, explosive snort of a laugh which sent flecks of spittle arcing across the table. Ripley tried not to move her hand as a droplet landed dangerously close to her fingers.

"Look around you," he exclaimed. "Everywhere you look there's proof. How stupid do you all have to be? If *I* can see it, why can't you?"

"Is that why you killed those people, then, Martin?" Dunn asked, her patience at an end. "To make them see?"

"I didn't kill anyone," Martin said, fixing Ripley with a steady stare, the first time she'd seen his eyes hold their focus. "He did it."

"Who?" Dunn asked.

Martin gave her a smirk as he tapped the leaflet on the desk, his finger hopping on the words Demon God.

"Fine," Dunn said. "This is a waste of time. Interview terminated at two thirty-three. We'll pick this up again later, when you've had a little time to think about your situation here. I would advise you, again, to accept some counsel from your solicitor."

"Could we have a word?" Cotter said to the solicitor, who had just looked up, surprised at the sudden termination of the interview.

She followed Cotter, Dunn and Ripley out into the corridor. Ripley left the leaflet on the table in front of Martin, deliberately. He would have a few moments alone in the interview room before being taken back to the holding cells.

"I need you to persuade him to talk to us, Diane," Cotter said.

"He's well within his rights at the moment, Detective. And unless you can present some compelling evidence for his arrest, you're going to have to release him soon enough."

"I know that," Cotter said, his voice gentle though Ripley could tell he was annoyed with this woman already. "The thing is, innocent people are dying here, and their deaths have almost certainly got something to do with these leaflets he's giving out. I just need to understand what."

Diane looked at him for a moment, and then patted his arm affectionately.

"Leave it with me, darling," she said.

As she walked back into the interview room to talk to her client, Dunn shuddered.

"You're a better man than me, Farm," she said, heading back towards their offices. "I don't know how you can suck up to her like that."

"If it gets him to talk," Cotter replied grimly.

"Yeah, smug bastard," Dunn said. "Did you see the look on his face when he tapped that leaflet. I could have swung for him."

"I wouldn't be surprised if he's just drawing this out a while," Cotter replied, holding the door for both Dunn and Ripley to walk through. "He's been arrested before, remember, he knows he gets a square meal and a warm bed. He's hardly going to be in a hurry to clear his name is he?"

"Right then," Dunn said. "Well, let's see what your lady friend can get out of him, and meanwhile let's keep digging for something that will force him to speak up."

"Fair enough," Cotter replied. "At least we've got a bit of time until we have to let him go anyway."

"If we're at a sticking point," Ripley said. "I might head off for the evening. My husband's moving up to a residential care place up here, and I want to make sure he's settled in alright."

Cotter looked a little crestfallen, a small frown furrowing his brow, and Ripley realised that she hadn't even told him that John was back. They had barely spoken about either of their personal lives since she'd arrived.

"Of course," he said, shrugging.

"We'll give you a call if anything big happens," Dunn said.

Ripley didn't know why she felt she should go after Cotter and explain, but she followed him down the corridor as Dunn peeled off to collect her things from their office and caught up with him just before he reached the men's toilets.

"Dan, wait."

He turned.

"I'm sorry I didn't tell you John was back," she said.

"It's none of my business, really, is it? But I'm pleased for you," Cotter replied. She immediately saw in his eyes that he wasn't so pleased. Emma had teased her before that Dan had a little crush on her, and she'd just dismissed it. Perhaps her friend had been right after all.

"He's not himself," she blurted.

"It's none of my business," Cotter said again, more softly this time.

"It's just a really difficult time," Ripley said. "For both of us."

Cotter smiled and touched her elbow.

"Well, you must go. I'll call you if anything urgent happens, but I think we could all do with a night to gather our thoughts."

And with that, he pushed through the door and was gone.

THE HOTEL BAR was quiet when Ripley arrived. An instrumental rendition of old piano bar classics burbled harmlessly in the background and, apart from a couple of businessmen around one table, the place was empty.

Ordering a glass of wine from the bar, Ripley found a table as far from both the bar and the businessmen and she could and settled down. She hadn't agreed to meet Adam until seven, so she still had over an hour to read a little more about Martin's background, and his time in the psychiatric unit. She wondered whether that was where he had begun to obsess about this theory of his.

She arranged the folders on the chair beside her, thanking the barman as he delivered her wine and a small bowl of peanuts.

"There was a messenger delivery for you as well, Dr Ripley," the barman said, taking an envelope from beneath his arm and handing it to her.

"Thanks," she replied.

The distinctive frank mark from the University of Manchester told her that her colleague in the library had come through with the search she'd asked him to do.

She tore the envelope open, taking a sip of her wine as she emptied the contents onto the table. Sure enough, there was a sheaf of photocopied pages marked intermittently with small coloured tabs to highlight the searches she'd requested.

She'd remembered, years before, reading about a papyrus manuscript that had been found near Beni Mazar, Egypt in the

1970s, which had only been translated in the early 2000s. The manuscript included, among other gospels, the self-titled Gospel of Judas, which had never been included in the canon of Christian Scripture, but which offered a different viewpoint on Christ's teachings. This would hopefully back up her suspicions about the origins of Martin's message, and perhaps give them something to throw at him in the morning.

She took her laptop out of her bag and fired it up, logging into the hotel wifi and opening a search page. Ready to go, she settled down to read the pages she'd been sent.

The Gospel of Judas had apparently been badly damaged, and it had taken years of painstaking work to piece together as many of the fragments as they could and arrive at some kind of meaning. The picture it painted of Judas Iscariot was far removed from the one that had become familiar in the rest of the Bible.

What was interesting about this Gospel – aside from the fact that it was an original text, and so was far less distorted by translation and politics than other gospels – was that it presented a very different understanding of Jesus and his relationship to God. This relationship was what Ripley had been vaguely reminded of by the proclamations in Martin's leaflets, and the more she read of this lost gospel, the more she believed that it was the basis for Martin's beliefs.

Judas in this Gospel was different from the betrayer depicted in the others. In this version, Judas's act of betrayal was actually done at Jesus's behest. Jesus asked him to release him from his human form, so that he could return to the divine realm he'd come from.

In the Gospel of Judas, the earth was an evil realm to be escaped from at all costs, and so Judas's actions allowed his friend freedom. Ripley wondered if this was what Martin had believed he was doing for his victims? It didn't quite tie up for her yet, though.

One of the passages Ripley found most interesting was quite near the beginning of the translation and set the tone for the whole Gospel. It described an altercation between Jesus and his disciples that started because he had laughed at them for thanking God for their food. When they grew angry, and asked him why he laughed when he was the Son of God, Jesus told them that no one of their generation would ever understand who he really was. What became clear in Judas's description of the ensuing argument was that Jesus's God was not the same God as the one his disciples were worshipping.

According to Judas, Jesus himself was from a higher realm of truly immortal, divine beings, and the Creator-God of the Old Testament was from a lower realm, who came along far, far later than these other divine beings. According to him, instead of the earth being a good creation of the one Almighty God, it was actually a corrupt realm created by his two helpers – the blood-stained, rebel angel Yaldabaoth and the fool Saklas – at God's bidding. These two apparently created the earth and its humans, and saddled us with this violent, bloody, selfish existence.

The argument Judas had put forward – which Ripley found resonated most with the words in Martin's leaflet – was that when people worship God, it's not the true God they're praising, but the Rebel and the Fool instead, thus celebrating corruption and evil.

It was a loose interpretation, but wars have been fought for less compelling reasons. Was Martin genuinely, in his own warped way, trying to save humanity from itself? Is that why he made his victims pray before killing them? To prove that their God revelled in their pain and death?

She ran the theory around in her head as she drained the last of her glass of wine. Perhaps, if she could show Martin that she understood what his message was about, she could get him to open up and talk to her. Maybe she could convince him that his message had been heard, if that was what he'd been trying to achieve.

She wondered about calling Cotter and seeing if they could talk to Martin again tonight, but, looking at her watch she realised that Adam was due any minute. She packed away the laptop and the research documents, and pulled open Martin's file, already feeling better equipped to talk to him tomorrow.

Martin's parents, both devoutly religious, had died in a car accident that he was responsible for. He would have heard his father praying the whole time he had been trapped in that bent and buckled vehicle, waiting to die. And he would have realised that those prayers had fallen on deaf ears, just as all of his own prayers for salvation had in the weeks before he had got behind that wheel, over the limit, and distraught, and killed his parents.

Ripley could see how the psychosis that followed could have led him to find alternative answers in the belief system he had now. What she couldn't see, was how to stop him from punishing everyone else for their own beliefs. If indeed it was him.

She hadn't had the chance to talk to Cotter and Dunn about their chat with the headmaster. He had a much closer connection with each of the victims, and had that studied, precise manner which she suspected the killer must share, and which Martin most certainly did not have. But did Morris Hanson have any kind of motive? Surely Cotter would have said something to her if he'd let anything slip in their interview?

She couldn't help feeling that there was someone else involved in this, beyond Martin. Was he the Fool to someone else's Blood-stained Angel?

"You look engrossed," a voice said behind her.

She looked up to find Adam standing at the table with a full bottle of wine and two fresh glasses in his hands.

"The barman assured me this was your tipple."

COTTER STRETCHED, LEANING back over his chair, arms above his head. The office was quiet, and he realised he'd lost track of time sitting here reading through the case notes and trying to make sense of what they knew, or rather, what they didn't.

He'd been frustrated that they hadn't got more from Martin Gibbs, but there was something niggling him about the case that made him question whether Martin even had anything to do with it?

The message in the leaflets was one thing, but why was Martin staging the bodies to recreate scenes from that doom painting? And why had he started his killing spree now, rather than when he'd been released back into the community? Had something happened to trigger this violence?

Cotter turned his thoughts back to the headmaster, Morris Hanson. All they really to go on there was the fact that he knew all four victims, and that he had made a few off-hand comments to Dr Ripley about how it made you question whether God existed at all. It was hardly the kind of evidence that would stand up to an arrest, let alone a trial.

There was definitely something about the guy, though, that Cotter didn't trust. He flicked open his notepad and ran over the notes he'd taken during the interview. He'd become hostile and ended the interview when they'd pressed him on Dylan Parker. It was all too easy these days to assume the worst of senior members of staff and young pupils, but Cotter had felt that there was something more to the way Hanson clammed up when they asked about Dylan.

Cotter reached across the desk and pulled over the folder of evidence gathered in Dylan's case. There was something they were missing, he was sure of it.

THE FIRST BOTTLE of wine had slipped down easily, and as the waiter brought the second, Ripley asked him for a couple of menus. The food in the bar was perfectly fine, and she knew that she needed something to soak up the alcohol she could feel coursing through her veins and fuzzying her head.

The conversation had been a little stilted to start with, as though he was a little cautious of talking to her, but once they had got onto Adam's work with the men at the rehabilitation centre, he had come alive. Charming, quietly spoken, but fiercely passionate and obviously intelligent, Ripley had genuinely warmed to him, and was sure that John was going to settle in just fine.

When she'd asked about him, all Adam would say was that he had arrived safely, and that Neil Wilcox was staying with him tonight in an adjoining room, to make sure he felt safe. Adam would begin with him in the morning on some one-to-one sessions.

"You should join us for breakfast," he said, cheerfully.

"I don't want to get in the way."

"Nonsense," said Adam. "It's his home for now. You should be as much a part of it as you can. Besides, I'd love you to see how we work properly. I think you, of all people, will really get it."

Ripley frowned slightly, unsure what he meant by that, but also never too comfortable taking flattery.

"Well, that would be lovely," she said.

"We start early, mind," he said. "Seven o'clock."

"I'll be there."

As they waited for their food to arrive, Ripley excused herself to go to the bathroom. As she stood up, she realised quite how light-headed she was feeling. Stumbling ever so slightly as she stood, she put her hand on his shoulder to steady herself and was surprised how warm he felt, despite only being in his shirt sleeves.

"You alright?" he asked, looking concerned.

"Fine. Sorry. I won't be a moment," she said, regretting skipping lunch.

In the bathroom off the bar, she splashed some water on her face and dried it away with paper towels. She hadn't slept well last night, and she hadn't eaten enough today, but she could usually hold her wine better than this.

Feeling slightly steadier, she made her way back to the table to discover that their food had arrived – nothing healthy, but a lot of carbs and starch to line her stomach. She also noticed that Adam had topped up both of their glasses.

"So," he said, as they tucked in. "Tell me all about your work."

"You already seem to know quite a lot," Ripley said, smiling.

"Ah yes, but it's different hearing it direct from the source, don't you think? So much of what is written is open to poor interpretation, don't you think?"

"Especially if it's in the tabloids," she replied.

"Exactly, so tell me, in your own words, how you really feel about all this miracle business."

He didn't take his eyes off her as she spoke, not interrupting her flow, but asking intelligent questions about how she reconciled her views on religion, God and miracles, with all of the evidence she had seen to disprove any of it.

"It's all about interpretation, as you said," she replied, feeling slightly interrogated. "It's less about religion and more about the history of politics, isn't it?"

"What do you mean?" he asked, sitting forward.

"Well, I mean, all of these scriptures – they were all designed to guide the illiterate masses into a way of living relatively peacefully alongside each other. But the rules have all been overblown. It's our nature isn't it, as humans, to try to justify the bad things we do to each other, or the bad things we think. Scriptures can be selectively used to justify almost any horror."

"Ah, but does that mean the messages are false, or the interpretation is misleading?" he asked.

She cocked her head, looking at his boyish smile. He seemed to know exactly the questions to ask to drill into her thinking.

"Probably both," she replied. "I mean, take the bible, for example. There are gospels which were dropped over time, others re-written, the whole thing translated and retranslated according to politics over time. How can any of it be seen as fact?"

Their conversation rambled on in the same vein until their plates were clear, and the more they talked, the more Ripley thought this was all so pertinent to what she and the team were investigating up here. She wondered what Adam would think of the case? Perhaps his keen mind would unlock something she hadn't seen. Struck by a sudden thought, she pushed her plate away and looked at him again.

"You know when I saw you, the other day, at the church meeting?" she began.

"Yes, sorry I didn't hang around, but I had another engagement. I hope you weren't too upset by Martin's behaviour."

"Well, that was what I was going to ask," she said, again surprised that he seemed to constantly know what she was thinking. "How well do you know him?"

Adam smiled benevolently.

"Well enough to know that he means no harm," he said. "He's a troubled soul, though. He was one of our early residents at the centre."

Ripley frowned. That hadn't been on his medical record. As far as she was aware, he'd been somewhat of an itinerant character since leaving the psychiatric unit. At least that made sense of that wild nervousness she had recognised in him.

"But not anymore?"

"No, though he does visit often. He's a good soul."

"He also suffers from PTSD?" Ripley asked. "Was he in the military too?"

"No, but traumatic stress is not exclusive to the military, as I'm sure you're aware. For most of us in the centre, yes, but not all."

Ripley hadn't even considered that Adam was a military man himself.

"You were in the forces?" she asked.

"I was," he said. "A lifetime ago now. I suppose it means I understand what some of my residents have faced, what they have seen. What horrors men can wreak on each other."

He fell silent, as though slipping back into a memory of his own, and Ripley drained the last of her wine.

"Have you read his leaflets?" she asked, trying to pull him back.

"Of course," Adam replied.

"What do you think?" Ripley asked. "Of the message? The whole Demon God thing."

"Well, it's another interpretation, isn't it?" he said, still looking serious. "The important thing is that he *believes* it. And he is willing to act on it."

"Act how?" Ripley asked, suddenly wondering how much Adam really knew about Martin.

"Well," he smiled. "To create his leaflets, to try and spread his message. To stand outside that church, day in, day out, trying to convince others that he's right. It's important to stand up for what you believe in, don't you think"

"How far do you think he would go to prove it, though?" Ripley asked.

He drained his own glass and moved it away from him.

"You're asking whether I think he would kill?" Adam said.

Ripley regretted having so much wine now. She desperately wanted a clear head to process this conversation. Too late now. She didn't really know Adam well enough to discuss details of the case with him, but she could share some of her theory.

"I suppose so," she said. "I'm helping the police investigate a case up here, and Martin's name has come up."

"I heard you'd arrested him," Adam said.

"Not me. But the police are questioning him, yes," she said, wondering how much he already knew.

"I shouldn't think you'll get far with that, he doesn't much trust the law. He's likely to clam up."

"Because of what happened after his parents died?"

Adam shrugged. "You should let me talk to him. He trusts me."

"It's just that the message he's written in those leaflets seems to chime quite strongly with the message we believe the killer has been trying to send."

"Oh yes?" Adam said. "Tell me more."

"I can't," Ripley said. "I shouldn't be discussing the case at all. It's just that you said you know Martin, and I wonder whether you think he's capable of the kind of organisation required to get away with this as cleanly as he has to date?"

Adam laughed.

"He may seem wild, but Martin is no fool. When he sets his mind to something, he really can be very focussed."

He leaned back in his chair, head tilted again with a quizzical look on his face, as though he were trying to read her thoughts.

"But as to whether he is a killer, I very much doubt it. The sight of blood tends to set him off. He's not a malicious man, Dr Ripley. He's no angel, but he's not your killer."

He seemed so confident in his appraisal that Ripley's heart sank. Were they back to square one? But that message in his leaflets. It had seemed to tie in so perfectly with the references to the doom paintings, attacking the innocent and the good.

"Perhaps," Adam said, as though sensing her despondency. "You should be questioning whether he is the author or the messenger."

"You think someone else is behind the leaflets?"

"Almost certainly," Adam said, as though it was obvious. "Martin is destitute. He is homeless. How would he afford to produce them?"

"Oh, God, you're right," Ripley said, feeling stupid that they'd overlooked the obvious. "But who?"

"I'm sure he'll tell you if you start asking the right questions," Adam said.

Ripley wondered whether she should ask Cotter if they could get Adam to talk to him. After all, there must be some kind of trust there, if Martin had been a resident. But then she remembered the way Adam had been so harsh and abrupt with Martin outside the church. She'd have a go herself first, but at least she felt like they hadn't been barking up the wrong tree altogether.

10

FEELING MUCH REVIVED after a good night's sleep, Ripley eased the old Audi into the car park of the residential centre just before seven the next morning. Hers was the only car in the car park, and the persistent drizzle meant she found a spot as close to the entrance as she could.

Adam opened the door before she could even knock, apron tied around his waist and spatula in hand. She hadn't realised he was going to be cooking the breakfast as well.

"Come in, come in," he said. "You're just in time."

She stepped inside and shrugged off her coat, as he bustled back through towards the kitchen. A delicious smell of bacon and warm toast carried on the air – far more appetising than the offering in her hotel.

"Smells great," she said, walking into the kitchen.

"Coffee's ready too," Adam said, pleasantly. "Help yourself, won't you?"

Ripley poured out a coffee, desperate to ask after John, but conscious of not seeming too overbearing. She topped her cup up with milk and leaned against the counter, watching Adam flip eggs in the frying pan.

"Ah, Alex," said Coxy's familiar voice from the doorstep. "I wondered if I'd catch you before I left."

"You're not staying for breakfast?" Ripley asked, happy to see her friend, and immediately deflated that he seemed to be leaving already.

"Got to run, I'm afraid," he said, indicating the overnight bag at his feet as though that were somehow an excuse.

"Everything alright?" Ripley asked.

"Yeah, just got to get back," he replied.

Ripley thought there was something amiss.

"I'll walk you out," she said.

Adam glanced over his shoulder at them both and smiled.

"Don't be too long," he said.

Coxy picked up his bag, thanked Adam, and promised to return on the weekend.

"Saturday's fine," Adam said, concentrating on the eggs. "Sunday will be a bit busy."

Ripley followed Coxy down the hall and out into the car park where a taxi had just pulled up. Coxy signalled for him to wait five minutes.

"Heavy night with our host?" Coxy joked. "I heard you were giving him the third degree. I don't blame you."

"How's John?" she blurted.

He wobbled his head from side to side. *So-so.*

"I'm sure he'll be fine when he's settled in a bit," Coxy said. "It was a rough night. Adam's given himself something to help him sleep, so he'll be out of it for a bit."

Ripley's heart sank. She'd been naïve to think that everything would just fall into place once he got here, but she really had been looking forward to seeing him this morning.

"What do you make of him?" Coxy asked. "Our host."

Ripley looked at him quizzically. Coxy was a good judge of character. Did he smell something off?

"I like him," she said. "He's calm, smart, he really seems to care."

She noticed the almost imperceptible rise of his eyebrow.

"You're not sure?" she asked.

He sucked his lips.

"I don't know," he replied. "There's something about him that seems odd, don't you think? Like he's outside, looking in. Like he's from a different time."

"I think he's very considered. It's not something you see often. He listens." Ripley said. "I think he'll be good for John. He's come highly recommended by your lot, anyway."

Coxy nodded.

"True."

"Besides, I thought all of you army types have something a bit distant and removed about you, don't you?"

"Cheeky bitch," he said, smiling.

"It'll be fine," Ripley reassured him. "I'm staying up here for the next few days, if not longer, and I'll pop in every day."

"Okay," Coxy replied. "But I'm still going to do a bit of background into his service history."

"You didn't do that before you came up?"

"I didn't know he was a serviceman until now, did I? According to everything I read, he's a civilian counsellor."

"But I thought the MoD was paying for this place," Ripley said.

"Oh no. They're paying for John to attend, and handsomely too. It's the least they can do. No. This place is private – entirely outside of our influence. I think that's why the Doc recommended it for John."

"Well, they wouldn't do that lightly, would they? Not in his state?"

"You're right," Coxy said, sounding resigned. "Just do me a favour, will you? Keep an eye on your new friend."

"Why? What's up with him, Coxy?"

"It's not him so much, just the way the guys here behave around him. It's hard to explain, but I saw it last night. They're different when he's here."

"Different how?"

"It's hard to say, but it's like he brings them to life. Like, they all want to please him. They were all just sitting around quietly, and then he came home and it all got a bit weird. Like kids showing off for teacher."

Ripley didn't really know what to say. Surely anything that pulled these men out of the darkness was a good thing. The taxi driver bibbed his horn.

"Look, I've got to go," Coxy said. "Just watch him, that's all I'm saying. I don't want John becoming part of some kind of cult."

"You think…"

"No," Coxy said, shaking his head and giving her a quick hug. "Look, I'll call you later, okay. We'll talk then. And I'll be back up on Saturday. It's probably all just a bit outside of my comfort zone."

And with that, he climbed into the cab and was gone. As she turned to go back in herself, Ripley noticed a shiny blue mountain bike leaning against the trees on the edge of the gravel drive. Not locked up. You'd never get away with that in Manchester, she thought, that'd be gone in an afternoon.

She walked back into the house to find Adam carrying two laden plates into the lounge room.

"Ready when you are," he said, beaming.

She followed him into the lounge and found a small table, laid for two.

"I'm afraid John is sleeping," he said. "So it's just you and me."

"Coxy – Neil – said he'd had a tough night," Ripley said, trying not to sound too worried.

"He did," Adam said sympathetically. "But it's to be expected. Change is hard to adapt to. A good sleep will help."

John had done little else but sleep since he'd got back, and he didn't seem to be getting much better, she thought, and immediately chastised herself.

"Baby steps," she muttered.

She sat down where he indicated, feeling touched by the effort he'd gone to. The table cloth was neatly pressed, orange juice freshly squeezed.

"This looks amazing," she said, taking a sip of her orange juice as he sat down opposite her. "Thank you so much."

"Look," he said. "I don't want you to worry about John, okay? This will be the making of him."

She smiled weakly. The tart sweetness of the juice was doing a good job of cutting into the grogginess of her mild hangover.

"I know you wanted to see him this morning," Adam continued. "Perhaps after breakfast you can at least go on up and see where he is."

"That'd be great," she said, tucking in.

She could hear movement from the rooms upstairs, faint and muffled. Feet thudding as someone moved about.

"No one else joining us?"

"They've already eaten," he replied. "Early risers around here. They've got things to be getting on with. To keep them busy."

He glanced at his watch, and then back at her. A tight smile.

Ripley tried to spear a piece of bacon with her fork, but realised that her vision was swimming a little. She leaned back, as though the distance would help, blinking hard.

"Are you okay?" he asked. "You look a little pale."

"I'm fine," she said, finally succeeding in getting the bacon on her fork. But as she tried to lift it to her mouth, she lost the strength in her hand and the fork clattered down onto her plate.

She felt like she was going to faint. Leaning back in her chair, she was aware that he'd stood up to come to her aid. She could feel his hands beneath her arms, easing her to a horizontal position on the floor. She could hear his voice, soothing, close to her ear, calming her. And the next time she tried to blink, she found her eyes wouldn't open again, and she disappeared into the darkness.

Just as her consciousness faded, she felt her phone buzzing silently in her pocket.

I CAN'T HELP feeling just a little disappointed. I'm not saying I've made a mistake in choosing her, not at all – she is still by far the best person for the job – but I just don't have the time to wait for her to understand what is required of her. I thought she would see straight away and seek me out, but I was wrong.

Still, we're here now, and this can still work. Divine inspiration goes a long way, but nothing beats meticulous planning. Shame I had to bring her husband into it, he would have been a fabulous challenge, but it's a little late for that now. He was my back-up – a means to an end. But the end is already upon us, so he will have to do.

The Good Doctor, on the other hand, will be my redeemer.

"YOU HAVEN'T HEARD from her this morning then?" Cotter asked, hurrying into the police station, his phone pressed to his ear.

"No," Emma Drysdale replied. "But when I spoke to her last night, I arranged to meet her over at your office at ten. She said she had something to do in the morning. Something about helping her husband settle into his new place. It's up North of here, not far. So we should be seeing a bit more of her."

Drysdale sounded happy at the thought. Cotter was too, he realised, though he was still feeling a little conflicted about his reaction to the news that her husband was home. He knew he liked Alex, but he hadn't realised quite the depth of his feelings for her until he was reminded that she was off limits.

"I hadn't realised that her husband had been found," Cotter said. "She'd mentioned he was missing-in-action when she was up in Kirkdale, but the way she talked about it, I just assumed she thought he was dead."

"I think we all thought that," Emma confirmed. "He was brought home just before Christmas, but I don't think it's been easy. She doesn't really ever want to talk about it, but God knows the damage that a couple of years held captive in Afghanistan could do to a man. I don't think she really knows how to handle it."

"I can't begin to imagine," Cotter said.

"Why did you need her so urgently, anyway?" Emma asked.

"I just wanted to run something by her," Cotter said. "I've tried her phone, but it's just ringing through to voicemail. I guess it can wait until she gets here. Although… maybe you'll remember."

"What's that?"

"At that Monday Club thing at the church, you know the guy that came back to help when Ripley found Martin outside? The have-a-go-hero who scared him off? Did you get a look at him?"

There was a moment's silence on the other end of the line while Emma thought. Cotter pushed the door open into his office and nodded a greeting at Dunn as he put his things down on his desk.

"Vaguely," Emma said. "I think so, yes. I didn't get a good look at him though. Why?"

"Because I've just got the sketch back from the police artist who's been working with the other teacher at the school to get a description of the guy Mr Sampson called in as suspicious the day before he died. I think he looks a bit like the guy from outside the church."

"What? Really? I saw Alex talking to him after the event, like she knew him. I teased her about it, and she snapped at me."

"But you saw the guy, right?"

"Yes."

"And he was wearing a scarf, right? A blue and green scarf?"

"I think so," Drysdale said, sounding unsure. "I'm not certain though. Why do you ask?"

"It struck me as odd because it's June, and it's not really that cold. I just thought he was a bit pretentious. But then the teacher I spoke to yesterday said that the guy hanging round the school was also wearing a scarf – green and blue – the school colours. Mr Sampson had commented that he might be an old boy. But I got to thinking – what if it wasn't his scarf?"

"Go on…"

"Well, Dylan Parker was wearing his school scarf when he left the choir rehearsal. The choirmaster remembered telling him to tuck it into his jumper so it didn't dangle free and catch in his bicycle spokes. They're long scarves."

"Right…"

"Well, Dylan was naked from the waist up when he was found. No shirt, no jumper, no coat and definitely no scarf. What if the guy we saw at the church was wearing Dylan's scarf?"

"As a trophy?"

"As a taunt. I don't know. It's just two vague threads that may be nothing. But, like you said, Dr Ripley seemed to know him. I just wanted her to take a look at the photofit and see if it was the same guy."

He could feel the excitement in his voice. He felt like he might be onto something.

"Where does that leave us with Martin?" Drysdale asked.

"Well, I'm going to question him again, ask him if he knows the guy, but I doubt he'll talk. Dr Ripley sent me a message quite late last night wondering whether Martin might be working with or for someone else. She said: 'If he's homeless and destitute, how is he affording to create and print all those leaflets?' She's got a good point."

"So you think this chap with the scarf may be the brains behind the message?"

"I don't know what to think," Cotter said. "That's why I wanted to speak to her. I'll send his image over to her phone now, but if you do see her before I do, won't you get her to call me?"

"Sure," Drysdale said. "I'll see you in an hour or so anyway."

"Okay. Meanwhile, I'm going to pop back to the church and see if the vicar recognises him and can give us a name. He must have been at quite a few of those events, and they all seem fairly social. Someone must know who he is."

"Send it over here too, will you? I'll see what the boys in the lab can come up with. They've got some pretty fancy face recognition software they love playing with. If nothing else, we might find him on the CCTV we've gathered from the different scenes."

"That would be great," Cotter said. "You said you thought she knew him?"

"It was just a feeling," she said. "The way he looked at her. I don't know. It was… familiar, you know?"

"But she didn't say who he was?"

"I didn't press her on it, though, because everything kicked off with Martin."

"Right, okay. Well, if you hear from her, tell her to call me."

As they hung up, Cotter realised that Dunn was sitting opposite him at her desk, listening in.

"Who was that?" she asked, as soon as the call was disconnected.

"Emma," he replied. "I was looking for Dr Ripley, but they've already parted ways."

Cotter was sure he saw her flush slightly at the mention of Emma Drysdale's name. He tried to hide his smile.

"What's going on, Farm?" she asked, "Sounds like you're on to something interesting."

"I think I might be," he said.

As he filled her in on the description of the guy from the school and his conviction that it was the same guy they had seen at the Monday Club event, she sat back in her chair, with one leg crossed over the other, her fingers gently tapping out a rhythm on her thigh.

"You think Martin knows him then?" she asked, when he'd finished.

"I'd say it's likely," Cotter replied. "That's why I wanted to speak to Dr Ripley. Firstly because I wanted to see if she could confirm the e-fit, and secondly because she understands all the stuff in those leaflets, and I want to know whether Martin is involved in the message at all, or whether he just gets to distribute the flyers."

"I'd say he's involved, either way," Dunn said. "Shall we go and have a word? See if he's willing to talk about his friend?"

Cotter looked at his watch. They still had over an hour before either Ripley or Emma were due to come in. Perhaps they could get a little more out of Martin, now that he'd been in the cell overnight, sobered up and had a couple of decent meals.

"Let's do it," he said, already standing up. He felt like they were close to piecing a few more links together, and he knew he wouldn't be able to sit still waiting for confirmation.

RIPLEY FELT HERSELF slowly creeping back towards consciousness. Her eyes weren't ready to open yet, but she could see some light beyond her eyelids. Her head swam, her tongue felt thick, her saliva tasted bitter, catching on the back of her throat as she swallowed.

What the hell had happened?

Her eyes flickered open for the briefest moment, shutting again automatically as the dim light hit her retinas. Her mind, dull and heavy, struggled to reconcile what she'd just seen in that brief glimpse. A man, broad and strong, sitting in an armchair in front of her, head down, hands resting in his lap. A big window behind him, higher in the wall, curtains half-drawn. *Where was she? Who was he?*

She kept her eyes closed, focussing on the memory of the image of him sitting there so peacefully, head bent, waiting. She shouldn't let him know she was awake until she had some of her faculties back – she knew that much for sure. In her self-imposed darkness, she dragged her mind back to her last conscious moments.

Sitting down for breakfast with Adam. She'd drunk her orange juice. They'd been talking about going up to see John. And then… nothing. Had he drugged her? Why on earth would he need to do that?

In the swirling fog of her memory, she saw his face smiling at her across the breakfast table. She heard his voice easing her into the darkness: "That's it, Doctor, you get some rest. We've got a lot of work to do." *What did he mean?* Nothing good, she was sure of that. How had she not seen who he was?

Her heart thumped hollow in her chest as more memories of him dropped into place from their meetings over the last few days. The way he'd rushed back to stop her talking to Martin. She'd thought he was trying to defend her from the homeless evangelist at the time, but what if he'd been making sure Martin didn't reveal anything to her? What if he was protecting himself?

Snippets of their conversation from the night before came flooding back, peppering her brain like shrapnel. *How had she not seen this?* He'd even told her that Martin was the messenger not the author. He'd been desperate for her to know it was him.

She was kicking herself for being so slow; for being duped by him. He'd seemed so charming. So personable. He couldn't possibly be a brutal killer, could he? Of course he could, if he believed his own version of the gospel enough.

So who was the guy watching over her now? One of the residents? Ripley forced her breathing to regulate, it wouldn't do to alert him before she was ready to face him. *Stop panicking, start thinking.*

She carefully began wiggling her toes, and gently flexing the muscles in her arms and legs, grateful to still feel her clothes around her, and shoes on her feet. Without moving, she tried to assess whether she was tied in any way, but she couldn't feel anything on her wrists or ankles.

She risked opening one eye, just a crack, trying not to move the rest of the muscles in her face. The guy was still looking at his lap, hands resting there, not looking at her, hands worrying each other as though he was repeating an imaginary rosary.

Whether she moved or he sensed her scrutiny, his head suddenly snapped up and he looked her in the eye. Head slightly tilted, like a curious dog. A smile crept across his lips, quiet and menacing.

"Welcome back," he said, his voice like cold metal, making her flinch.

There was no point pretending that she was still out of it now, she needed to get herself together, just in case he tried anything.

Stretching, she allowed her body to move for the first time in what must have been hours, judging by the stiffness in her muscles. How long had she been unconscious? It was light outside, but the heavy grey clouds meant it could be anytime during daylight hours. Was it even the same day?

"Take it slow," he said. "There's no rush, Dr Ripley."

She froze, not wanting to move anymore, hating the attention it drew from him. He seemed calm, quizzical. Whatever his plan for her, he seemed in no hurry to get on with it.

"Where is Adam?" she asked, the words cracking from her dry throat.

The man cocked his head to one side, looking at her, before smiling and hauling himself upright. He was tall, broad-shouldered, scraggy-bearded. She didn't recognise him from the session she'd sat in on, but there was definitely something familiar about him.

As he stepped across the room, closer to her, she felt herself tense. She had no idea what this guy was capable of. Why had Adam left him to watch her?

She lifted her head, feeling the leaden weight of it straining the muscles in her neck. Too heavy to hold, she let her head drop back onto the pillow. She had no chance of defending herself.

Fortunately, he walked straight out of the door, not even glancing at her again. She strained to hear if he'd locked it, but heard nothing. She tried to lift her head again but could barely lift it.

She flexed her fingers, feeling the blood flowing through them again with that sharp prickling sensation. Coming back to life.

Feeling her pockets for her phone, she realised that it was nowhere to be found. Too much to hope for that he would have left it for her to call for help.

She could hear voices down the corridor, a door closing firmly. A shout, deep and guttural – more frustration than pain. She knew that cry, too. *John!* Was bringing him here all a ploy to get to her? Had Adam used her poor, broken husband to draw her close to him? But why? If he was the killer they'd been hunting, she hardly fit the profile of his other victims. She could hardly be called either good or holy.

Footsteps approached outside the door. A pause. And the door opened. Ripley held her breath. *Here we go.*

Adam stepped into the room and closed the door behind him. He still moved with that calm demeanour that she'd trusted and enjoyed. Now it simply felt sinister. He was carrying her leather satchel, and she noticed that he put it down well out of her reach before coming back over to her.

Had he been though her bag? Had he read her notes? Everything she'd written about the case, Martin, the missing gospels, the doom paintings. It was all in there. He would know that she knew. A little wave of panic hit her. Is that why he'd knocked her out? Had he spotted her notes over dinner yesterday and decided he wanted to find out what she knew? She felt far too woozy to figure it out yet.

"How're you feeling?" he asked, sitting on the edge of the bed beside her. She flinched away, realising with relief that the hand reaching towards her held a small water bottle rather than anything more sinister.

"It's alright," he smiled. "It's just water. I promise."

He cracked the seal on the water bottle and, though she tried to resist, he cupped his hand gently, like a lover, beneath her head, raising her chin just enough to feed a sip of water into her mouth. She wanted to spit it back in his face, but her body overrode the desire – she needed water. He fed her another sip with the soft touch of a carer helping a patient. The heat from his hand felt as though it was burning the back of her head and neck, but there was little she could do to pull away from him, and the warmth radiating from him was easing the pain shooting from her head.

"There," he said. "I'm sorry I had to do that to you, I know it's not the best way to start a friendship."

"What do you want?"

The water had helped, but her voice was still rasping and dry. Still cupping her head, he put the water down, out of her reach and helped her into a sitting position, leaning her back against the cool wall, bolstered by a pillow behind her head.

"I need your help," he said. "But I'm going to let you have a moment to come around. I need you to *hear* me properly this time."

He moved away from the bed, taking the precious water with him, and sat in the chair opposite, smaller than her previous guard, but somehow far more intimidating.

Coxy had been right to be suspicious of him. She should have seen it earlier. She remembered her plan to meet Emma back in the police station after her breakfast with John. Surely enough time had passed now that they would already be missing her? Would they try to phone? Why hadn't she told Emma exactly where she was going? How long would it take them to start looking for her properly if they got no answer? And would it be too late by then?

"What do you want, Adam?" she asked again.

She eased herself into a more comfortable position, feeling as though every move was being scrutinised. Was he taunting her? Daring her to try to make a run for it? She looked at him again, disarmed by his gentle smile.

She couldn't believe she'd been so wrong about him. She'd been so focussed on Martin and his leaflets, and how that message related to the murders they were investigating. And yet it had been Adam all the time.

"You were in the church, weren't you?" she asked, suddenly assaulted by yet another memory of him. The handsome man who had been praying in the small chapel when she'd first gone to look at the scene of Reverend Tom's death.

"Of course," he said. "I had to be sure you'd finally got my message."

He tossed the bottle of water back towards her, aiming it perfectly to land beside her thigh.

She was already feeling stronger. Picking up the water, though, she realised quite how much her hand was shaking, partly in fear and partly because the muscles were still struggling to understand the instructions from her brain. *Take it slow.*

She noticed the small smile that traced his lips as he watched her struggle to steady the bottle to her lips.

"What do you want from me?"

"You know what I want," he replied, looking a little deflated.

It was the first time she detected that same hint of mania just itching below his skin. He was a ball of anticipation and excitement.

"You want me to endorse your message," she made no effort to hide her contempt. This guy had viciously murdered at least three people, he'd tricked her, used her husband as bait to get her to trust him. She was in no mood to pander to his ego.

"It's not a message. It's the truth. I want you to tell the world what I am," he said.

"A murderer?" she snarled. "No problem."

He surprised her by smiling. A patronising, slightly disappointed smile.

"Come now," he said. "You don't have to be like this. You know what I mean."

He leaned over and lifted her satchel, reaching in and pulling out her dog-eared notebook. Taking a deep breath, he began flicking through the pages.

"When did you realise?" he asked, not looking up.

She wasn't sure what he meant, so said nothing, resenting his intrusion into her thoughts. He smiled as he read her notes.

"You're very good," he said, with a slightly lascivious tone. "You've got almost everything covered here. I'm impressed."

She scowled, wanting neither his praise or his attention.

"I'm glad you came," he said, eventually. "To Penrith, I mean. I hoped you would come. That's partly why I chose this place."

She hadn't been expecting that.

"You should be flattered," he purred. "It's a lot of work to go to, just to have this little tête-à-tête."

"You could have just called," Ripley replied, guessing as soon as the words were uttered that it was the wrong approach to take. He wouldn't want her to be hostile to his advances. As he'd said, he'd gone to a lot of effort to get her up here.

"Don't be facetious, Dr Ripley," he said, a niggle of annoyance in his tone. "You're better than that."

"What do you want?" she asked again.

"I told you," he said. "I want to talk."

"About your message?"

His smile was broad, but manic and completely chilling.

"I knew you'd understand," he said. "I just knew it. From the moment I first read your work, I knew I wasn't alone. You see it too, don't you?"

Here we go.

"That God has abandoned us?" she asked, testing the waters.

He actually laughed, and then a deep frown crossed his brow.

"You've been talking to Martin?" he asked.

"He gave me one of his leaflets," Ripley said. "Or are they yours?"

"No, they're his," Adam said, smiling benevolently. "Well, almost his. The core of the message is mine. He understands it in part. But he's not got it quite right."

"How so?" Ripley asked, feeling her brain beginning to click back in through the haze.

"Their God hasn't *abandoned* them, he's still very much here, he's just not a very nice guy."

Ripley didn't say a word, knowing he would feel compelled to elaborate. All she allowed him, by way of reaction, was a small raise of her right eyebrow.

"You know this already, Dr Ripley," he said. "You understand it. It was all written, a long, long time ago."

His hand waved casually towards her notes in his lap. He was trying to get her to say what he wanted to hear – to confirm his conviction that she was on his side, or at least that she understood his message.

"The lost Gospels," he said, triumphantly. "The truth."

"You're talking about the idea that Jesus was from a higher realm, right? You think people have been worshipping the wrong God for all this time."

He smiled.

"Very good, Dr Ripley. I knew I could count on you to understand."

Ripley knew she had to play this very carefully.

"Those leaflets are very informative."

"Hmm," he said, standing up, pacing. "Yes, they are. But, as I said, they are not entirely accurate. They've served a purpose until now, while people weren't ready to understand the whole truth. But now, we need to move on. I'm running out of time."

His pacing was making her anxious. The room was not big enough to contain his excitement and anticipation.

"And that's why you killed all those people? To properly get their attention?"

"Oh no," he said, stopping his pacing and sitting down again. He shook his head sadly, pursing his lips. "No, I did that for them. To free them from his tyranny. I did it so that they could finally see. They needed to recognise the truth. The truth you and I already know. They all need to see it, to believe it."

He looked at her, quizzically, as though trying to figure out whether he'd overestimated her. His pupils reduced to little more than pinpricks in a sea of ice blue. She met his gaze. She needed to keep him talking.

"What do they need to see?" she asked.

He held up both hands.

"All in good time, Dr Ripley. It doesn't do to rush these things. I've been waiting a long time to talk all this over with you. I've been looking forward to it. You'll have to indulge me a little before we get to the nub of it."

She closed her eyes in a slow blink, nodding her concession. Good. If he thought she was on his side and was keen to discuss his theory, she still had time to regain her senses and figure out a way to get herself out of this mess alive.

"Is John alright?" she asked.

"Your husband? Well, no, I'd say he's far from alright. But he is alive, if that's what you're worried about. He's sleeping right now."

"Why did you bring him here?"

"He was my back-up plan," he said. "To get you to help me. And now, he's my guarantee that you will."

"Help you with what?"

"All in good time," he said. "There is a lot to do, but first we've got to make sure we're both singing from the same hymn sheet, as it were. Not like poor old Martin – he wasn't really ever disciple material, was he? I think I can do better."

"Is that what you want? Followers?"

"It's not what I want," he said, happily, leaning back in his chair. "It's what I *need*. It's not like the old days, you know? People – the masses – seem to need a bit more persuading these days. The rot has been there too long already."

There was something about the way he said it that rang alarm bells for her. She suddenly had a sense of the depth of his delusion. *Surely not.*

"You've done this before?" she asked.

He smiled.

"Oh, I've tried," he said. "Several times, in fact. I've tried being nice – I've given them miracles and kindness, forgiveness and love. And look where that got me."

Her heart sank. *Now* she knew where this was going.

"No," he continued. "Nice wasn't going to work this time. This time, I realised, people would need to be scared into believing in me. Terrified in fact."

"Jesus," she said, the exclamation escaping her lips before she could stop it.

"By any other name," he said, clapping his hands in glee. "I am he! I knew you would understand."

COTTER WAS SURPRISED at the difference in Martin since last night – the power of a safe, dry bed and a couple of square meals. His eyes were bright, his skin less sallow. He still looked like a vagrant, but at least he looked engaged and alert.

Dunn was already at the table in the interview room when Cotter brought Martin in. She didn't look up until he was seated opposite her and ready to begin. They had agreed that Cotter would play good cop on this one, which meant that he would probably be leading the majority of the interview. Martin didn't seem to respond well to hostile women, but they'd agreed that Dunn would keep that particular persona alive for now, just in case it helped to break down whatever wall Martin had built around himself. If Cotter couldn't coax it out of him with kindness, she would have to scare it out of him.

Cotter started the recorder and announced who was in the room, his voice level and calm.

"Martin," he began, as soon as they were all settled. "We need to ask you a few more questions before we can let you go. I hope that's okay."

"It's your show," he said, shrugging.

"Great," Cotter replied, opening a folder and flicking through some notes.

After a slightly exaggerated pause while he read, he looked up at Martin and smiled.

"So, Martin. I wonder if you could explain a bit about your leaflets? Tell me about the message you're trying to share."

Martin huffed loudly.

"If you can't understand what's written in there, then there's little point me trying to explain it to you. You wouldn't understand. Why are you keeping me here?"

"I'd like to understand," Cotter said, ignoring his question. "It's obviously important to you. You've spent a lot of time creating these flyers. You spend hours each week handing them out. And they must cost a bit, nice glossy ones like that. I'd have thought you'd be happy to talk to someone who was interested in understanding your message."

Martin fixed his eye, cold and suspicious.

"I would, ordinarily," he said. "But I don't think you *are* interested. I know what *you lot* are like. You just want to twist my words to make sure you can lay the blame for everything on me."

"The blame for what?" Dunn asked, and Cotter saw Martin retreat slightly. She'd gone in too quickly. He nudged her under the table and, out of the corner of his eye, saw her look down. *Stick to the plan.*

"Is that what happened before, Martin?" Cotter asked. "When your parents died."

They had agreed to reveal what they knew about his history – hoping to use Martin's past trauma to force any information out of him. Despite now thinking it unlikely he was the killer, both Dunn and Cotter were sure he had something to share with them. They just needed to take him close enough to the edge to get him to start talking. Looking at the shadow that crossed Martin's face now, Cotter hoped he hadn't played the parent card too early.

"It was an accident, wasn't it?" Cotter continued, when it was clear Martin wasn't going to give him an answer. "But you still ended up serving time in prison? Was that because the police twisted your words?"

He noticed the shake in Martin's right hand. Small. Little more than a tremble, but the memory of his past had triggered it – he'd been quite still before. A flicker of pain in his eyes before the cold, suspicious stare returned.

"They said I'd been careless," he said, quiet and low. "They had no right to say that. All I did was care. I cared for both of them, when they needed me. I drove them everywhere, I made their food, I helped them clean, and wash, and dress. Every day I cared. And they said I was careless, and that's why I killed them."

His voice wobbled towards the end of his sentence. Cotter knew he'd pressed a raw nerve and was watching Martin for any signs that he might flip into mania and stop giving them anything useful. Martin needed, more than anything, to feel believed and listened to – that much was obvious. Dunn cleared her throat, and Cotter shot her a cautionary look. *Don't say anything yet.*

"But it *was* an accident, wasn't it?" Cotter pressed. "I've read the report. You nearly died yourself. You couldn't have meant for any of it to happen, could you?"

Martin shook his head sadly, bottom lip pushed out slightly.

"Who knows what is *meant* to happen? Who knows what fate has in store for us all," he said, leaning back on his chair, tilting it slightly.

"Do you think it was fate?" Cotter asked. "Do you think there is some kind of plan for us all? Is that what your leaflets are about?"

"In a way, yes. But not the way you're thinking," Martin said, a cryptic little smile twitching half of his lip.

"You don't think God has a plan?" Cotter asked.

Martin's snort of laughter left a tiny fleck of spittle sitting on the table between them. The laugh was derisory, entirely without mirth.

"I knew you wouldn't understand," Martin said, giggling. He was walking a thin line – about to topple into mania and, if he fell, it would render any information he provided all but useless. Cotter knew he had to tread carefully.

From Ripley's explanation, Martin's hatred for God was clear, but this belief that God was a demonic force, determined to corrupt and destroy his believers, was what Cotter found most difficult to understand. He wished again that he'd been able to get hold of Ripley before coming back to interview Martin.

"I do understand that you think God is a demon," Cotter said, tapping the headline to that effect in Martin's leaflet. "And I know from your statement that you blamed this Demon God for what happened to your parents. Why don't you tell me about that? Why would He want your parents hurt? Your father was a vicar, wasn't he? One of God's servants."

Martin had begun shaking his head when Cotter had said the first line. By the time he got to the end of the question, Martin's head was like a metronome, his bearded chin pinging back and forth from shoulder to shoulder.

"Well that's exactly it, isn't it?" he exploded. More spittle. "That's the whole point. If God was good, and just, and pure, why would he let all of this happen? Why make humankind, only to cause them so much pain and suffering? Why set them at each other's throats, why create disease and destruction? Why all the darkness? If God is not a corrupt force? Why let all that happen? Don't you see? This – all this darkness – *that* is his plan."

He gestured around him wildly, as though even the interview room – this situation – was evidence of his point.

"I was always told these trials were sent to test us, to make us stronger," Cotter said. He could almost feel Dunn's internal eye roll, but Cotter was on fairly firm ground here – after all, he'd grown up in a community that had taken faith and twisted it to control the majority of the villagers, to build fear and cause division. He knew how easy it was to create an interpretation of any part of the bible story to suit your needs and, by presenting it properly, get enough people to believe it until it becomes the truth.

"Well, that's just the perfect excuse, isn't it?" Martin said bitterly. "Why are you all so determined to deny the evidence around you? You think He has your happiness at heart? If He did, He would let us all live long happy lives, in a beautiful place, and He would grant us all a gentle, peaceful death. Instead, we suffer this Hell he created as though it is a gift, and we accept the pain, the torture, the corruption as our rewards. *That!* That's what makes no sense."

His speech was erratic, words occasionally running into each other, others lingering on the consonants, like a suppressed stutter allowing time for the mouth to catch up with the brain. His final point was explosive, rocking him back so hard his chair nearly flipped over. His hands grabbed the edge of the table, and he clattered upright again, eyes wild, staring at Cotter, hoping for that confirmation that his message had been understood. But Cotter wasn't going to let it end there – he was just starting.

"So," he said, flipping the folder on the table in front of him closed and leaning forward, elbows and forearms resting on the table, forcing his body language to express fascination. "You think God had it in His plan for your parents to die in that accident, and for you to take the blame? For your father to suffer for hours waiting for death to claim him, and for you to watch, helpless, knowing that you had caused it?"

"Exactly!" Martin stood up triumphantly. The uniformed officer at the door made a step forward to stop him, but Cotter gave him a nod. *Let him be for now.* Martin had noticed it too, though, and quickly retook his seat, but his face was glowing now.

"Exactly," he repeated, quieter. "What kind, benevolent, creator God would do that to one of his most loyal subjects? And he was loyal, my father, right until the very end. He prayed, so hard, for all of us, for himself, for my mother, for me. And look what happened. She died, he was wracked in agony for hours and then died, and I would have been tortured for the rest of my miserable life, if I'd continued to believe the lies."

This time when he sat back, it was with a kind of confidence. Arms crossed over his chest, head cocked slightly to one side, the look on his face challenging Cotter to contradict him. Cotter didn't move, still leaning forward into Martin's space.

"So what changed?" Cotter asked, his own head tilted to mirror Martin's. "Why did you stop believing?"

"Because I listened to my father begging that God of his for forgiveness, for peace, *for his life*. His prayers went unanswered. Everything he begged God to prevent, happened anyway. It had been raining all afternoon. A huge, angry storm. But when they finally got him out and carried him away, the sun actually came out. And do you know what he thought? He thought it was God's blessing. He was dead an hour later, and I knew then what that sunshine had been – it was his God laughing at him for his foolishness."

"So that was the moment you stopped believing?" Cotter asked.

Martin leaned forward, his hands clasped, fingers interlaced beneath his nose, crossed thumbs framing his mouth, gently stroking the wispy hair over his top lip. He closed his eyes for a moment, reliving everything. Finally, he shook his head.

"No. It took me a lot longer to see the truth," he said. "If I'm honest, what I realised that day was only the half of it. I had to go through a whole process of being angry at Him for what He'd done, before I finally realised that He was actually only fulfilling every promise He'd ever made."

Cotter frowned, trying to remember any promises from his own bible studies that could be useful but nothing came to mind.

"He made humans in his own image," Martin said. "Didn't he? It took me years to remember that simple, key, detail. If we – who are brutal, and selfish, and corrupt, and evil – are made in his image, then he must be all of those things and far worse. I can't tell you the hell I went through before I figured it out. I can't explain that feeling of jubilation when I learned the truth. The special knowledge that so few of us ever get to hear and understand. In that moment, I became more than a man. In that moment, I became a disciple."

The word made Cotter sit up straight. Now they were getting to it. So Martin *was* just the messenger. A disciple, rather than a prophet. He noticed Dunn shift in her chair beside him – she was getting tired of all this religious chatter. He knew she would prefer to ask Martin outright who he was working with, who had killed those people, but Cotter had convinced her that aggressive questioning would only make Martin clam up. Whoever he was connected to, Martin was clearly enraptured, and wouldn't betray him to a hostile detective. Especially not one that he didn't deem worthy of hearing the message in the first place.

"You haven't told me how it happened," Cotter said. "How did this 'truth' present itself to you?"

"What is your understanding of the bible, Detective?" Martin asked.

"I'm not sure I have one, anymore," Cotter said, and realised that it was the first time he'd expressed it aloud. He had never questioned his own faith, having been brought up in the community he was, and yet, since his last case there and, perhaps more so since moving away, he'd actively put distance between himself and the church. The smile he and Martin shared in that moment was almost conspiratorial.

"But you believed once?" Martin asked. "You listened to all of those stories, and you thought that you were on the good side?"

"I suppose I did," Cotter admitted.

"And what ended that trust for you?"

Cotter wasn't sure he wanted to talk about it. Could he sum that whole tragic situation up in one short sentence?

"I saw how much pain faith could cause, when guided by the wrong hand."

Martin raised an eyebrow as though impressed with his insight.

"Well, you are a wiser man than me," Martin said smiling. "You are able to see through the lies and walk away from them. That means you're already over halfway to true salvation."

Dunn tutted. Cotter nudged her knee with his own, trying to let her know this was all part of them getting to the bigger picture.

"How so?" he asked, before she could say anything.

"You've already walked away from the bad God," Martin said, smiling warmly, yellow teeth – snaggly and stained – bared under thin lips. "But you've yet to hear the teachings that will lead you to salvation."

"Is that what this is?" Cotter asked, lifting the leaflet.

"That is my distillation of those teachings," Martin said, proudly. "But if you want the truth, you have to meet the prophet himself."

Finally he felt Dunn sit up and start paying attention. This was exactly what he had been working towards throughout the interview – the name of the man they were actually looking for.

"And who is the prophet?" he asked.

"Jesus, of course," Martin replied.

"For fuck's sake," Dunn muttered, and the look Martin bestowed on her was one of absolute hatred, so intense that Cotter wondered whether he might actually be their killer, after all.

Cotter raised a placatory hand, knowing that he had no authority over her, but also aware that her bull-in-a-china-shop approach would shut this conversation down even further. He had read everything Ripley had sent them about her theory, and though she'd promised to flesh it out for him when she saw him, Cotter had still understood enough to know what Martin meant.

"I'm sorry to seem slow," Cotter said, calm and steady. "But am I right in thinking that part of your belief is that Jesus is not the son of the God *we* all know, but he's actually the son of another, higher God, right?"

Back in her box for now, Dunn settled into her chair, arms crossed aggressively, lip curled in distaste. Martin continued to stare at her, though his face had softened as soon as Cotter had asked his question.

"You aren't like the others, are you, Detective?" Martin said, eventually swinging his gaze back to Cotter and gifting him with a smile. "But you are absolutely right. The Jesus we were taught about was not a 'son', but a physical embodiment of a much higher deity, as you have said. *Jesus* was simply a name the people could understand at the time. He has walked among us many times, using different shapes, shades and names, but he has always struggled to find people who would understand his message."

"And you think he's among us again now?" Cotter asked, feeling like he was entering the madness himself.

"Of course he is," Martin replied. "You've seen his teachings. You have them in the photographs papered all over your walls. You're almost ready to take the next step yourself, Detective."

"What name is he using now, Martin? It's not Jesus, is it?"

Martin giggled again. "He has many names."

"Where did you meet him? How did you become a 'disciple'?" Dunn's question was harsh, rapidly put, the word disciple snarled. Cotter bit his tongue, sure that she had just closed the door he'd so gently prised open.

Martin's expression changed instantly, running through suspicion, to anger, to a superior smile.

"You think I will just give him up to you like that? History will not repeat itself, not in my hands. I found him at the darkest point in my life, and he lifted me up and showed me the truth. I will never betray him."

Unfortunately for Martin, he'd just done exactly that. Cotter looked at Dunn and nodded. Interview over.

RIPLEY WISHED SHE knew how much time had passed since she'd arrived at the house, but by now, it must surely be hours after she'd promised to meet Emma and the others. Surely, they'd come looking for her?

For now, all she could do was string out this odd conversation with Adam, and try to learn as much about him as he was willing to share, and hopefully more that he wouldn't realise he *was* sharing. If she was lucky, she might even talk herself out of here.

Every time she had tried to draw him on anything – the murders, Martin, his message – Adam had become defensive. She'd realised, eventually, that he had been planning this whole conversation for a while, and she would have to let him lead it. The murders – although he would never see them as such – were just part of his bigger plan to get his message across to the whole world, and Ripley had just realised that she was also an integral part of his plan.

It broke her heart that he had chosen Penrith to lure her into his scheme, because he knew she'd be called in by her friend Emma Drysdale to help investigate if he made the murder scenes religious enough. He'd admitted that recreating images from the Doom Painting was little more than a contrivance to ensure that the police would feel out of their depth enough to call her in. He had been disappointed that he'd had to make it so obvious in the end, but it got him the result he wanted.

"So why did you keep killing, after I'd been called in? We'd already met. You had John here. What was the point of killing that poor teacher?"

She watched him consider his answer for a moment, as he had with every other response he'd given.

"Because they'd arrested poor Martin," he said. "And he has a habit of claiming responsibility for deaths that had nothing to do with him. Dear boy."

She noticed that every time he mentioned Martin, there was a softness to his voice – a genuine fondness for the man – but it seemed to also be tinged with a creeping annoyance that Martin needed so much guidance. Like a much-loved pup, who still needed to learn to relinquish the thrown ball after he'd brought it back. Ripley had at least established that Martin was less of a disciple and more of a protégé.

"So you murdered that teacher just to make sure we didn't assume Martin was our killer and pass the whole thing off as the work of a madman."

"He's far from mad," Adam said defensively. "He's actually an incredibly enlightened man."

Don't poke the bear, Ripley reminded herself for the umpteenth time.

"I know," she said. "I could tell. But you know what the police are like. If the cap fits, and all that."

He settled again. He was constantly on edge, ready to fight, but quick to settle when he heard what he wanted to hear. Ripley felt like they were on a seesaw. As long as she could keep appearing to agree with his worldview, she knew she would keep him talking. Although, if she managed to draw him out on the details of his killing spree, she wasn't sure she'd be able to keep up the pretence any longer. Whichever way he wanted to frame what he'd been doing, it still boiled down to little more than religious mania, and nothing made Ripley angrier. That's where he'd got her all wrong.

"The thing is," he said, looking deeply into her eyes. "Those victims, as you call them, they were already too far gone for salvation. They'd believed the lies for too long. The poison has settled so deeply into their bloodstream that this world seemed normal to them. The death, the anger, the brutality – they are all seen as things to lament. But it's locked into the way they treat each other. What of justice, honour, purity? What of true faith? Their version of Christianity is a farce."

She desperately wanted to argue that she had met countless Christians who were nothing but kind, honourable and just. She wanted to remind him that the people he had killed were those kinds of Christians – good people, who hadn't deserved to die to prove his crazed message. But while he was effectively holding her hostage, there was no point opening that particular can of worms. She would wait until she was in an interview room with him, with Dan Cotter by her side. Again, she wondered whether they would be looking for her yet.

"Isn't there another way to stop people believing in this wrong God, rather than heaping more violence onto to them?" Ripley asked, knowing that it would probably set him off again.

"No," he said, quiet and earnest. "No. That's no good, is it? Because his game continues, regardless. Their belief is no longer relevant. The rot is too deep. All that can stop them now is fear. Something that wipes out the vulnerable, the weak, the innocent. Plagues, pestilence, and apocalypse. The time for a new prophet – a new testament – is now. If people don't hear the truth soon, and *listen*, the end will come quickly, terribly, painfully, with every clever weapon and missile that the Demon God gave them to use on each other. Minutes. That's all we have left. That's why I had to come back now. One last battle to finally end the war."

His mania was worse than Ripley had imagined. He actually believed he was Christ. Not a second coming – that would be too Christian – but another incarnation of that divine Christ that he believed in, the one from that higher realm, that had featured in the Gospel of Judas.

"Can I ask you something?" she asked.

He frowned slightly, but nodded.

"When did you know?" she asked. "That you were him? Did you choose to come back, or were you sent?"

In part she was fascinated with the psychosis that would undoubtedly underpin his delusion, but she was also intrigued to meet someone with such a cold, clear conviction that they were an embodiment of the true Christ.

In the past, she'd dealt with at least two cases of people claiming to be the second coming, and one case of a fundamentalist group claiming they had cloned a Christ child from one of the holy sacraments. In both cases she'd been able to unpick the claims and prove them false. This time, with Adam, it felt like she was dealing with something different.

Adam wasn't interested in wealth or power. He was only interested in turning people to his version of the truth, sharing his message. And he didn't care if they only actually believed for the briefest moment – just before he killed them – as long as they believed. Their deaths would force others to believe sooner. The more devout they were the more he wanted to make them see his version of the truth just before they died – praying for salvation to a God who not only wasn't listening, but who was actively gaming for their death and suffering.

"Have you always known?" she asked.

She watched him ponder the question. Had he ever been a normal child? Was he once a young man without this level of anxiety and paranoia? What had triggered this psychosis? Because Ripley was certain that's what this was.

"I'm not sure what you mean," he said, eventually. "I was created this way. I have always been thus."

"Well," she said. "We all know the stories of the birth of Christ, marking him out as a son of God…"

"Son of *a* God," he corrected her.

"Indeed," she said. "But there are stories of his childhood, his life as a young man, his early sermons, the way he built his following."

"Yes…" he said, beginning to sound impatient.

"So what's *your* story? Were you born this way, or did you arrive as a fully formed man? Why are you only just beginning to build *your* following now?" She, too, was running out of patience, getting increasingly frustrated with having to pander to this strange egomaniac.

He chewed his cheek, eyes distant. Thinking.

"Because the time is now."

"The time for what? A new religion? A new world order? A change?"

He smiled.

"Time for the truth to be told. That's why I needed *you*."

"Why would *I* help you?" Ripley asked.

"Because it's what you've been working towards all your life. People listen to you. People trust you. You will give them the answers they need when the end comes. When I am gone, you will show them the truth."

"What do you mean 'when the end comes'? What end?"

"Oh, it's all planned," he said proudly. "The most spectacular display of pointless destruction to prove, finally, that their God only delights in the devastation of his followers. Fire and brimstone. The end of days. And when it's over, and I am gone, you will tell everyone who I was and why I did it, and they will listen. Only then will they hear the truth."

"What are you going to do?"

He crossed the room, sitting on the bed beside her. She tried not to recoil from him, from that smell of camphor wafting from his clothes. He didn't move for a moment, looking at his hands in his lap. The strange intimacy of him sitting so close made her want to shudder, but she managed to suppress it. This man had killed all those people just to get her to buy into his message – to get her attention. Well, he had it now.

"A chorus of innocents," he said, spreading his arms as though conjuring the image for her. "Suffer the children to come unto me."

He beamed at her, the smile fading as he realised she didn't share his excitement.

"What are you going to do?" she asked again.

"It's better if I show you," he said, standing abruptly. "I'll need you to come with me now, Dr Ripley. We can't stay here. There is simply too much to do to sit around here any longer."

He lifted her coat down from the hook by the door and held it out expectantly for her. She hesitated to move. Would going with him mean she would be complicit in whatever horror he was planning? Surely, she'd have a better chance of stopping it, and of escaping herself, if she was out of this room.

She swung her legs off the bed and stood up, feeling as though she was fighting a massive hangover. Her head felt foggy, and she waited for a moment before the wooziness passed.

"That's it," he said, as she took her coat from him. He paused just before opening her door, turning back to look her in the eye.

He reached into his jacket and lifted a small, sharp-bladed knife from his pocket, turning it slowly in front of her face.

"Please don't disappoint me by trying to run away," he said. "That wouldn't help your husband. We are in this together now, you and I. No matter what."

She nodded. What it actually was they were in, she had no idea, but she was certain she had a better chance of controlling the situation from within. She just had to make sure she kept him thinking she was on his side.

"Good," he said. "Off we go then."

As he guided her down the corridor towards the stairs, keeping himself just a couple of paces behind her, Ripley put her hand in her pocket and relief surged through her as her fingers locked around her phone. How long before she'd get the opportunity to use it?

"SOMETHING'S HAPPENED to her," said Emma Drysdale, the worry clear in her voice. "Alex never misses an appointment without calling, and definitely not by this long."

Cotter had already come to a similar conclusion. It was clocking off time, and Ripley had been due to meet them over four hours ago. He'd tried her phone countless times across the afternoon, and each time it had rung through to her voicemail.

"Maybe she's got caught up in the library or something," Dunn suggested. "You can't have your phone on in there."

It wasn't Dunn's first suggestion. They had already run through most of the options for her sudden disappearance. Emma had checked with the hotel, and they had confirmed that Ripley had left her room key at reception earlier in the day on her way out of the hotel. Emma had asked them to try phoning her room, but there was no reply there either. The bar manager had called back when he'd started his shift to say that Ripley had spent the evening before in the bar with a young man. But that everything had seemed amicable enough between them, and they had parted company after settling their bill. After some persuasion, the hotel had agreed to send over some stills of the man from the CCTV footage in the lobby.

"How long do you think it would take to get a read on her phone," Cotter asked. He hadn't had much call for triangulating mobile signals in his career so far, but he knew it was both possible and accurate.

"Not too long," Emma said. "I'll get the guys onto it as soon as we hear back from the hotel that she's not in her room."

"Perhaps she had to go back down and see her husband again," Dunn suggested. "Maybe there was an emergency."

"She would have called," Cotter and Emma said in unison. Cotter appreciated what Dunn was doing – trying not to think the worst – but all three of them had begun to suspect that somehow Ripley had come into contact with their killer and was in some kind of trouble.

"What if he's taken her?" Cotter said, finally voicing what they all feared.

"She doesn't really fit his profile, does she?" Dunn said, causing both of her colleagues to turn on her with expressions so angry she recoiled slightly. "I just mean she isn't the devout religious type that the others have been. Which is a good thing, isn't it? Killing her doesn't fit his message, does it?"

Emma stood up suddenly.

"That's it, isn't it?" she said, excitedly.

Cotter was yet to understand.

"What was it that Martin said at the end of your chat there?" Emma asked.

"That someone else had shown him the truth," Dunn said. "But we have no idea who."

"He also said he had become a disciple. Didn't he?" Emma said.

"Yes, but…"

"A disciple spreads the word, right? Retells the message?" Emma was on a roll. "So, this guy has a message to spread and he needs help to do it. So he finds Martin, who turns into a devoted follower, but his reach is pretty limited, and this guy obviously wants to go big. So, if you're trying to deny that God cares any more, or worse, if you're trying to suggest he's deliberately destroying humanity, who better to get on side than someone who's become a celebrity for proving that miracles don't exist – that people's proof of God is nothing more than smoke and mirrors. Ripley is the most high-profile cynic we have. If she says God is a delusion, or worse, people will listen. That's what he wants."

She looked at them both in turn, eyes wild.

"You might be right," Cotter said. "Ripley has made a career of proving that God doesn't move the way we think He does. She'd be exactly who I'd turn to if I wanted together this kind of message across."

"But what does that mean?" Dunn asked. "You think he's going to try to force her to speak publicly about all this crazy Demon God stuff?"

"She would never agree to that," Cotter said.

"He may not give her the choice," Dunn replied.

"Jesus," Emma said. "We need to find her. This guy is ruthless and clinical. God knows what he will do if she knocks his theory. And if I know Ripley, she's not going to take any of this lying down."

"If we're going to find her, we need to know where he would take her," Cotter said. "Martin also said that he'd met this guy at the darkest point of his life. What if they were in St John's together? I mean, it stands to reason that someone who's capable of all this would have been sectioned at some point in their lives."

"Good shout," Dunn said, firing up her computer. "I've got the patient manifest from his time at St John's right here."

Cotter and Emma crowded around her screen, looking over her shoulder as she brought the document up, running through the list of names.

"Did he mention a name?" Dunn asked, already staring at the list dejectedly.

"No. Are there any photos?" Cotter asked.

They crowded closer as Dunn called up the list of names with thumbnail photos beside them. Black and white mug shots of the secure prisoners at the time Martin was on the ward.

"There," Cotter said, excitedly tapping her screen. "Who's that?"

"Adam York," Dunn read aloud, calling up a bigger version of the photograph.

Cotter stared at the mug shot on her screen. He was younger, thinner, rougher looking, but it was a good enough match for the e-fit they'd been looking at.

"That's him," Cotter said, clapping Dunn on the back harder than he'd intended. Now they could start hunting him down.

HE ISSUED THE directions quietly, knife turning gently in his hand as though it were the needle on a compass. They were back in Ripley's car and he was guiding her through the back streets towards the centre of town.

At almost every turn, she could feel his eyes scrutinising her movements. They passed very few people but, each time they did, he moved slightly closer to her, saying nothing, but making sure she knew he was there, and he still had that knife.

She needed to level the playing field. But what could she do? How could she make him believe she would help? And, even if she could convince him, how would that end? Hopefully, marginally better than if he thought she wouldn't help. But she still had no idea what he was planning. She followed his directions as he guided her into the public car park behind the church, and then following his pointed directions to the furthest corner, away from the barriers, ticket machines and, presumably, any cameras.

"Adam," she said, as calmly as she could muster. "I don't mean to question you unnecessarily, it's just the way I am. What you've said makes sense. In fact, it answers a lot of the questions I've been asking myself for years."

She glanced across at him, but he waited long enough to meet her eye. When he did, he blinked rapidly. Was he nervous or dangerously on edge? Either way, she had to tread carefully. Parking the car where he'd instructed, she killed the engine. As its rattle died away, she turned in her seat and looked at him.

"I just want to understand what you need from me," she said. "Tell me what you want. What have you got planned?"

"Out you get. Come on," he said, smiling as though they were off on a trip to the zoo.

She locked the car and joined him at the passenger side. "Where are we going?"

Linking his arm through hers, he guided her along the path towards the church, as though they were any normal couple out for a stroll. She felt his hand tighten on her arm as they passed an elderly couple, as though he was fearful that she would call for help. But still, he said nothing.

They passed the front of the church and headed out across the square. There were cameras here – Ripley had seen them. Would her friends be running any face recognition, searching for her? She wasn't even sure they had anything as sophisticated in place up here.

She considered tearing herself away from him and making a run for it, but she had come to realise that he wasn't intending to harm her. In fact, it sounded like he needed her. And she really had to find out what he was planning. They were heading towards the bog park, that would come out on the other side of the school gardens. The path they were walking up was festooned with banners for the Whitsun Parade, and a couple of council workers were half-heartedly unloading crowd barriers from the back of a pick-up truck. Again, she felt Adam's hand tighten on her arm as they passed the men.

"It's going to be hard to make people change their views," Ripley said. "You must know that?"

He turned to face her as they walked. His eyes were cold and hard.

"But I have to try," he said. "Otherwise all this was for nothing."

"I know you do," Ripley replied, locking her own eyes on his and willing him not to look away. "And I want to help you. But I don't know what I can do. What you did to those people is wrong. That is not the way to do it."

He looked down, like a schoolboy chastised, and for just a moment, she thought she might be getting through.

"If I understand you correctly, you're supposed to be the true light – the path away from death and destruction. Can you see why I am confused?"

It was this duality to his nature that she was poking at here, trying to find the crack that would let her break through whatever wall he'd built around himself and make him see that he needed to stop. The danger was that if she got it wrong, he may flip altogether and take her out with him.

"You still don't understand," he muttered, angrily. "But you will."

"I *want* to understand," Ripley insisted. "But right now you don't seem any better than this God you're trying to turn people away from."

She held her breath, waiting for him to react. The silence that hung between them like an invisible thread, tying her to him. He had already told her that he had framed his crime scenes specifically to get her attention, to draw her up to Penrith to see his version of the truth. What didn't chime with his message was the fact that he'd killed so many people. In everything she'd read, this higher divinity that Adam was claiming to represent was nothing but good, and yet Adam had killed and tortured people, whether he thought they were innocent or not. What Adam had done was the work of a vengeful soul, not a peaceful one.

"The problem is," he said, his voice tense, verging on impatient. "You're still looking at those creatures as people, as innocent beings. I healed their souls and released them from their prisons. They are my angels now."

Ripley didn't respond, leaving the space for him to fill. He sighed.

"I thought we'd covered this," he said, tutting as he guided her down a narrow cut through between two houses. The alleyway was damp and dirty, and he was forced to move her in front of him again, this time keeping hold of her elbow. His voice was right by her ear, quiet and tight. "I really thought you, of all people, would understand straight away, but part of you still believes their story. Is that why you have been searching for a real miracle all these years? To prove that this so-called Creator God actually *does* exist?"

The challenge in his eyes was clear and bright. This was the moment where she won or lost him.

"No, not at all. I just want people to stop their faith to hurt each other."

"Ha!" he exclaimed.

The alleyway opened out a little and he came up alongside her, guiding her out onto another road where council workers were cleaning the quiet street and erecting crowd control barriers.

"And that's exactly what I want," he said, insistently. "Can't you see? That is why I chose those people in particular," he said. "It was the only way to free them from their ignorance. But what I did wasn't wrong. I did them the greatest favour. I stopped them from pulling even more people into their web of lies. The only way the world will believe me is if they can see their own God sitting back, laughing, while His most devout, innocent followers are killed. That is why I came back. The time for temperance and goodwill is gone. Tough love. It's what I should have done the last time."

He laughed mirthlessly to himself. "Ah, the hindsight of two thousand and twenty years. What damage could have been avoided. Never mind. I'm here now."

His mania was high. The warped logic of his statement showed just how deep his delusion ran. How had he become this way? Where had this delusion – this absolute conviction – come from?

They stopped in front of a tall, dark brick building. Faded copperplates told of a doctor's surgery and a solicitor's office, long gone now judging by the grime on the windows of the ground floor and the smell of urine in the entrance porch.

"What are you planning to do, then?" she asked him again. "How are you going to make them see your point now?"

"Not just me, we," he said. "Come on."

He pushed the door open and escorted her inside. The hallway was dark and dusty, a dim light flickered on once the door had closed and he'd located the switch, but it did little to lift the gloom. There was no sign of life in the building. Piles of unopened mail, now yellowing and crinkled, sat on the dirty floor, leaning against doors that looked like they hadn't been opened for months.

He guided her up the stairs, creaking and worn, carpet long since removed, but the painted sides revealing its ghost. At the top of the stairs, he opened the door to an old office. A desk and bookcase stood empty and forlorn, a hat stand leaning like a broken skeleton in the corner. A large metal cupboard in the corner, locked with a small padlock.

"Sorry it's not the most glamorous environment, but it's private and, well, needs must," he said, closing the door behind them and pulling the chair out from behind the desk for her.

She sat, keeping her coat on, still waiting for a chance to use her phone and not wanting it to be out of her reach when that opportunity arose. He didn't seem to notice. He crossed to the window and peered out through the grime, briefly watching the workers below.

Turning back towards her, he bent over his duffel bag and took out another bottle of water and a packet of chocolate biscuits. He handed both to her.

"I know it's not a proper meal, but you must be hungry by now," he said.

She had been trying to ignore the gnawing feeling in her stomach, wishing she'd had a decent breakfast before leaving to see John that morning. Not even a day had passed, and it felt like a lifetime ago. Was John even aware of where he was, or what danger she was in? What would that do to his recovery? Ripley was suddenly overwhelmed with guilt for inadvertently getting him involved in any of this.

She rested the water bottle between her knees and opened the biscuits, taking two and eating them quickly. They were dry and hard but, washed down with a bit of water, they would do the job. *Hardly the loaves and the fishes,* she thought to herself, recognising the defensive gallows humour. Taking another two, she handed the packet back to him and watched as he neatly folded the top and tucked it into his duffel bag.

The water was cool and refreshing, and she felt it hit her stomach almost instantly. It made her realise how dehydrated she'd felt. Finishing the bottle in a few gulps, she laid it on the floor and finished off the two biscuits. Anything to give her a little strength for when her chance came.

Without a word, he crossed to the large metal cupboard and fiddled with the lock, lifting it off and putting it in his pocket. His movements were precise, she noticed, as though he was taking special care to do everything in exactly the right order.

Humming tunelessly as he worked, he lifted out another, identical duffel bag – black canvas, silver zip, no badges –and put it on the desk. She craned to see what was inside as he unzipped it, but the contents were too deeply buried.

He didn't lift anything out. Instead, he carefully checked the contents: moving, counting, nodding. He zipped the bag up again and placed it by the door in the same gentle precise movements.

She blinked slowly, feeling strangely tired in the dim light. He pulled open the drawer of the desk and removed two heavy metal objects and placed them on top of the desk. Only when he moved away, did Ripley realise that they were two identical automatic handguns. She felt her stomach drop – more violence was clearly inevitable.

"Adam," she began. "You don't have to do any of this. I can help people understand without you having to kill anyone else, you've done enough."

Her voice slurred a little as she finished the sentence. She sniffed, her sinuses feeling tight and her tongue thick. This wasn't good. *Not again.* He laid a calming hand on her shoulder as he passed her. It felt distant and strange.

"Don't worry," he said calmly. "It's all part of the plan."

"What is? What are you going to do?" It was the third time of asking.

He crouched down in front of her, taking both her hands in his. She wanted to pull away, but her arms felt heavy, leaden.

"I already told you," he said. "A chorus of innocents. It's the only way."

As her vision began to fade, she grasped at the straws of understanding. Nothing came. Her mind swum in and out of darkness. She was fading fast.

"Please don't," she said.

He smiled, genuinely and sincerely. That face she'd once seen as handsome, now nothing but a flimsy mask for the madness that lay within.

"This is the beginning and the end," he said, quietly. "I have much to prepare, and you? Well, you need to sleep again for a while. At the end, you'll be the only one who can make them see."

As he stood and gathered the two automatic weapons from the desk, she felt her head slump and the darkness took her.

11

COTTER DRUMMED HIS fingers on the desk, anxiously waiting for results. It was long past clocking off time, but none of the team were showing any sign of leaving. Ripley had been missing for four hours now, and they were no closer to finding her.

Emma had just got the CCTV footage from the hotel and was trawling through it to see if she could spot Ripley leaving the hotel again. The hotel had confirmed that the hotel room was empty, her bags were still there and there had been no sign of any kind of struggle that they could see.

The footage they had provided covered the lobby only, with a single static image taken every two seconds. Cotter had left Emma to the search after they had both confirmed seeing Ripley leaving the lobby via the rear entrance towards the car park. She didn't seem in a hurry, and there was nothing about the way she moved that suggested she was in any trouble.

They had also put a rush request in for any footage from the streets and buildings surrounding the hotel. Emma's team would run it through their face recognition systems to speed up the process, when it eventually arrived, but Cotter knew that it would still be a while before anyone came up with anything useful. *Where the hell had she gone?*

Dunn was still going through everything they had on Adam York to see if they could find anything more current than the details on the old patient manifest from St John's. Cotter could tell by the angry tapping of her fingers on the keyboard – and the odd muttered expletive – that she wasn't getting very far. Neither, for that matter, was he.

For his part, Cotter had been on the phone to Reverend Judith Clay, to see if she knew any more about Adam – he'd attended a number of church events, but she reminded him that they had been mostly Reverend Tom's domain. Beyond vaguely recognising his face, she could tell Cotter nothing about the man.

And, as for their biggest hope, Martin had clammed up and refused to tell them any more about his friend and mentor. When they'd pressed him, he just shook his head with a disappointed little smirk, as though they were too stupid to understand. Dunn had thrown the book at him, but none of it made any difference. He would not tell them what they wanted to hear. *Who was this guy? And where would they find him?*

So they were back to good old – slow as hell – detective work, and Cotter was feeling the pressure. He was inordinately fond of Alex Ripley, and the thought of her being in close quarters with someone capable of the horrors they had seen in these recent crime scenes filled him with dread. He tried to remind himself that she was tougher than he could ever imagine. She'd spent a large chunk of her life dealing with religious fanatics, just like Adam, and though many had tried, none of them had stopped her yet. He couldn't help but wonder whether this would be the one.

"Oi, Farm!" Dunn called. "I've got those details of his trial here."

"What was he in for?" Cotter asked, joining her at the screen.

"Double murder," she said. "Joseph and Camilla York. His parents."

"Jesus," Cotter said, looking across the desk at her. She was reading from her screen, eyes scanning quickly across the details in front of her. "What happened?"

"Fire," she said, reading. "He apparently discovered it and called the fire brigade, but by the time they got there it was too far gone. His defence was that he'd been out for the night and came back to find the fire already raging. Several eye-witnesses, however, contradicted that. There was a statement from a neighbour saying they had heard fighting throughout the evening. It had all died down for an hour or so before they heard the sound of the fire engines.

"No one saw Adam going out, but a couple of witnesses stated that they had seen and heard him inside that evening. More importantly, there was not a single witness to corroborate his alibi. No one saw him go out, or come back.

"Fire investigator ruled it as arson, with accelerants placing the start point in the parents' bedroom. The forensic report said they had both been alive, but probably unconscious, when the fire had taken them. He got sixteen years. Pled diminished responsibility – no details on that, by the way – and had the sentence reduced to ten."

"Wait, even if he only got ten years, how did he get out so quickly?"

"New evidence came to light that compromised the prosecution's case. The sentence was overturned on appeal – he'd done just under a year in there by then. The chief psychiatrist spoke up at the appeal and made a strong case for the prosecution, claiming that Adam still required psychiatric care and was not fit to be released into the community. The judge ordered that he should get some therapy and turned him loose."

"Brilliant. And I assume he just dropped out of sight after that?"

"Looks like it," Dunn said. "I've left a message for the psychiatrist to call me back. Hopefully he hasn't left the office yet. We need to know how his illness manifested itself, what makes him tick. Anything that might help us figure out what he's going to do. Meanwhile, I'll keep digging, see if I can find out what happened to him after he got released."

"Hey guys," Emma called from across the room. "Come and look at this."

"What is it?" Dunn asked, as she joined Cotter behind Emma, all peering at the screen.

"This is from the hotel bar last night," Emma said, setting the video playing. "Look."

The grainy footage from the hotel lobby flicked and stuttered through its series of still images like a bad animation. Black-and-white snapshots stitched together to show a number of people moving in and out of shot. Only one person in the bar, at one of the low tables.

"That's her," Dunn said.

The view was momentarily obscured by another person's back as they arrived at Ripley's table. As the figure sat down, Emma paused the video.

"And that's him," she said. "Adam York."

Emma spooled forward through the video, the three of them watching Ripley and the man they were sure was the brutal killer they'd been hunting, sharing a bottle of wine, some snacks, laughing – deep in conversation.

Cotter felt a creeping anger – somewhere between jealousy and panic – rising in his gut. *What was she doing?* He watched Ripley finally say goodbye, saw Adam York leave the building, and then watched her take her time finishing her wine, pay the bill after a chat with the barman, and head towards the lifts. Done for the night. He really hoped that wouldn't be the last time they saw her alive.

"The next time we see her is first thing this morning," Emma said, bringing up another feed.

Sure enough, Ripley left the lift, dropped her key at reception and headed out through the rear doors to the hotel car park. She looked calm. She was in no hurry. *So what happened? Where are you now?*

"The lads at the lab say they've been running their AI on the footage that's come in today. No sign of her after she headed out of town on the main road. They're almost up to speed though, and if either her face or reg number pop up anywhere, we'll know straight away.

"Boss," one of the uniformed sergeants called through the door. "There's a Captain Wilcox here to see you."

Dunn glanced up, frowned and looked at Cotter questioningly. He shrugged. *Never heard of him.*

"He says it's about Dr Ripley," the sergeant added.

"Stick on this, Emma," Dunn said, her hand fleeting on Emma's shoulder. "Farm, come with me."

THEY FOUND CAPTAIN Neil Wilcox pacing in a waiting room out the front of the building. He exuded military confidence, Cotter thought, but when he turned to face them, Cotter could see that he was full of anxiety.

"DI Dunn," she said, extending a hand which Wilcox shook. "This is DS Cotter. How can we help?"

"I was hoping to see Alex – Dr Ripley," he said, looking deflated. "She said she'd be here most of the afternoon."

"She was supposed to be," Dunn said, and Cotter could hear the tension in her voice.

"How do you know Dr Ripley?" Cotter asked, trying not to let his own nerves affect his tone.

But Wilcox had clearly made a career reading people.

"She's not here, is she? Do you know where she is? Is she okay?"

Dunn leaned forward, assessing this new face.

"We don't know," she said, clearly having decided he was one of them.

"What do you mean you don't know?"

"She was meant to be here at lunchtime and she hasn't turned up," Cotter said, and Dunn gave him a sideways glance that told him to shut up.

"We haven't been able to reach her," Dunn added.

Wilcox finally slumped into a chair.

"Shit," he said.

"What is it?" Dunn asked, sitting down herself.

"I think her husband's in danger," Wilcox said, fixing them both with a solid stare. "And now that she hasn't turned up here today, I'm worried that she is too."

He explained that he'd seen Ripley that morning, at the halfway house where her husband had just taken up residence. "It's a program to support guys in the force with severe PTSD. It's had some good results." He sounded like he was defending it a little too much.

"So, what do you know?" Dunn asked. "Why do you think either of them are in trouble?"

"The guy who runs it," Wilcox said. "He's not all he seems."

Wilcox went on to inform them that he'd been the one to recommend that Alex's husband, John, try the residential place out as a more radical solution to his PTSD. It was only when they'd turned up that John had recognised the guy running it.

"Only vaguely," he said. "But you know when a face sticks in your mind. It wasn't 'til I got back to base and looked him up that I realised who he really was. I never served with him, but John did. It was something John said that made me look him up. When we arrived at the halfway house, John called him Padré. It seemed odd – it's a nickname we tend to use for a chaplain in the unit. Seemed strange for John to use it. And he was pretty upset. I thought it was just the shock of the move. The guy himself said it."

Wilcox ran his hands over his head, as though equally frustrated and annoyed.

"I let him give John a bloody sedative," Wilcox said. "I left him there. In his care."

"Who is he?" Cotter asked, feeling anxious.

"He's using a different name now, so it didn't ring any bells. But he's the same little psychopath bastard who went apeshit in the field out in Afghan."

Wilcox ripped open his briefcase and thrust a dossier at Dunn. "What's this?" she asked.

"Everything we know about Adam Nathaniel Spicer," he said. "Military Chaplain, dishonourably discharged. Went berserk. Killed five friendlies in the field in 2012. Spent a year in military care, discharged to a civilian psychiatric unit in 2014. St John's."

Dunn exchanged a glance with Cotter, eyebrow raised. Dunn opened the folder, flicked through a couple of pages, and tossed the whole lot over to Cotter.

"Adam York," she said. "Shit."

Cotter looked at the now familiar image of the handsome young man they were searching for. "Shit," he repeated.

"Where was this place you dropped John at?" Dunn asked.

"Not too far out of town. I can take you," Wilcox replied.

"And you say you saw Alex there this morning?" Cotter said, already standing up.

"Yes, she was going to have breakfast with John," Wilcox said. "Only he'd had to be sedated. I told her to keep an eye on the guy, for Christ's sake. I knew there was something off about him."

"Right," Cotter said, itching to get moving. "I'll go with you to this halfway-house then." He looked at Dunn. "Is that okay?"

"Perfect," Dunn replied. "Call in when you get there. Don't take any risks. If he's got her there, we'll send backup, okay?"

Cotter said nothing.

"Dan," Dunn said, using his first name for the first time since they'd met. "I'm serious. Don't do anything that might endanger her life."

"I won't," Cotter said, heading out of the door with Wilcox in tow.

ON BALANCE, I am pleased with the way the day has gone. The good Dr Ripley has finally understood my message, and when all this is done – and I am gone – she will be the one to share it with the whole world, and they will all see that I am the light. This time, my sacrifice will not be in vain.

The streets are already beginning to quieten down from the post-work rush, now just the early Saturday shoppers bumble along the streets, oblivious and ignorant. For the first time, I don't mind their ignorance; I don't care that their sin washes over them like a celebration, because tomorrow they will all be saved.

Tomorrow will be the beginning and the end, just as I told Dr Ripley. The beginning of a new dawn for earth and its inhabitants, and the end of my internment in the physical form. My work here is almost done, but they will only truly understand when the Spirit touches them with fire and light, baptising thousands and adding them to the number of believers.

For now, I'm quite enjoying strolling along the pavements, checking that none of the council's preparations have interfered with any of my plans. Everything, so far, is still intact. I manage to resist the temptation to check each one too closely. I have planned this for so long. I have to have faith in the prophesies.

"SO, WHAT'S THE plan then?" Cotter asked, stepping up to one of the downstairs windows of the isolated property on the outskirts of Penrith, and peering in, hands cupped around his eyes. There was no sign of life inside, but everything looked in order – nothing out of place.

"Her car's gone," Wilcox said, crouching down to inspect the gravel in the drive. "Not in any kind of hurry though." He stood up. "It was right here when I left this morning."

Cotter climbed the steps to the door and rung the bell. Insistent, repeated, ineffectual. There was no answer. He turned back to Wilcox, who was already heading off around the side of the building, looking up at the windows on the first floor.

"John!" Wilcox yelled. "John! Can you hear me?"

Cotter followed him. Peering through all of the windows he passed on the ground floor. There was no movement anywhere. There was also no handy fire escape, no open back door, no window left ajar.

Wilcox tested the back door. The handle didn't budge. He stepped back into the garden, found an old brick under the hedgerow and hefted it in his hand.

"If you would rather not be party to breaking and entering, I suggest you step away now," Wilcox instructed.

"I think we have reasonable cause," Cotter replied. "Go for it."

Wilcox smashed the brick into the small pane of glass nearest the door handle. It took a couple of goes to get through the toughened double-glazing, but he smashed through easily enough and knocked the chips out of the way before slipping his hand through the gap, locating the key on the inside of the door, and unlocking it. They were in.

They both paused in the doorway, listening intently. Not a sound from within. No reaction to the glass smashing. No movement. Wilcox was first to cross the threshold, and though Cotter knew he was the only one with even the vaguest authority in this enterprise, he let the soldier take point – it seemed the natural order of things.

Following Wilcox through the kitchen – crouching low for no explicable reason – Cotter smelled burnt coffee, disinfectant, and something else he couldn't quite place for a moment. It reminded him of his grandmother. Mothballs. Camphor. *Strange.*

Wilcox made some unintelligible signal with his hand and Cotter suddenly realised he'd had enough. This was ridiculous.

"This is ridiculous," he said, and Wilcox spun quickly to shush him. Cotter shrugged. They'd just smashed the door in, after all. What was the point in being circumspect?

"Mr York," Cotter called, loud and official. "This is the police. Show yourself."

No reply, unsurprisingly. Wilcox shook his head – eyebrows raised, lips tight.

"You take upstairs?" Cotter suggested.

"God's sake," Wilcox tutted, but nodded. Heading towards the stairs through the hallway, and taking them slowly, still pressed against the wall as though sniper fire was imminent.

Cotter hurried through the downstairs rooms with less precision. The dining area, the lounge, the therapy room – all empty. Everything felt strangely normal. Disquietingly normal. Back in the kitchen, he saw two glasses, two plates, two mugs set on the draining rack. *A last breakfast?*

Upstairs, he heard Wilcox opening and closing doors, with increasing speed and less care. Finally he heard his boots on the stairs and the captain arrived back in the kitchen looking concerned.

"No sign of anyone," he said, flummoxed. "There were at least half a dozen men here this morning. John took the only remaining room. He was heavily sedated when I left him. Where the hell is he? Where are they all?"

Cotter took out his phone and dialled Dunn.

"What's up, Farm?" she asked straight away.

"We're at the house," he replied. "There's no sign of anyone here. She's not here."

He saw the curious glance Wilcox gave him, but didn't care. She was his friend too.

"There's no one there at all?" Dunn asked. "Any sign of trouble?"

"No," Cotter said. "The place is just empty. Like they've all just gone out."

"Tell her that there are at least seven vulnerable men missing," Wilcox said, his voice loud enough for Dunn to hear anyway.

"You get that?" Cotter asked, not sure why he was feeling any animosity to this man. There was no need for it.

"I heard," Dunn said. "I'll send a team out to go over everything there. Where the hell could he have moved seven grown men?"

"I'm less worried about the men," Cotter said, earning himself a disdainful glance from Wilcox. "Alex is still missing and we're running out of daylight. What's he planning?"

"I know," Cotter replied. "What else have we got?"

"Emma's lads have found her car," Dunn said. "In the public car park behind the church. She's trawling the CCTV now with whatever fancy whotsit they've got, to see if they can see where she went after she parked up."

"Okay," Cotter said. "I'll get up to town then, see what I can find. Call me if you get any leads."

He hung up and turned to Wilcox. "She's sending a team to go over things here. They've found Alex's car in a car park near the church in the town centre. I'm going to head in there. Maybe you could stay here, wait for the team to arrive."

"Bollocks to that, son," Wilcox said. "We need to find her, and we need to find John. I promised him he would be safe. Come on."

EMMA PRESSED HER phone to her ear as the call connected to Ripley's voicemail again, strangely relieved to hear her friend's voice, even though she knew it was only a recording. Emma hung up before the beep, finger hovering over the dial button again, when her own phone rang, startling her. It wasn't a number she recognised.

"Alex?" she asked.

"No, it's me," Dunn's by now familiar voice said. Emma realised she hadn't taken her number yet, despite having spent a couple of nights together now. At least she had it now.

"Ah," Emma said. "What news?"

"Dan's found nothing at the house. The guys who were staying there are all missing too. He's heading into town, now. To the car park," she said. "I don't suppose you've got an update for him?"

"Not yet. The first of the footage has only just come in. The lads are running it through the system."

"Are you still in the building?"

"Yes, why?"

"I'm on my way upstairs. That psychiatrist from Martin's trial is coming in. He reckons he can get Martin to talk. It may be the best shot we've got of figuring out exactly what this Adam guy is up to and why he's taken Dr Ripley."

"That's great," Emma said.

Having only just discovered the real identity of their killer, she had been going through the files Dunn had sent over while they tried to trace where Ripley had gone. Although Adam's first crime – the fire that had killed his parents – had seemed far less calculating and far more passionate than any of the murders they'd been working on recently, she could almost see how he'd got from who he had been back then, to the man they'd been tracking recently.

The files painted a picture of an only child, gifted and intelligent, raised in a strict Christian household, sent away at the age of seven to a religious boarding school – one that had since come out very badly in a series of abuse scandals. Adam's name was not linked to any of the victims in the report, but realistically, that might only mean he hadn't come forward. Perhaps everything that he now believed about God being cruel and corrupt and evil could have been formed in his young mind by both of those negative aspects of his religious childhood.

Emma had seen how clinical his crime scenes had been, how calculated his murders were, and now one of her best friends was trapped somewhere with him and she couldn't bear to think about what he might be doing.

"Look, I don't know her like you do," Dunn said, bringing Emma's attention back to the call. "But Dr Ripley's pretty tough. If anyone knows how to deal with a guy like this, it's her, right?"

"I suppose so," Emma said. "Will you let me know if there's anything I can do to help?"

"Just keep scanning that footage – Dan's waiting for news. I've got guys on the team looking at past addresses, cars, anything we can to find where he might have taken them all. If we find anything, I'll let you know straight away."

"Likewise," Emma said. "And Helen, just be careful, okay?"

"Sure," Dunn said, clearly a little embarrassed by the familiar and tender expression. "I always am."

Emma hung up and stared at her phone. There was no point calling Ripley again – her phone was switched off. The guys had promised her they would let her know as soon as it was switched on again.

Feeling restless and fidgety, she turned back to the files on her screen with renewed determination. Somewhere in this lot would be a clue as to why Adam York was doing what he was doing right now, and why he needed Alex Ripley to achieve it. There was always a clue. She just had to find it in time to save her friend.

DUNN FOUND DR Sathianathan waiting for her in reception when she got there. She'd guessed from his tone on the phone that he was keen to talk to her about Adam York. In the message she'd left him, she hadn't mentioned why they wanted to know about him, but had said it was in relation to a case they were investigating.

Given that it was late on a Saturday, she hadn't really been expecting to hear from him until Monday, if at all. But he had called back within the hour.

He'd told her on the phone that Adam was an extremely volatile character with a dangerous series of complex conditions. When she'd told him they would be looking at Adam for murder, he had insisted on coming straight down to talk to her. When he'd heard that she already had Martin under arrest linked to the same crime, she'd noticed that he sounded genuinely upset.

"Dr Sathianathan?" she asked, extending her hand to shake his as he stood up. "I'm DS Helen Dunn. Thank you so much for getting back to me."

"It sounded urgent," he said. "I'll be glad if I can help."

He was a tall man, hazel eyes and a round face framed by surprisingly dark hair for a man his age, the soft curls half-tamed by some kind of pomade. He had small, steel-rimmed glasses perched midway up his nose. Kindly but anxious. No time for small talk. Dunn was glad.

She led him through reception and down the corridor towards the office. The floor was quiet now, with just a skeleton staff sticking around on the overtime bill, still trying to follow any leads on where Adam York may have taken Dr Ripley.

Dr Sathianathan stopped dead as they walked into the office and he saw the crime scene photographs posted on the board.

"Oh God," he said, stepping closer. "Did he really do this?"

"We believe so," Dunn said, offering him a seat facing away from the board. He craned over his shoulder as he sat, unable to tear his eyes from the images there.

"You thought he was capable of something like this, didn't you?" Dunn asked, sitting opposite him. "That's why you spoke at his appeal."

He turned back to face her, soft eyes damp.

"Yes," he said, quietly. "Yes, I told them that it wasn't safe to let him out. I told them he was likely to kill again. But his lawyers were good, and the police... well, there had been some mistakes."

He tailed off, obviously not wanting to apportion blame at the police's door while standing in their house.

"What is he like?" Dunn asked. "When you worked with him. Was he particularly religious? How did his illness present itself?"

She realised she was asking too many questions too quickly, but she could sense Dr Sathianathan's energy was high too and she just wanted answers to the many questions they had.

"It's funny that you ask about religion," he said, steepling his fingers in front of his lips in a calm, studied gesture that had obviously become a habit over years of choosing exactly the right questions to get into his patients' minds. "He had some very radical views about God and the Bible. On the whole we try to steer the patients away from religion while we work things out, but Adam was quite, well, singular, I suppose."

"How so?"

"Well, you couldn't draw him on any other subject. On everything else he was silent. But on the role of God, he suddenly came to life. But not in a healthy way."

"Go on," Dunn said.

"He has a dissociative condition, and it's more serious than any I have seen. He even denies his own existence."

"What?"

"As a human being, I mean. He was never able to acknowledge that the two people he killed were his parents – his flesh and blood. He refused to answer to his name, claiming his body was just a host. He claims – no, he believes – that he is from another realm. A divine realm. And that he is sent by God."

"To what? Maim and kill? How does that work?" Dunn asked. "Because the theory we've been working on is that he is killing these people – good, innocent, devout Christians – to prove that God is evil and wants them to die. Is he saying that God sent him to kill? Isn't that the opposite of all that religious stuff?"

"You clearly didn't study ancient history. Brutal murder and oppression seem the only constants. Forgive me, I am a scientist at heart."

Dr Sathianathan took his glasses off and rubbed his eyes, wiping each in turn with the back of his hand. Hooking the frames back over his ears, he looked at her, full of sadness and guilt.

"I should have known something like this would happen," he said. "I should have fought harder to keep him contained."

She let him have a moment, knowing he would come back to her question. He had come here to help, after all.

"He thinks he is the next incarnation of Christ," he said.

She laughed. She couldn't help it. Not a big laugh, but a short angry snort.

"What the hell?" she asked, collecting herself.

"It's incredibly complicated," he said. "But to put it as simply as I can, he believes that he is the real Christ, and that everybody else has been following the wrong God all this time. He also believes that the God in the Bible is a malicious force."

"This coming from a man capable of the brutality we've seen," Dunn snorted.

"He would often say that the time for kindness and goodwill was gone, and it was time that people saw their God for who He really was – someone who delighted in the suffering of his people."

"That ties with everything we've seen in these recent killings," Dunn said. "We think he's trying to send exactly that message by targeting the specific people he has, but we can't figure out to what end. How will killing these people make anyone believe his version of anything?"

"He's an incredibly intelligent man," Sathianathan replied. "Bordering on genius, I would say. The problem is, he can't remove himself from this fiction that he lives in. All of his focus, his full attention, is on proving his version of the truth. I warned them that his behaviour would escalate dramatically without treatment, and it looks like it has."

He turned back to the images on the incident board, standing up and moving closer. Dunn gave him a moment to look before joining him herself.

"The problem is," she said. "We think he's moving even faster now, but we don't know what's next. He's killed two in the last ten days, and now it looks like he's taken a consultant of ours captive."

"Oh no," Sathianathan said. "I'm so sorry."

"She's not lost yet," Dunn said defiantly.

"No, of course," he said, turning to her with a renewed optimism. "You said on the phone that you'd arrested Martin Gibbs?"

"That's right," Dunn replied. "He's still in a holding cell, although technically we have to charge him or let him go now. Our time is up."

"Has he told you anything yet?"

"Not enough. He says he is a disciple. It sounds like this Adam guy got to him while they were in St John's together."

"Quite possible." Dr Sathianathan took his glasses off again, repeated the same eye rubbing technique. It was clearly a tic he'd developed to buy himself time to think.

"Would it be possible for me to talk to him?" he asked. "I think we built something of a rapport during his time at St John's."

"He's had a lot of time with Adam York ever since," Dunn said. "He seems defiantly loyal."

"I did a lot of work with him," Sathianathan said. "I have ways of getting him to tell me things. Please. I'm so worried about what will happen."

"We need all the help we can get, Doctor," Dunn said. "I'm happy for you to talk to Martin. I'm just warning you that he is quite resistant. But you seem very worried, if I may say. Is there something else you know?"

He lifted his hand to his glasses, but caught her eye and obviously decided not to go through the routine again.

"He always spoke of the End of Days," he said. "Adam, I mean. He always said that this would all end in a spectacular event through which he would reveal his message to the whole world."

"Jesus," Dunn said.

"If he's spent the last six months with Martin, then I think, I'm sure, I can get him to tell us what that event will be."

"Right," Dunn said. "Let's do it."

I FEEL STRANGELY content. For now, I'm still relatively safe in this pathetic human form, if I keep my head down. I won't need it for much longer, but it will only delay me to get caught by the police now, and I know they'll be looking hard for their dear friend. They will also know my face by now, for sure.

Night is finally drawing in. These long days dragged out the light, helped by the streetlights, but at least the roads are quieter at this time of night. Most of the Saturday night revellers have gone home. It's time to call my disciples to me.

With Ripley, I now have my twelve. Martin is my Judas – he was the only one who could be. It's why he's never been included in the plan for this final moment. Martin has to betray me for them to truly see. It's all part of the plan. Pathetic and unoriginal though it is, the cycle must repeat – parallels must be drawn – for the masses to understand properly.

Arriving at the tall office building, I lean back to look up at the sky, stretching my arms out to the sides. Why not enjoy the moment? These weak physical forms have their base pleasures, if you listen to the flesh and bone.

This is one of those moments. My heart is alive with anticipation, my skin warmed by the lingering evening heat, the stars are clear and home is calling me. Not long now.

Stepping through the door and into the dimly lit room, I am greeted by a small cheer from my friends, my followers. They have clearly made an effort to do everything I've asked. A dining table laid with a red cloth, food spread across its entire length, wine in the cups I gave them. It makes me happy to see them so dedicated. This will not be for nothing.

Their place was already safe – these people that have been shunned by the rest of society – the lost, the homeless, the hopeless. They are the ones who heard my message and understood it straight away. They are my disciples.

I half-wish that Dr Ripley could join us this evening, but things have to be different this time. The eleven can celebrate with me tonight, the twelve will unite tomorrow. Her role is far greater than any of these men and women gathered here. Besides, she is only one storey above them, so she's close enough in spirit.

As I take my seat at the centre of the table, I feel like I have come home. My final instructions can wait until the feast has been enjoyed. Everything is in place now. I just have to let it flow.

EMMA REWOUND THE video clip again, triple checking that the figure she'd seen turning the corner and crossing the road was indeed Alex Ripley. The route she'd been led on was very clever indeed – he obviously knew where the surveillance cameras were in the town and how to avoid them.

She had been able to track them both leaving the car park behind the church, crossing the square and heading towards the long road that would lead them away through the park and on towards the school.

It was the briefest glimpse, but it was definitely them. Walking quickly, with Adam York a pace behind Ripley at all times. From the way she hesitated to cross the road, it looked like she was waiting for instructions from him.

There wasn't even enough of a glimpse to study her body language? Why was she sticking with him? Did he have a weapon on her? Why wasn't she trying to run?

Emma kicked herself, not for the first time, for letting this psychopath get so close to them. He had obviously been watching them all along, playing them into his sick game, coaxing them to a point where he could get Ripley on her own. But why?

She quickly typed in a bunch of street names, calling up any footage from the surrounding roads and pavements. Of course, there was nothing of any help. There were three possible routes from that corner alone, and no official cameras on any of them. Someone may have a doorstep camera that had caught something, but it would take far too long to source and review. They were running out of time, she felt it.

She picked up her phone and dialled Cotter's number. It wasn't much to go on, but at the moment he was walking blind. At least they had a direction.

"What have you got?" he said by way of answer. She could hear the urgency in his voice. No time for niceties.

"I've found a glimpse of them at the bottom of Princes Street," she said. "Crossing West Lane. It looks like they turned towards Castle Drive, but I can't be sure. There are no other cameras around there to check."

She could already hear his footsteps as he broke into a run.

"Great," he said. "I'm on my way over there. Check for anything around the castle. I can't get into the park – the school have got some event going on in the morning. But there are cameras over most of the exits. Check those as well. Call me back if you get anything."

And with that he was gone. Emma called one of her colleagues over and divided the search among them, focussing on the park exits herself. She had a horrible feeling that he was deliberately leading them, and Ripley, on some goose chase, but she had to keep following the crumbs he left. They had to find her before the worst happened.

MARTIN GIBBS WAS already sitting in the interview room when Dunn lead Dr Sathianathan in. His eyes widened when he saw the psychiatrist, and he flinched as though he wanted to stand up and run away.

"Hello Martin," Sathianathan said, his voice immediately taking on that calming, almost monotonous tone.

"What is he doing here?" Martin asked, addressing his question at Dunn, and sounding, for the first time since they'd arrested him, like a rational human being whose rights were being violated.

"Dr Sathianathan just wants to talk to you," Dunn said.

She indicated for the psychiatrist to sit and joined them at the table. No tape, no official announcements.

"I'm not going anywhere with him," Martin spat.

"No one's asking you to go anywhere, Martin," Sathianathan said. "I just want to talk to you about Adam."

Martin sat back and crossed his arms, head tilted to one side.

"I don't know any Adam," Martin said defiantly.

"Adam York," Dunn said, sliding a picture of him across the table. She saw the recognition in his eyes.

"That is not Adam," he said, as though they were genuinely stupid.

"His name is Adam York, Martin. He was with you in St John's. Do you remember? He was part of our therapy group."

"You look and look, but you do not see," Martin said.

"Don't start that, Martin," Dr Sathianathan said sharply, surprising Dunn. He sounded like a cross teacher reprimanding a silly schoolboy. Martin made a sign of zipping his lips.

"You told this officer that you were a disciple now," he said, ignoring the gesture and heading down a different path. "Why don't you tell me what that means?"

Martin shook his head like a petulant child.

"Martin," Dr Sathianathan sighed. "I'm sure you know how much trouble you're in here. You don't want to have to come back to the hospital with me, do you?"

Dunn noticed the fear flick across Martin's eyes as he shook his head.

"So tell me what has happened. What has he asked you to do? What is your part in all this?"

As Martin sat mute, Dunn felt that same rising frustration that they were wasting their time trying to get anything out of Martin. But Sathianathan had obviously asked the right question. Martin sat forward, uncrossing his arms.

"I'm to tell you three things," he said plainly.

"What things?" Dunn asked.

"A name, a time, and a place."

"Go on," Sathianathan said.

Martin smiled sadly, shaking his head.

"What day is this?" he asked.

"Saturday," Dunn said.

He checked the cheap, blue plastic watch on his arm. A little digital display that they'd left on him since there was little he could do with it to harm himself.

"It is time," he said. "So you can know this: His name is Jude, and he is Christ. Adam died, that Jude could rise. And through him, we will all be saved."

"So Adam changed his name to Jude?" Dunn asked, not wanting him to get into any of that preaching stuff again. "What do you mean we will be saved?"

"You listen and listen, but you do not hear," Martin said.

They looked at him blankly. He sat back, smiling, arms crossed.

"Martin, what do you mean we will be saved? What is he planning to do? Why has he taken Dr Ripley?"

"He needs his twelfth," Martin said, "It couldn't be me. I had to be here, you see?" He sat back and pretended to zip his lips again.

No matter what they asked, or how they tried to coerce him, he would give them no more. He just kept looking at his little watch.

"You said you had to tell us three things to tell us," Dunn said. "But you've only told us one – his name. What about the time and the place?"

Martin shook his head. "Not yet," he said, tapping his watch. "Too soon."

COTTER AND WILCOX had walked each of the possible routes individually and together, and come up blank every time. It was fully dark now, and even the streetlights couldn't provide enough light to see any clues Ripley may have left. She could literally be anywhere.

"This is useless," Wilcox huffed. "They must have more to go on by now."

Frustrated and at a loss, Cotter took out his phone, dialling Dunn's number.

"Tell me you've got something?" she asked.

"Nope," Cotter said. "Emma found a single glimpse of them heading towards the castle and the park, but I've gone down each route and there's no sign. I'm just chasing my tail out here. What about you?"

"I've been in to see Martin with this psychiatrist guy, Dr Sathianathan," she said. "Apparently, he has three things to tell us, but will only reveal them at an appointed time. I swear to God, I'm going to wring his neck."

"What has he told you so far?"

"That the guy's name is now Jude, and that he is Christ, and through him we will all be saved. Which basically means nothing and is unlikely to help us with anything."

"Did he say anything else? Anything about Alex?"

"He said something about this Jude having to take her because he needed the twelfth. I mean, the guy just talks in riddles the whole time."

"I don't know," Cotter said. "Didn't he say he was a disciple before?"

"Yeah, but he's said so much mad shit."

"Well, there were twelve disciples in the original story. And with Martin in with us, perhaps he needed to replace him for whatever he's got in mind. Whatever he's doing you can guarantee it's going to be symbolic. And, as we said earlier, he would love someone like Ripley on his side, sharing his message."

"How does that help us find her?" Wilcox snapped.

"I've got the captain with me still," Cotter said. "There was no one left at the halfway house, so the guys there must all be part of Adam's plan."

"John included," Wilcox said. "And he's in no fit state to be part of anything. He shouldn't be out on the streets."

"Whatever he's got planned, Ripley would never go along with it," Dunn said. "Would she?"

"Of course not," Wilcox said. "Unless he had something over her to force her to."

"Like her husband's safety?" Dunn asked.

"Exactly," Wilcox replied. "But even then, he'll have a hard time containing her."

Cotter could agree with that. It was the first time he had felt a glimmer of hope in hours. Ripley was tough, and she dealt with people like this Adam character day in, day out. She would know how to handle him, wouldn't she?

"Right," said Dunn, still sounding annoyed and frustrated. "But none of this helps us find her, or figure out what this psychopath is up to next."

"No," Cotter said. "But it does mean that there are at least eleven other people following him, if Ripley was the twelfth."

"And?" Wilcox sounded frustrated.

"Hmm," Cotter said, suddenly urgent. "Dunn, can you see if there have been any strange reports come in over the last few days that we may have missed?"

"Strange how?" Dunn asked.

"Plagues, rats, locusts, floods, I don't know, end of the world stuff."

"What?" Wilcox looked perplexed.

"If he's rewriting the story, enough of it has to be the same for people to understand. He's been doing it all along. The parables – the seeds, the messages. He's re-writing the book. Or trying to. Somewhere local there will be a report of something out of the ordinary. See what you can find. Especially online, on those conspiracy sites we keep hearing about. If he's about to bring the apocalypse, we'd better figure out what he's planning."

DUNN HAD TO admit to being impressed with Cotter's initiative. Perhaps because he'd had such a religious upbringing, all of these strange phrases and shared knowledge of scriptures came easier to him. Dunn felt completely out of her depth.

Cotter was right though, the more clues they unravelled, the clearer it became that Adam York, or Jude, or whatever he wanted to call himself, had been playing them all along.

Even now, he was playing them, getting Martin to drip feed them pointless information, obviously trying to keep them distracted with wild goose chases rather than tracking him down. But Cotter was on to something with his apocalypse theory, especially knowing that Adam York had used the halfway house as a place to start his little cult and build a following of fragile souls gullible enough to fall for his promise of greatness. But what was he building up to?

She checked her watch. It was nearly midnight, and with no sign of Ripley, she decided to press on with Cotter's query.

She grabbed her keys and pass, deciding to go downstairs and see how Emma was doing, and see if she and her team could help with finding anything out of the ordinary that had gone on in the last few months that might help them.

"Boss," a uniformed officer said, sticking his head around the door, looking harassed.

"What's up Mike?" Dunn asked.

"Your man down in the holding cells is kicking off. Something about the time. He's going nuts, ma'am."

Dunn grabbed Dr Sathianathan on her way down to the cells. He looked like he'd been asleep in the family room, but he'd insisted on staying to help with interviewing Martin, no matter how long it took, and she had to admit she was grateful to have someone at her side who understood Martin's condition and how to get anything out of him.

As they got down into the corridor, they could already hear him shouting. The two officers on duty looked frazzled.

"What happened?" Dunn asked.

"Nothing, ma'am, he just started kicking off. Screaming and hollering. We thought it best to call you down, before we have to restrain him.

"Thank you, Mike," she said.

She slid the small metal window open on the cell door and looked inside. Martin was pacing inside, shouting at the sky.

"Martin," she called over his shouting. "Martin, it's DS Dunn."

He turned at the sound of her voice and strode across to the door, face close to the gap.

"The time," he said. "Will be the third hour."

He took a step back and made a deep bow, arms spread wide.

"What does that mean, Martin?" Dunn asked. "The time of what?"

Martin sat down on the slim bed in the corner.

"I'm cold," he said.

"The time of what, Martin?"

"I will tell you, I promise," he said, lifting his legs onto the bed and curling himself into a foetal position. "Before the third hour."

Dunn turned to Dr Sathianathan, exasperated. He stepped up to the little window.

"Martin, you're doing very well," he said. "But it's important that you tell us now. You are a good man, Martin. You don't want anyone to get hurt, do you?"

"Through him, we will all be saved." Martin muttered, so low it was almost inaudible.

Sathianathan turned to Dunn and shook his head, and she mouthed a series of expletives.

"I'm cold," Martin shouted, as they slid the metal window cover shut again.

"Get him another blanket will you, Mike?" Dunn asked as she passed the officer. "And give me a shout if he kicks off again. I'm getting sick of this little game."

As they made their way out of the holding area, Dunn was itching for answers.

"What the hell is the third hour supposed to mean?" she asked.

"Three in the morning, maybe?" Sathianathan suggested.

"Who does anything big and symbolic at three in the morning?" she asked. "What is the point of him drip feeding us these bloody riddles?"

"This is not Martin's usual pattern," the psychiatrist said. "It's like he's been given a script to deliver, and he's sticking to it no matter what we ask. Adam York can be very persuasive. I could see that in the brief time he shared our group therapy sessions. He was very popular. He must have a real hold on Martin."

"A regular little cult leader, by the sound of things," Dunn muttered. "I just wish I knew what he was planning next."

"I fear it won't be pleasant," Dr Sathianathan said.

"That's an understatement," Dunn said. "Listen Doc, it's been amazing you coming down here and working with us to get anything out of Martin, but it looks like he's on a schedule with his information, so I'm not sure there's any point you hanging around any later."

"Maybe you're right," he said. "He seems intent on following his script now, come hell or high water."

"I'll call you if we need you again, okay?"

"Please do."

"Thanks again."

He shook her hand formally and made his way towards reception. Dunn watched him go and then headed down to the forensics lab to see how Emma was doing.

12

RIPLEY WOKE UP slowly, cold and alone, trying to understand where she was, and rapidly filling in the spaces in her memory. She had been drugged, twice in twenty-four hours. She had that same thick-headed feeling she usually woke with when she'd taken a sleeping tablet. Something she'd been doing quite regularly since John had come home.

She remembered fading into sleep as Adam had made his way out, carrying two automatic weapons and God knows what else in that duffel bag he had checked so carefully. *What was he going to do? Or had he done it already?*

It had been heading to sunset when he'd left her here, but now, looking outside, it was clear that dawn had long since broken and the sun was making its way up the sky, pushing in determinedly through the grimy windows.

She listened for a moment to nothing but silence close by. Distant noises on the street below told her nothing. Just the sounds of the town waking up and beginning another day. *Was he here?*

It didn't feel like there was anyone else in the room but, for now, Ripley was too scared to look around her in case he was there. She needed time to gather her thoughts, but she guessed that time was something she might have already run out of.

A dull cheer from the floor below startled her. Now that she focussed, she could hear voices chatting. Perhaps there was a working office down there after all. Should she shout for help?

She stopped herself at the last moment, suddenly realising that she had no idea whether she was even locked in here. No need to shout for help if she could just walk right out the door.

She stretched her shoulders, tried to uncrick her neck, and stood up. The faintest creak of the floorboard made her stop still. *What if that was him downstairs?* She didn't want him knowing she was awake and functioning. This could be her only chance to get out of here and away from Adam.

Treading slowly, she carefully made her way to the window, trying to get a bearing on where she was in relation to the part of the city she knew.

Despite the grime covering the windows, she recognised the trees that marked the edge of the park. She leaned closer to the window, looking left and then right. Sure enough, the open grounds of the castle ruin were just in sight to the right. The park opening into the school grounds was out on the left.

The road below the window was quiet, the pavements separated from the carriageway by temporary barriers. She remembered that the workers had been erecting them last night when Adam had brought her here.

She peered in both directions, wondering what was going to be happening there? Each of the lampposts had been hung with banners, intermittently dark green and blue stripes with a small crest in the centre, or a deep red pennant with the words Whitsun Walk picked out in gold.

Ripley gripped the window sill to steady herself.

"Of course," she whispered. "Shit."

The secretary at the school, Maureen had said they needed to hurry through their chat because they had to go over preparations for the Whitsun Walk. If today was Sunday – and she assumed it was – then the boys of the school would be parading through the park, past the castle and into the town square, finishing at the church to celebrate the descent of the Holy Spirit on the disciples.

Hadn't Adam talked about disciples? Hadn't he mentioned a parade of innocents? Hadn't he said the words 'suffer the children'? He'd left the room with a bag he was carrying delicately, and two automatic weapons. Ripley was suddenly very alert.

She reached into her pocket and took out her phone, switching it on and having to wait for a series of messages and missed call alerts to flash across the screen before she could call up her message app. Before she could begin typing, a notification popped up to tell her that her battery was critically low and her phone would switch off shortly. Typical. Would there even be enough battery to make a call?

She decided to send a text first, and if that went through, at least they were warned. Pulling up Emma's number, she typed: "I'm okay. Battery low. He's going to attack the Parade." Pressing send, she watched the blue bar show the message's progress. As the bar cleared, the phone screen went black. Dead. Had it sent in time? And would Emma understand it? Ripley needed to get out of here.

She crossed to the door, being sure to tread lightly, and turned the handle, expecting exactly what she found – locked. She skirted the edge of the room, heading back for the window, but that was locked shut too.

Peering down, she realised that an escape via the window would be futile, anyway. Perhaps she could arm herself somehow and rush him when he, and if, he came in.

But what if he didn't come back before it was too late? She had no idea what time the parade started, or even what time it was now.

EMMA GRABBED HER phone as soon as the message alert came in. She hadn't slept at all, and was still in the office, with Dunn at her side almost mainlining coffee from the machine in the corner.

"Oh my God," Emma said. "It's from Alex."

"What does it say?"

"She says 'I'm okay. Battery low. He's going to attack the Padre'." Emma frowned, shrugging.

"What the hell does that mean?" Dunn asked. "I thought he was the Padre. Wasn't that what Captain Wilcox said?"

"I don't know," Emma said, pressing the button to call Ripley back and holding the phone to her ear. The call cut straight to voicemail.

"Shit," Emma said, hanging up and trying again, with the same result.

She tapped out a message: *What does that mean?* Holding the phone at arm's length, she watched the screen, waiting for that little 'delivered' confirmation notice. It didn't come.

"Her phone must have died," Emma said, staring at the message. "He's going to attack the Padre. What the hell is she talking about?"

"Maybe he's going to attack another priest?" Dunn offered.

Cotter walked in, balancing more coffees on a cardboard tray and looking exhausted. Clocking both of their faces he stopped.

"What's going on?"

"We just heard from Ripley," Dunn said, while Emma turned to one of her colleagues.

"That phone number you've been triangulating should just have made another hit. Let's get it traced. Quickly!" Emma implored.

"What did she say?" Cotter asked, almost dropping the coffees on the desk. "Is she okay?"

"Her phone's gone dead again," Emma replied. "But this is what she sent."

She handed the phone to Cotter and he read the message, looking up, confused, before looking back at the phone.

"That doesn't make any sense," he said.

"No, but the contact at least gives us a chance to trace her," Emma said. "She can explain it when we find her."

IT'S SIX IN the morning. Three hours until the beginning of the end. I made sure to bless each of my disciples as they left the room, sending them on their way in my name. They have all secured their place in the divine realm. They will be the new Apostles.

Should I go back upstairs and check on Dr Ripley? She's safe in her room, but she will probably be waking by now. It's far too early for her part yet, though. I need Martin to enact his final betrayal first, and that won't happen for another hour yet.

No, I should stick to my plan. Leave Dr Ripley alone for now. Her time will come.

Instead, I allow myself a moment of quiet reflection – a farewell to this human form that has carried me so well.

"GOT IT!" COTTER called excitedly. The triangulation of Ripley's phone had provided a small area of the city, near the park and the school, and he'd just confirmed that there was an empty office building – a converted townhouse – which was being rented by one of the names on the list he'd just got from the halfway house.

"Brilliant," Dunn said. "Let's go and get her. I'll get SWAT mobilised. We can meet them there."

"Boss, you'd better come," Mike, the duty officer from the holding cells said urgently, leaning through the door.

"What is it?"

"Your man down in the cells," he said. "He's hung himself."

"Oh Jesus," Dunn said, sprinting after him, Cotter and Emma following right behind.

RIPLEY HEARD THE front door slam closed and peered out of the window to see Adam leaving the building wearing a long coat and a green and blue cap – school colours. So he *had* been in the building all along.

She considered banging on the window to get him to come back upstairs, but to what end? Not only was he stronger than her, he was totally deranged. If she'd challenged him now, he'd be as likely to kill her rather than let her get in the way of what he was planning.

She still didn't really know what her role was meant to be in all of this. He'd said he wanted her to explain his message to them all when it was over, but what was he hoping? That she would defend him after he'd attacked those children? That she would try to convince people that they should follow his teachings? Or what? Where would this stop? What if he was planning to martyr himself at the same time? Would she be the one left trying to explain how they had failed all of those kids?

She watched him disappear into the gathering crowd and was suddenly overwhelmed with panic. She turned back to the desk, picked up the chair she'd been sitting in, and hurled it at the window.

The chair just bounced back and hit the floor. Toughened double-glazing. She picked it up again, holding on to the legs this time, and took a fierce swing at the glass. Nothing, but a crack of the wooden chair back. She swung again. She was going to smash her way through that window and call for help. It was all she could do.

Down below, no one even looked up. The sound of her efforts dulled by the thickness of the window and the bustle on the street as the crowds began to gather for the parade, slowly making their way towards the park, unaware of the danger they were all in.

THE COMMOTION OUTSIDE the holding cells confirmed that the worst had happened. Martin's limp, lifeless body was hanging from the bars of the high window in his cell. He had managed to strip and bind the blanket they had given him to make a thick rope, and he'd obviously managed to tip the bed on its end and use it to climb up and tie the rope to the window frame. The mattress and pillow were on the floor, the bed now upside down on the floor beneath him. Martin hung, facing them, legs reaching across the floor in front of him. He'd have had to drop himself with some force, given that he could have reached the ground and lifted himself at any point.

"Jesus, how the fuck did this happen?" Dunn turned to the duty officers. "What is this? Didn't you check him?"

"We did, ma'am," Mike said. "He had requested a pen and paper about half an hour ago. He'd been talking all the time, chuntering on, you know? He was fine. I did the rounds, came back and realised he'd gone quiet. I thought he'd finally worn himself out, ma'am. He wasn't due another check for another half hour."

Emma walked past her into the cell, bending to look at Martin's limp body.

"There wouldn't have been enough distance to get a proper break on the neck. He'd have strangled himself like this. Would have taken a while."

"There was no sound, ma'am, honest."

"It's okay. If he was committed to doing it, he would have gone quietly," Emma said, standing up and giving the distressed officer a small smile. It wasn't his fault, but he would be the subject of a horrible inquiry now.

She lifted a slip of paper from Martin's hand.

"A note," she said, handing it to Dunn.

"The spirit of Christ will be upon us all. At the third hour. Suffer the children to come unto me," Dunn read. "That's it. What the hell is this now?"

"Oh shit," Cotter said, taking the note and reading it again.

"What?" Dunn and Emma asked in unison.

"Ripley's message. Must have been bloody autocorrect," he said. "The parade. Not the padre. He's going to attack the school's Whitsun Parade."

RIPLEY SLUMPED TO the floor, more frustrated than exhausted. There was no way out of this stupid room, which meant she had no way to stop that madman. The street below was too busy, and no one would be looking up to the third floor to see a deranged woman hammering on the pane with a half-broken chair. It was no good.

This was the real reason he'd chosen Penrith. She should have figured it out straight away – he knew it was one of the few places in the country to still celebrate the descent of the Holy Spirit with a full Whitsun parade and a fete.

The school always made a thing of it. Whatever he was going to do to the people on that parade, Ripley could guarantee it would be on a grand scale. This was going to be his big moment.

If Adam believed he was the reincarnation of Christ, and he was rejecting every celebration of his so-called Demon God, then today would be the perfect day to rewrite the story everyone had believed for all these years.

She should have seen it earlier. Each of the other murders had tied with some part of the Christ story: Dylan Parker had died during Advent, Sister Francis during Holy Week, Reverend Thomas on Ascension Thursday. Even Mr Sampson, the teacher, had been killed during Pentecost. Adam had been laying the signs all the way. No wonder he was disappointed that she hadn't seen his message earlier. Even she was disappointed.

Ripley felt desperate. She pulled herself up again, holding the now shattered stump of the chair leg in her hand, and began smashing pointlessly on the window again.

From downstairs, she heard an almighty smash. Raised voices shouting. Feet clattering up the stairs. A voice shouting her name. It was Dan Cotter.

"I'm in here!" she called out. "Quickly."

"Stand back!"

She moved away from the door just in time to be clear when it smashed inwards, splintering around the lock. Armed officers ran into the room.

"He's not here," Ripley called.

"Clear," one of the officers shouted. "Move out."

Dan Cotter ran in as they piled back out of the room, fully shielded in body armour. He swept her into his arms.

"Are you okay?" he asked, holding her back. "You're okay!" He hugged her again. "Thank God," he muttered into her shoulder.

"I'm fine, Dan," she said.

"Alex," Wilcox charged in after the armed squad had moved on to check the other rooms. She jumped back guiltily from Cotter's embrace, but if Wilcox had noticed, he didn't show it. "Where are they? Where are the others?"

"What do you mean?" she asked.

"John?" he said urgently. "And the other men from the halfway house. Where are they?"

Ripley wracked her memory. Nothing. She hadn't seen John. Adam had assured her that her husband was alive, but she hadn't actually seen him. Wait.

"I heard voices, downstairs with him. I heard them laughing. But John wouldn't—" she didn't bother finishing. None of them knew what John was capable of.

"We found enough cocaine in that centre of his to feed a rave," Wilcox said. "Amongst other things. There's no telling what any of them will do if he's turned them."

"But John had just arrived," she said, feeling desperate. "He can't—" Again, she couldn't bring herself to finish the thought.

"Sir," one of the SWAT team leaned around the door. Both Wilcox and Cotter turned to answer. "You're going to want to see this," the young officer said.

They followed him out into the corridor, with Ripley close behind. She noticed that Cotter was the only one of the two men to look back and check she was okay to follow them. Wilcox was in full combat mode. Ripley nodded her confirmation and Cotter held back just enough to put his hand on hers again.

"You okay?" he asked as he let her pass in front of him down the stairs.

"Let's just get this done," she said, giving his hand a squeeze in return. "But we can't hang around: we've got to move, now! He's going to do something terrible to those kids. To everyone."

"The parade," Cotter said. "We know. We figured it out, thanks to your message."

"So you've stopped him?"

"Not so easy, but we're working on it. The start of the parade has been delayed, we've got full tactical down there, with dogs, everything. We're trying to move people off the route, but it's a bit like evacuating the whole town. We don't want to start a stampede. We'll find him, though. You can count on that."

THERE ARE MORE police – different police – than I'd been expecting. What are they doing here already? Has Martin told them too early? Has my most faithful servant betrayed me too soon? No matter, really. The more the merrier.

It's already almost nine o'clock, and though the children are all beginning to gather outside the front of the school, it doesn't look like the parade is ready to start anytime soon. Another wrinkle that will need to be smoothed, but I'm not too worried.

Standing amid the gathering crowd, hidden among them, I watch as the police close down the side routes and move people along towards the more open areas. Exactly as I'd assumed they would.

No need to worry. One way or the other, today will be the end and the beginning. The beginning, and the end.

RIPLEY FOLLOWED WILCOX into the downstairs room, shoving the energy bar Cotter had given her down her throat in two gulps. She was starving, and grateful of the small burst of sustenance. Stepping around Wilcox, she stopped dead, feeling Cotter step in close behind her. The scene in front of them was quite surreal.

"What the hell?" Cotter asked.

A long table, adorned in a rich red cloth, and covered in the remains of a feast. Platters, chalices and candlestick that all looked like they'd been lifted from a stage show of the last supper. The wall behind the table was a dark, brutal mural. Roughly – manically – painted in blacks and reds, almost completely filling the white of the wall. A doom painting of a very different kind. A portent. A depiction of the darkness that lived in Adam York's mind.

Hundreds of figures – little more than a black stripe for a body and a blob for a head – spread out from the centre of the wall to the far corners, perspective giving the sense of infinite numbers of bodies in a long procession. Each had a small red cross on their chest, painted with a thinner brush. And surrounding them, a crowd of taller figures, looming over them. No crosses for the crowd.

All along the bottom edge of the wall, red and orange flames licked at the feet of the crowd, the figures closer to the edge were already on fire, those on the sides of the procession being swept away by winds, bodies circling in the air – angels and demons.

Vivid red bursts – blood-like splashes, explosions, fire – all threatened to overwhelm the crowds standing either side of the procession, some were on fire, some torn apart, some flung skyward.

The only part of the wall that remained white formed the shape of a man, floating omnipotently at the back of the procession, as though the figures were all souls pouring out of his body. Lines of white light surrounded his body. But instead of being a beatific presence, he looked like a macabre puppet master, his hands seeming to have swept figures from the crowd, only to be tossing them away, discarding them like so much waste.

A swirling column of white travelled from his head up to and across the ceiling. A tornado of souls, and destruction, all seemingly beings sucked towards the angry, dark-clouded heavens.

"What is this?" Wilcox asked, stepping around the spilled detritus of the table and making one of the metal chalices clatter across the floor.

"This is the message he wants to send. This is what he has planned for the Whitsun Walk parade today." Ripley stepped up to the wall, pointing. "These are the boys from the school. And look at the crowd – look at these guys—" She was moving quickly now, urgently pointing out what they were supposed to see – the four horses surrounding the crowd, large and imposing. "The Four Horsemen."

"The apocalypse," Cotter said.

Despite, or perhaps thanks to her drug-induced sleep, Ripley felt suddenly alert and ready – adrenaline pumping through her veins.

"Exactly," she said. "We need to get everyone off the streets."

"They're working on it," Cotter said. "But we don't even know when he's going to strike. All Martin gave us by way of a time was the third hour, but we have no idea what that means."

"The third hour?" Ripley asked, looking at her watch. "It's figurative. The Holy Spirit descended on the disciples at the third hour. It was taken to mean nine o'clock, given the translation to the Roman clock and seasons and all that. It's already half-eight."

"The parade was due to begin at nine," Cotter said. "We've delayed it. We've tried to get the whole thing stopped, but the powers that be weren't buying into this as a terrorist threat because we couldn't give them any details apart from our best guesses. Adam isn't on any lists, and they're not willing to commit the kind of resources we'd need to evacuate the city centre."

"Well, we have to do something. Everything he's done so far has been a literal representation of either a doom painting or his interpretation of the Bible. This will be no different."

"Meaning?" Wilcox asked.

"The Holy Spirit descended in a flash of light, a sucking of air, fire and thunder."

"Sounds like a bomb," Cotter said.

"Exactly," Ripley agreed. "And he was carrying two automatic weapons when I saw him leave. God knows what the others have, but if they're acting as his agents and disciples, they will all be part of this destruction."

"But John's with him," Wilcox said, desperately. "He wouldn't be part of this."

"From what Adam told me, John and the other people he's been recruiting are perfect for what he needs them for. He knows exactly what they have been through. He knows what horrors they have seen, and he knows how to dig through the cracks in their armour to turn their minds to his way of thinking. He also knows that all of them are on the verge of suicide, and that, too, makes them the perfect candidates to be disciples in his crazy cult."

"But not John," Wilcox protested. "I know him. He wouldn't—"

"John's gone, Coxy. That John is gone." Ripley said, feeling both completely deflated and filled with an impotent rage. "With the right voice in his head and the right drugs fuelling him, neither you or I know what he's capable of anymore."

Wilcox looked as though he was about to protest, but stopped himself. He just stared at her, head still shaking like he wasn't ready to fully accept what she'd said.

"Besides, John was just the final lure to make sure he got my attention. It's me he was after all this time."

"What?" Cotter said, just before Wilcox could.

"He wants me to explain his message to the world when this – whatever this is – is done. John was his final bargaining chip. Whatever he has in mind, I'm not sure he's planning to survive the day. Not as Adam York, anyway."

"This is a suicide mission?" Wilcox asked, incredulously.

"No," said Ripley. "This is Judgement Day. He's going to take them all with him."

13

BY THE TIME they reached the park and began pushing their way through the crowds, Ripley realised exactly what they were up against. Despite the police being out in force, erecting new cordons, trying to limit access to the park, and move people away from the site, there were still hundreds of people there.

She could feel the tension from the police, and the innocent confusion from the crowd. This would be exactly what Adam would have wanted – the blind faithful stumbling to their deaths.

"We're going to be too late," Cotter said desperately. "There's no way they'll move all these people in time. If he's set timed charges, we're done for."

"I'm sorry, Dan," Ripley said. "I should have figured it out earlier."

"We all should. But it's not done yet. Come on, we can still get him."

Wilcox had gone off into the crowd, searching for any sign of John, or any of the others from the halfway house that they had managed to get photographs of. He'd taken two tactical officers with him, who didn't seem too phased to have been co-opted by a civilian. They were all after the same thing. Stopping anything before it happened.

Dunn waved Cotter and Ripley over as she spotted them.

"God, are you a sight for sore eyes," she said to Ripley. "Good to have you back Doc. We've already primed all the tactical leads with everything you've told Farm here. We've just got to hope we find Adam York before he can do anything. Do you really think he'll be here himself?"

"He has to be," Ripley said. "It wouldn't be right if he wasn't here. And he will want to get it right. He will want to make sure that the message is perfect. Besides, I think he's planning to die here today."

"Jesus," Dunn said. "Could he be wearing a vest?"

"I would doubt it," Ripley replied. "I think that would dilute the message."

She stopped, her stomach dropping.

"But the others might be," she said. "God, why didn't I think of that before. John. Shit." She scanned the crowd, desperately searching for her husband. What would he be wearing? She saw Neil Wilcox moving slowly through the crowd, searching for his friend.

"We'll find him," Cotter said, his voice solid and reassuring.

Ripley saw Dunn's confused expression and heard Cotter mutter that John had been taken as part of the plan to embroil her. She just wished she had looked into the centre when Coxy had first suggested it. But then, she'd fallen for Adam's charms as well, hadn't she? She hadn't realised how she was being played by him.

"I'll let the bomb squad know," Dunn said. "They've got the dogs with them. If there's a rig in the crowd, they'll find it."

"And why are *they* still here?" Cotter asked, pointing to the growing mass of schoolboys, all in their uniforms, carrying banners and flags. They had been kettled at the top of the park, separated from the crowds by the flimsy metal barriers. Parents and Grandparents lined the barriers, oblivious and tutting that they were being made to wait.

"The Head is insisting that they will not deviate from their path. He says they're doing this for Dylan."

Cotter frowned, cocked his head to look at Ripley. She knew what he meant. They had brought Morris Hanson in for questioning. Ripley had questioned him herself.

"Shit!" she said. "I should have seen it when I spoke to him."

"Seen what?"

"No time to explain," she said. "I think Mr Hanson might be one of them."

"We need to get those boys away from him," Cotter said, even as Morris Hanson walked to the front of the crowd and began gathering the boys into some kind of formation.

Dotted throughout the rest of the crowd were a number of people in school caps or waving school banners – old boys showing their support for the kids who still had to perform this ritual every year.

"He was wearing a school cap," Ripley said to Dunn, suddenly remembering. "When Adam left the house, he was wearing a cap like that."

Dunn relayed the message to the teams again.

"Suspect last seen wearing a school cap, expect others on the list to be wearing the same."

Ripley heard an order barked across the radio, obviously from the tactical team leader. "Keep your eyes peeled, check your lists again. Any of those faces show up, we contain them straight away. Controlled fire only. I don't want any of these civilians hurt on my watch. And get those people out of there!"

The church bells began their distant chimes, counting down nine o'clock. One. Ripley felt herself holding her breath. Two. What was he going to do? She watched as a gathering of people were rushed back by the police line. Three.

A space had opened up between the schoolboys and the barriers. Four. Ripley saw Morris Hanson arranging them into neater lines, closer together. And the bells rang on. Five.

A police line, in full riot protection gear, appeared from the side of the school gardens, moving solidly towards the boys. Six. Ripley let go the breath she'd been holding. As the column of boys, ranked in age order with the youngest at the front, began to move forward, she looked up. Seven. On the balcony outside Hanson's office, overlooking the school she saw Adam step into view. He was dressed in white, from head to toe, and he raised his arms. Eight. Exactly the image they had seen daubed on the wall. Without the bloodshed.

"Come and see!" Adam's voice echoed over loud speakers rigged around the park and gardens, and it felt like the world stood still. A crackle over the police radio, calls from the crowd as the police line tried to push them back, the clatter of horses' hooves as the mounted police closed in from all four corners.

"No!" Ripley said, seeing the horses add to the tableau. "They're doing exactly what he—" But her warning came too late: As the ninth chime tolled, the first explosion sounded. The far side of the park erupted in screams and commotion, but the people running from the explosion were all running towards the school gardens, towards the parade, towards danger.

Ripley was transfixed, Adam motioned with left hand, as though conducting an orchestra. A second explosion responded, tearing through the crowd to Adam's left. And a third bounced off the surrounding buildings in quick succession.

Over Dunn's radio, Ripley heard the first reports coming in over the screams and howls of the crowd: *"Small explosions just off the corner of King Street. Multiple casualties. Paramedics in attendance. Arrests made."*

Ripley wasn't the only one who heard it. Was John one of those arrested? Officers in the park were still trying to herd the panicking people away from the parade start area, but there was nowhere to move them on to.

Crowds had gathered at all the entrances, and the central run was cordoned off for the parade itself.

A strange silence hung in the air. Nobody knew what to do. Run or hide? Stay with the police or make a break for safety? But which way was safe?

And then a series of screams sounded from somewhere outside the park, painful, visceral cries of terror and anguish. And above the screams, gunfire – short, rapid, conclusive.

"We got one. Man down. Suspect down." "Confirm, confirm." "One of the twelve, Sarge." "Take York down. He's on the balcony." "Clear shot." "Take it, fire at will."

A staccato burst of gunfire rang out, one-two-three, tearing high above the heads of the crowd, resulting in more screams. Police on the ground charged the crowd again, driving them back towards the park exit – towards the site of the first explosion.

Ripley and Cotter both had their eyes fixed on Adam, who stood on the balcony with his arms raised at his sides, still orchestrating the pandemonium. The gunfire had no effect.

"The screen," Ripley said. "It's bulletproof."

Another flick of his wrists right and left and another two explosions tore through the crowd. Agonised screams. Desperate calls. Pandemonium as the crowd now found themselves the wrong side of the barriers to get out of harm's way, panic took over.

More gunfire, just outside the park now. *"Two down, repeat, two down. Both wearing vests. IUDs. Unlit. They're not rigged to auto-trigger."*

"Shit," said Dunn.

Ripley felt Cotter give her hand a squeeze. She had frozen to the spot. Had John just been shot? Was he one of the two taken down?

"Take him down!" "We're inside the building. On my mark."

The voices coming from Dunn's radio were urgent but in control. Ripley saw Adam bring his arms closer together in front of him, and as he did so, two flashes burst on either side of him, filling the balcony with bright red smoke – flares.

As the smoke consumed him, two more explosions burst, on both flanks of the parade line. The boys had been being shielded by what they had all thought were members of staff, but two of them had just triggered their vests. Screams rang out, some in pain, most in fear. The boys who could tried to scatter, helping each other, some limping, all looking shocked and battered.

"Clear!" "Clear!" "No sign." "He's gone." The voices on the radio were more desperate now.

Ripley looked up to see the police arrive on the balcony, the thinning smoke revealing that Adam had, indeed, disappeared.

A single shot sounded, parting the boys who had been fleeing back towards the school. Adam was striding out of the front entrance of the school, those two guns Ripley had seen him packing now held aloft, picking out children as they turned and ran from him.

"Take him down!" "No clear shot!" "Negative."

There were boys on the floor around him, and cries of agony and terror followed him out of their midst. A swarm of riot police, with shields aloft, closed the gap between Adam and the fleeing, terrified boys and their teachers, shouting to them all to stay down.

The remaining spectators were trying to escape the park, but now the police were almost boxing them in. Adam had planned this, too, Ripley realised. Coming from inside the crowd meant the onlookers had nowhere to run. Her eyes flashed around the crowd, looking for his followers.

"Dunn, look," she called. "They're following him."

Sure enough, coming through the fleeing crowd were a handful of bedraggled looking men and women, all in long coats, all in school caps, and uniquely identifiable by the fact they weren't afraid.

Adam smiled, fired off one more bullet into the group of cowering boys, and Ripley saw a spray of blood arc over their heads as more screams issued forth.

"Someone take him down!" "Not safe, guv." "I've got a shot!" "Take it!"

The sound of the shot clipped just before Adam's shoulder jerked backwards.

"Hit!"

Adam had been struck in the chest, just below his shoulder. He didn't even break stride, barely glancing at the mark where the bullet had gone in. Another pumped into his chest, closer to the centre, this time knocking him back a little. But still he smiled. And Ripley saw that there was no blood.

"He's wearing a vest!" "Wing him!" "Get a head shot." "Negative, not clear."

The rag tag group of disciples following Adam began to fan out. Right at the back, barely shuffling forward, Ripley saw John. He looked bigger than he had for months. He was wearing a vest too, she realised, but not one that would protect him from bullets – one intended to destroy the innocent, John included. She needed to get to him, but how?

Adam tucked the gun in his right hand into his waistband, and lifted a mobile phone from his pocket. He slowed his walk, gun casually picking off innocents as they scurried away from him, still effectively trapped too close to him by the barriers.

Adam's disciples were spreading quickly around the outside of the group. Ripley took a step forward but Cotter held her back.

"No," he said.

"I have to," she replied, pulling her arm away, breaking free of him and pushing her way through the police line.

"Adam, stop," she called.

He stopped. His expression rolling from surprise to sadness to anger. She wasn't supposed to be here. This obviously wasn't part of his plan. She saw that straight away. Ripley could hear all sorts of conflicting orders being given over different headsets behind her, over the top of screams and whimpers of the injured.

She took another step forward and Adam levelled his gun straight at her.

The crowd had thinned enough that she was directly in front of him, still some distance away, but at least it would buy more time to get more people out of the way. There were still more than enough innocent lives to be lost here.

"Adam, please," she said. "This isn't the right way."

"I am the way," he said in a sing-song voice. Taunting and crazed. He moved his finger to hover over the green call button on the old-fashioned phone. Ripley heard Cotter behind her hiss to her to get back.

"That's a group trigger," Dunn said. "He can set off all remaining charges with one button."

Which means he'll take John out, she thought.

Ripley stepped forward again, hands raised peacefully.

"Adam," she said. "This isn't right. This won't work."

"You weren't meant to be here," he said, voice thick with sadness and anger. "Why have you betrayed me?"

She saw straight away that he had gone completely. Any hope of appealing to the man he had once been was lost. She stopped in her tracks, not willing to back off yet, still thinking that she must be able to do something. But whatever that something was, she wasn't going to get any closer to Adam.

Over his shoulder she saw Neil Wilcox pushing through the police line, saying something firmly to the officer in charge and sprinting across the narrow bit of space to tackle John to the ground in a flying leap.

She needed to buy Coxy some time to get that vest off John, or they would both be lost. She was desperate.

"If you press that button," she said. "I will tell them all that you were just a madman. The wrong God will win. They won't change."

He frowned now, and wiped his nose roughly against the back of the hand holding the gun, the phone still held aloft in the other.

"No matter, Dr Ripley," he said. "I will rise again."

He pursed his bottom lip like a petulant schoolboy. His finger shaking over the button. She could feel the tension behind her of several guns raised at a target she was currently standing in front of.

"There is another way," she said, taking another step towards him.

"Alex, please. Get out of the way." It was Cotter's voice, a low whispered hiss.

Not yet.

She saw Wilcox land two hefty punches on John's left temple, and saw her husband slump. Wilcox immediately signalled the guy from the bomb squad, who ran – low and fast – across the clearing.

"Headshot clear."

Ripley raised her hand behind her to the side, hoping they would listen to her. She didn't want him pressing that button as they shot him.

"Hold. Hold."

"If you do this, it will all die with you here, today."

This was a big call, but she hoped it would get through. The look of hatred that crossed Adam's face in that moment was shocking, even for Ripley. There he was – the man behind the delusion, and she had really pissed him off.

His remaining disciples were already around the edges of the area, but the crowd had mostly dispersed, and the boys of the parade were being filtered out the back into the school, with Morris Hanson pinned in place by two armed policemen.

Ripley did a quick mental count. Two shot, John and Morris Hanson down. The remaining seven disciples stood, zombie-like, around the edges of the scene, seemingly undisturbed by the bodies of children and adults all senselessly killed for their leader's cause. And she – the twelfth – would be the one to betray him.

Adam followed her gaze, over his shoulder, to his beloved disciples. She didn't want him to turn back far enough to see that the bomb disposal guy was already working on John's vest.

"Dr Ripley," a voice she didn't recognise, full of authority, called from behind her. "Step aside. Right now."

No.

Adam turned back to look at her. He'd dropped the phone to his side, finger still on the button. The last of the crowd had been shepherded from the area or was being partially protected by a wall of police shields.

Dunn's voice echoed around the space. "It's over Adam, give yourself up."

"You betrayed me," he said, raising his gun at Ripley. "You betrayed everything."

"Dr Ripley, please. Get back." It was Dunn this time, but Ripley heard Cotter swear too.

Taking a deep breath, Ripley turned her back on Adam. She saw a look of panic cross Cotter's face. He shouted something, but it was lost in the sound of a series of loud blasts. Adam had pressed the button.

Ripley turned back instinctively to check on John. Her bluff had failed. Before she could take in the scene, she saw Adam's gun fire and, at exactly the same time, a single shot burst through his head. A spray of dark red blood erupting above his ear.

Ripley was knocked to the ground, an incredible pain in her shoulder, and a resounding thud as she hit the deck. Daniel Cotter had bowled her to the ground from the side and was lying half on top of her now, covering her, keeping her safe.

The gunfire tailed off, the explosions faded and all that remained was a breath of silence followed by chaos. Heavy-footed, armed police clattered past, surrounding the place where Adam had stood, but Ripley could already see that there would be no more threat from him.

He lay on his back, peppered with gunshot, his own weapon on the ground beside his splayed hand. He'd fallen with his arms stretched out to his sides, Christ-like. Ripley guessed he would have enjoyed the image.

She wriggled out from beneath Cotter, about to tell him off for squashing her, only to realise that he wasn't actually moving. Only when she bent down to check he was okay, did she see all the blood. Bullet holes in an arc across his back. So much blood. The world closed in around her. She felt herself go, knees hitting the ground as she bent to cradle him in her arms.

She looked up, desperate for someone to help, and saw Neil Wilcox get to his feet, blood covering his face and clothes. He looked at her quizzically as though trying to process odd information. Was John gone, too? She couldn't cope.

All around her the chaos receded to a dull roar, she felt hands on her, scooping her away. She tried to hold on to Cotter, but she couldn't stop them lifting her off. Paramedics in green and yellow swamped the young detective – her friend – blocking her out as she was pulled backwards. *So much blood.*

RIPLEY SAT IN the hospital corridor with Emma by her side. Her friend had not left her since Ripley had been given the all clear, but they'd barely said a word.

Dunn was pacing, unable to settle at all, while Ripley didn't feel she would ever be able to move from that spot.

The doctors had been working on Cotter for what felt like hours. He'd still been alive, just, when they had arrived at the hospital, but they'd had no news since, and it was impossible to tell what was happening inside from the faces of the staff hurrying in and out of the operating theatre.

The paramedics who'd brought him in had come across to try to offer some reassurance once they'd handed him over. His body armour had taken the worst of the shots to his back, but one had caught him in the neck and nicked his artery. He'd lost a lot of blood, but was in the best place now. The words had felt hollow and empty, though they were well meant. Ripley just couldn't erase the sight of him lying on the ground, lifeless, as the blood pumped out of him.

It was her fault. That's all she kept thinking. He'd jumped across to save her. Adam had been firing at her, and Cotter had saved her. She couldn't bear the thought of him dying for that. For her.

Emma reached over and squeezed her hand, as Dunn finally sat, legs bouncing, on Emma's other side and took her other hand. They sat there in silence, the three of them, eyes fixed on the doors, waiting for news. Not daring to hope.

When the doctor finally came out to see them, they almost leapt on him, firing the same question in different ways: How is he? Is he alright? Is he dead?

The doctor held up his hands, stopping them in their tracks.

"He's stable, but still critical," he said, and any relief at the former statement was tempered by the latter. "The surgeons have done what they can, and he has been moved to the ICU."

He wouldn't be drawn on questions of prognosis. All he would say was that Dan Cotter was a fighter. After he left them, Dunn and Emma hugged, happy and relieved that he had made it that far, reassuring each other that he would pull through, that he was already over the worst of it. But Ripley couldn't shake her dread and guilt.

And she knew there was still more to come. Neil Wilcox, still blood-stained, stepped into the corridor, keeping a sort of distance. Emma saw the change of expression on Ripley's face, and looked behind her to see Wilcox approaching. She turned back to Dunn.

"Come on. Let's get you cleaned up," she said, taking Dunn's hand. "I'll be right back." She fixed Ripley with a look that told her she knew what was coming, she knew that her friend would need her, and she would always be there.

Taking his cue, Neil Wilcox approached as they left. He sat down heavily and Ripley waited a moment before sitting beside him, as though the action in itself was acknowledgment of the truth he was about to share. John was dead.

When she sat beside him, it was her that took his hand. He was shaking.

"He's gone, isn't he?" she asked.

Wilcox nodded, and a raw, gasping sob erupted from him. He was broken. She gathered him into her arms, and they held each other like their lives depended on it. Or, if not their lives, then their sanity.

HOURS LATER, ALONE in her hotel room, Ripley tried to find peace in a bottle of wine, her mind pouring over the events of the past days. Adam's psychosis had been so peculiar. He had all but eliminated any memory of his previous life; he was so determined he had been sent to deliver humankind from its corrupt ways.

She wondered whether it had struck him, as the police bullets had taken him down, that he was merely mortal after all. Or had he still believed that his spirit would ascend, and that people would finally understand his truth.

What did it matter, in the end, which version of the story anybody believed? What Adam had done to spread his version of the truth was as bad as any war or any killing in the name of any God.

Ripley realised, with a huge sigh, that she was sick of it all. People she loved – John, Dan Cotter – had been damaged by the same warped logic that she seemed to spend all her time fighting against: That somehow one interpretation of God was better than another, and worse, that it was worth killing for.

She downed her wine, swore violently at the walls, and lay back on her bed. Alone now. And strangely, released from that awful anxiety she had felt ever since her husband had first gone missing. The worst had finally happened. And she found she was relieved. But she would never be the same again.

RIPLEY MET DUNN in the corridor of the hospital as she was coming out of Cotter's room. The Detective smiled broadly as she saw her.

"How is he?" Ripley asked.

"Getting there," Dunn said, touching Ripley's arm reassuringly. "Go see for yourself."

Ripley took a deep breath before walking into the hospital room. She was dreading seeing Dan Cotter injured. He'd always seemed so strong. Young and vital. She didn't know if she wanted to see him reduced in any way.

Realising it was her guilt stopping her from opening the door, she tutted. Dan Cotter smiled broadly as she came in.

"I was wondering when you'd come to apologise," he said. His voice was a little croaky, and he was wired up to a drip and a bank of monitors, but otherwise he looked strong.

"I brought grapes," Ripley said, holding up a bag.

"I hate grapes," he laughed.

"I know," she said. "They're for me. You can have the choccies."

She bent down and kissed him on the cheek. A tender, lingering kiss that she hoped told him how sorry, how grateful and how relieved she was.

"Thank you," she whispered.

THE CUCKOO WOOD

Samantha Jaynes took her life in the cold lake. Now Rosie Trimble has done the same. Both claimed they had seen an angel. And they're not the only ones.

A spate of teenage suicides rattles the rural community of Kirkdale, in England's Lake District. Before they died, each of the girls talked about seeing an angel. Is this collective hallucination, or is something more sinister leading these young girls to their deaths? That's a question for Dr Alex Ripley, the so-called Miracle Detective.

Brought in to help the police, she finds a community rooted in fear and suspicion, bound by their strange faith, unwilling to help, unable to forgive.

Because the people of Kirkdale have buried their dark past once, and they're not about to let Ripley dig it up again.

A HOLLOW SKY

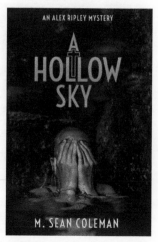

Jane Hewitt had a miraculous healing. After one meeting with a faith healer, Jane rose from her wheelchair and walked, seemingly cured of a terminal cancer and believing that her lifetime of devoted faith had been rewarded.

She was wrong. She died just days later. Her husband, Ian, blames her hastened death on the faith healer she visited and turns to Dr Alex Ripley, the so-called Miracle Detective for help.

Fascinated by the case, Ripley finds herself on Holy Island, off the coast of North Wales, caught up in an investigation that will prove more sinister and dangerous than even she could have imagined.

Ian is not the first person to complain about this particular faith healer, but he is the only one still alive. For now.

ABOUT THE AUTHOR

Born in the UK and raised in South Africa, M. Sean Coleman developed a love for reading and writing novels in his early teens, thanks to two incredibly passionate English teachers who infected him with their love of words and stories.

Over the intervening years, he has written film and television drama, cross-platform series, an interactive children's storybook and even a graphic novel series.

He finally found his niche as a thriller writer when he was asked to write a novel as part of the cross-platform project, Netwars. His first book, The Code, was published six months later, with the sequel, Down Time, hot on its heels. There was no going back.

He is obsessed with crime, mystery and thriller stories, especially those with a fresh or surprising angle.